THE REIVER

THE REIVER

MIKE ROUTLEDGE

Matador
9 Priory Business Park,
Wistow Road, Kibworth Beauchamp,
Leicestershire LE8 0RX
Tel: 0116 279 2299
Email: books@troubador.co.uk
Web: www.troubador.co.uk/matador
Twitter: @matadorbooks

ISBN 978 1838595 272

British Library Cataloguing in Publication Data.
A catalogue record for this book is available from the British Library.

Printed and bound in Great Britain by 4edge Limited
Typeset in 11pt Garamond by Troubador Publishing Ltd, Leicester, UK

Matador is an imprint of Troubador Publishing Ltd

Preface

My tale came about because on researching the local history of Carlisle in World War I, I came across numerous interesting stories and inspirational characters often little known by the general public. I shared these informally with friends and colleagues attending the lunchtime lectures that I organise at the city's Tullie House Museum. Then one day it was suggested that I should do a talk based on my findings. I started to collect information with a view to doing just that and, as it came together, I noticed that in many instances events and people were linked, even though sometimes the links were quite tenuous. Slowly the idea of a fiction book incorporating them all grew and I decided that this might be an ideal vehicle to celebrate some of the wonderful characters of that time. In a sense it is, therefore, also dedicated to those unsung heroes of the Great War from the city I am proud to call home. I don't pretend to be a Bernard Cornwall, Simon Scarrow or Allan Mallinson, but I hope the end product is both enjoyable to read and informative.

Although most of the people, places and events in this story are factual, sometimes details and timelines have been adapted to suit the storyline. Any factual inaccuracies are either changes of my doing to support the storyline – and my apologies to true historians for playing with history – or errors for which I take the blame.

Location Maps

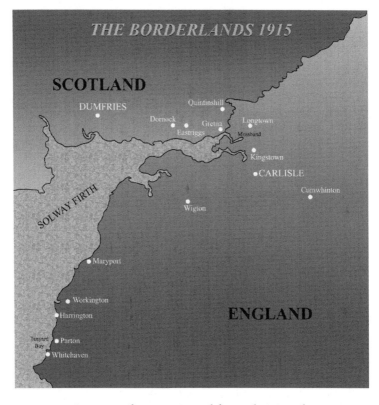

Courtesy of Martin Sproul fstop Photography

Irish (Caldew) Gate   Annetwell Street   Carlisle Cast

The Globe Inn

The Biscuit
  Factory

Canal Bank

To the
Cumberland
Infirmary

Holy Trinity
Church

Parhambeck

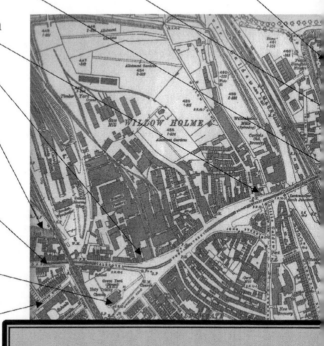

Jack Johnstone's
Carlisle, 1915

Courtesy of Alan Godfrey Maps

an Tait's Lane   Victoria Park   Finkle Street

To Eden St.
& Kingstown

Peter Street
Gym

To Strand Rd

The Methodist
Central Hall

Kings Head PH

Market Cross
& Town Hall

Carlisle
Cathedral

The Citadel
& English
(Bochard) Gate

The Railway
Station

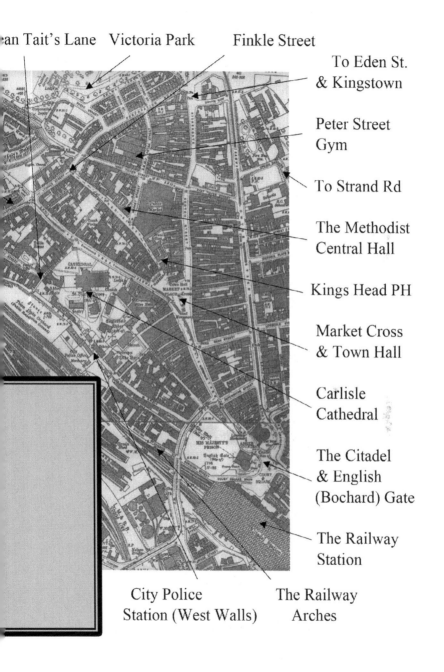

City Police   The Railway
Station (West Walls)   Arches

Introduction

Cumberland and South West Scotland were a long way from the battlefront during World War One and it would be easy to think that this meant that the fighting had little impact on these predominantly rural areas. Nothing could be further from the truth. Their very isolation made them ideal places to prepare new recruits and produce munitions. Here they were out of sight and out of mind of the Oberste Heeresleitung or German Supreme Command. Or were they? Many of the people, places and occurrences in this story are true and much of what is described actually happened. Whilst historians recorded these facts and reported them, the fiction writer can look at them, interpret them differently and pose the question 'What if?' So … what if these separate events were not isolated but linked together and what if historians simply chose not to explore this possibility?

Prologue

I curse their head and all the hairs of their head. I curse their face, their brain, their mouth, their nose, their tongue, their teeth, their forehead, their shoulders, their breast, their heart, their stomach, their back, their womb, their arms, their legs, their hands, their feet, and every part of the their body, from the top of their head to the soles of their feet, before and behind, within and without.

The Reivers' Curse
Gavin Dunbar, Archbishop of Glasgow, 1525

Solway Bank, Scottish West March
Mid-March 1604

Despite the darkness, only occasionally interrupted by a half moon poking through a cloudy sky, the twenty men rode confidently across the rough countryside. They knew the land well and most could have followed the rough track to their destination blindfolded. At their front rode a heavy set man whose once-athletic frame had given way to a late-middle-aged spread that made the wearing of his protective leather jerkin uncomfortable. The light drizzle ran off his steel bonnet and trickled down onto his face, catching in a greying beard which he occasionally stroked to rid himself of the cold, dripping moisture. He grunted with discomfort as his horse slid down a muddy bank and jerked to a halt in the shallow stream at the bottom before kicking on up the other side. His body ached with both age and the impact of the long ride, but he allowed himself a grim smile as the animal reached the top. The small group had crossed the frontier using the Sulwath Ford at the mouth of the River Esk then followed the Kirtle Water north for an hour before turning east towards a band of low hills. No one who lived in these 'debatable lands', long fought over by England and Scotland, really took much notice of the boundary, as it had frequently changed over the years. However, he knew that his presence in the Scottish West March would be seen as unlawful and the consequences could be dire. So this would be his last raid. It had to be. After King James had united the crowns of the two old foes almost a year ago he had made it clear that he intended to put a stop to the lawlessness that was endemic in the region. Feuding had become common place and the Border Laws had done little to prevent cattle-rustling, the destruction of property and murder. The new monarch was determined to put an end to this violent, criminal activity and ordered that offending raiders – or reivers, as they were known – should be executed or deported. There'd been warnings before, of course. His father had told him that the church had once tried to put a stop to the anarchy. The Archbishop of Glasgow had gone so far as to excommunicate the reiver families and issued a curse that he insisted was read out from every pulpit in the diocese. But to men with little time for religion or the church, it had caused amusement rather than fear. This time it was different. Many of his friends had ignored the threat and suffered the dire consequences. He was aware that the same thing would happen to him if the band were caught. It was a shame, really, the family he was raiding were only taking back what his idiot of a younger son had stolen from them on a drunken excursion, but the transgression could not be allowed or his own reputation would be diminished. He pulled his cloak closer around his body, but, like the rest of him, it was soaked through and offered little extra warmth. The border weather was an unforgiving foe, even in early spring. As he crested the top of a gentle rise he reined his horse to a stop and looked down into the valley below him where a small Pele Tower stood in splendid isolation.

The fortified stone building was designed to withstand attacks and even short sieges. Square in shape, it consisted of three storeys. The ground floor had no windows and was used for storage and to house the animals in winter. The first floor, consisting of a dining hall and kitchen, was accessed through an iron-reinforced wooden door at the end of a steep, external stone staircase. The top floor was the living and sleeping space, whilst the battlemented roof was flat for look-out purposes and to allow the occupants to hurl missiles or fire arrows down on unwanted visitors. Lights shone out of the upper windows and he could see a handful of men standing on the crenelated walls. It didn't surprise him that they were prepared for his arrival. They knew he would come and news travelled fast, even in these isolated lands. Normally the idea of attacking such a well-prepared fortification without the element of surprise wouldn't have been considered. An attempt up the narrow stairway would be suicidal and in most instances the raiders would settle for threats against the inhabitants and taking or destroying anything left outside the protective tower. This time he'd prepared for the possibility although it had cost a deal of silver to bribe one of the servants. The money had come from his son's purse by way of punishment for the crass stupidity that had created this situation. He hadn't been happy, but his father didn't care. The boy had to realise there were consequences to acts of folly.

The group rode down into the valley and stopped just out of range of the odd arrows foolishly wasted by the defenders. Time seemed to drag and for a moment he thought that the traitor had double-crossed them and decided to keep the money, hoping to stay safe within the walls. However, after what seemed like an age, the heavy door started to open and he shouted the order to attack …

'Now! Go now before someone realises what's happening. Up the stairs and kill them. Kill them all and burn the building.'

The rider next to him looked across and said, 'What about our man? Do we —', but his leader cut him off mid-sentence.

'No one gets out alive. No one can know we were here,' he paused, 'and if you can find the money, bring it back to me.'

His men raced up the steps and through the gaping door. For a while he sat listening to the screams coming from within the blazing building until they stopped and all that was left was the crackling of the flames. With a nod of the head, he turned his horse and headed home. The others would follow in due course. There was a grim satisfaction in the successful completion of a well-planned raid. He would miss that but he realised that times were changing and men like him would soon be history. The law was being re-established and people would sleep safer in their beds secure in the belief that there was much less likelihood of them being 'bereaved'. The day of the reiver was passing.

CHAPTER 1

Parton North of Whitehaven on the Cumberland Coast

Early Morning, Monday 16th August 1915

In the early hours of the late summer morning, on the cliffs high above the nearby Cumberland town of Whitehaven, the two men fought. The battle was vicious and each man knew that to lose meant death. For one it would be immediate; for the other it would come at the end of the hangman's noose or a bullet from a firing squad. The only observers of the confrontation were half a dozen seagulls, who, disturbed from their nests by the unwanted intrusion, screeched and soared on the thermals rising over the headland.

It was a dramatic location for their final confrontation. Above them an awakening sun lit up a powder-blue sky across which high, wispy clouds floated eastwards. After a grey and dismal dawn, the brightening day promised much. Below them at the foot of the cliffs, the rough sea roared in, sending waves crashing over the west coast railway line and spray high into the air, soaking the two-hundred-foot sandstone bluffs. The soaking often caused landslips blocking the London and North West Railway trains running from Carlisle southwards through Whitehaven to Furness. To the south the town's harbour nestled between two headlands that jutted out into the Irish Sea, the colourful fishing boats in stark contrast to the drab, grey port buildings. To the north the nearby chimneys of the local chemical works sent up an impressive plume of dark smoke, whilst inland the majestic Cumberland Mountains could be seen in the distance rising to over three thousand feet, the purples of heather and bright green of bracken visible on their upper slopes.

One of the protagonists was a tall, well-built young man in his early thirties with short, cropped, light brown hair, blue eyes and a clean-shaven square jaw. Standing over six feet tall, he wore a black roll-neck wool sweater and dark cord trousers. His outfit was completed by a pair of heavy-gauge military boots with a ring-tipped heel and 'gripper' studs. During the violent exchanges he had used them to good effect on his opponent's now battered and bruised legs.

The other man was slightly older, approaching middle age and at least a head shorter. He wore an ill-fitting checked green and brown suit over a faded white collarless shirt. With oiled back black hair, yellowing teeth, twinkling hazelnut eyes and a sharp nose, he looked like someone more comfortable working the black markets of a war-ravaged city than fighting for his life on a wild and windy clifftop.

The taller man held a savage-looking knife in his right hand. A long, double edged stabbing blade ended in a brass knuckleduster handle. It having been designed by the military to aid soldiers in close combat, he had made good contact on the smaller man, whose left arm showed the damage done. The sleeve of his jacket displayed the effects of several slashes and was ripped to shreds where he had tried to defend himself from the lethal blade. Blood oozed through the gaps and trickled down his fingers. On the ground beside him, a truncheon lay where it had been knocked from his hand.

Both men were breathing heavily and for a moment they stepped back and faced each other. Sweat glistened on their faces and ran down their backs. Neither said anything but despite their heavy breathing both were thinking what to do next. The older man knew he was tiring and could not keep up the fight much longer. His body was losing blood as a result of the numerous cuts he had received and his left calf was swelling where he had been kicked repeatedly. The metal studs on the other man's boots had left their mark and the damaged leg was hindering his movement. The taller man knew he was gaining the upper hand, but time was running out; he needed to finish things before others came, otherwise all was lost and it would be him who would lose his life.

Slowly they circled, each man's stare never leaving the other's eyes. Any attack would start there. Suddenly the younger man tossed his knife from his right to his left hand. For a moment the other's glance followed the movement. It was a fraction of a second's distraction but all the chance the tall attacker needed. Stepping quickly forwards, he pushed the smaller man hard in the chest and, as he over-balanced backwards, he pushed again. Panic flared in his eyes as he toppled over and fell, banging his head as he hit the hard ground. For a moment the air was knocked out of him by the impact and immediately his opponent took his opportunity and rushed forwards. Kneeling over the prostrate individual, he raised his knife and brought it down towards the other's chest. The older man flinched, expecting a searing pain. Instead, before the blade found its mark the air was rent with a massive explosion, lifting both men into the air and sending them tumbling across the clifftop. They landed, dazed by the noise with their ears ringing. Rocks and soil pattered down around them. As they gathered their senses and looked around to see what had happened, a second closer explosion went off and blackness engulfed both men.

CHAPTER 2

Berlin

Mid-Morning, Thursday 25th March 1915

The Abteilung IIIb, the intelligence section of the German Supreme Command, was located at 76/78 Tirpitzufer, south of Tiergarten across the road from the Landwehr Canal in Berlin. An imposing grey structure, it had offices on seven levels, one of which was below ground and another within its bright red roof. On its canal-side, the east and west wings, each about seventy metres long, spread out from a magnificent south-facing main entrance designed like a modern Roman temple, with four columns supporting a triangular pediment inset with the German Eagle. On each of the six main levels rows of rectangular windows reached almost from floor to ceiling. From one of these on the third floor a dark-haired man looked out onto the bustling street below. Leaning forwards to place his hands on the windowsill he pushed down, locking his elbows to take all his upper bodyweight, and sighed. Rain drizzled on the glass panel and as he watched, men and women walked quickly along the canal-side pavement, hurrying to get out of the March downpour. His thoughts drifted for a moment and he reflected that Berlin could be a miserable place even in early spring.

Colonel Walter Nicolai had been born in Braunschweig on 1st August 1873, the son of an impoverished Prussian army captain and a farmer's daughter. He grew up with few luxuries and was happy to join the 82nd Infantry Regiment in 1893. He had been promoted to major in 1912, a somewhat belated event, before moving into the intelligence service. In early 1913, after working in Konigsberg, which he had helped turn into a major centre for espionage against the Russian Empire, he had been chosen to be the Head of Abteilung IIIb. He was proud of his achievements but, given the lack of interest in intelligence matters within the German army and a consequent lack of funding, his position and influence had become increasingly under pressure from a navy that was keen to prove the independence and effectiveness of its own agency, and that had a desire to see it become the main agent of German intelligence. Although he had pushed senior officers to recognise intelligence as an independent section within the army a year previously, the reality was that he still had less influence on intelligence and counter-intelligence matters than the more political soldiers on the general staff. They had the advantage of direct access to senior officers in the Supreme Command. He was aware that he needed a big success or his career was doomed to be directed towards censorship and war propaganda or possibly something even worse. He wouldn't be the first person within the service to simply just disappear.

Nicolai was aware of the importance of the morning's meeting and, although internally fuming, outwardly he projected an air of calmness and kept his breathing even. He had already taken great care with his appearance. His hair was combed back, revealing a high forehead. His moustache was freshly clipped in the latest fashion and although he could do nothing about his Roman nose, which he hated, his eyebrows had also been trimmed and shaped. His dark uniform was freshly cleaned and pressed, and he hoped that overall he gave the impression of someone fully in control of both his emotions and responsibilities.

Behind him, sat around an oval mahogany table, were four of the very officers who had resisted his efforts to influence matters of intelligence. The body language of all four reflected their collective annoyance at having to attend the meeting. However, they were aware that regular intelligence gatherings were expected from which a report would be sent to the Supreme Command. The most influential of the group was Major Max Bauer, a bald man with a round face and a small moustache. A chemist before the war, he had risen to command the operations section at Supreme Command responsible for heavy artillery. Today he gave the bored expression of someone entirely indifferent to this army intelligence group meeting. He looked across the table at his colleague Colonel Heinrich von Kirchberg.

'At this rate, my friend, you are going to miss your weekly meeting with your pretty Marlene at the little flat near Potsdamer Platz. Instead you will have to make do with your wife this evening.'

Von Kirchberg scowled and the others laughed. Although short and overweight with round glasses that gave his face an owl-like look, the colonel played on his vulnerable appearance and attracted women like moths to a flame. They did not see him as a threat and seemed happy to become his friend, which he in turn was happy to turn to his advantage. Marlene was his latest conquest. She was a young waitress in a café he frequented near his office, and they had been seeing each other for over a year.

'I hear the popular artist Ernst Kirchner has been painting street scenes near there, perhaps you could persuade him to entertain her in your increasingly frequent absence,' continued Bauer.

The others laughed again.

'I mean, of course, that he could paint her, nothing more. At least it would remind you what she looks like.'

'Bugger off, Max,' replied Bauer. 'You're just jealous that you didn't pick her up yourself.'

He looked at Nicolai's back and shouted, 'Hey, Walter. Are we going to sit here all morning? Some of us have other things to do.'

'Yes,' said Bauer. 'Marlene doesn't like Heinrich to keep her waiting, you know, Walter. It cools her passion, which in turn disappoints him.'

The other two members of the group were Major Hans von Haeften, a personal aide to General Helmuth Moltke on the general staff, and Lieutenant Heinrich Gunter, who preferred to be called an intelligence officer rather than spy, which was actually what he was. With his blond wavy hair, bronzed good looks and immaculate uniform, von Haeften was the embodiment of the perfect German military man. He sat with his feet on the table, inhaling slowly on an expensive cigar and blowing occasional rings into the already smoke-laden atmosphere. In contrast Gunter was a tiny, weasel-like man with a narrow face and pencil moustache. He had just returned to Berlin, having been arrested in Norway on suspicion of espionage. However, after diplomatic pressure from Germany, he had been set free and deported, but not before he had spent several months in an Oslo jail.

Nicolai raised his hands, balled them into fists and brought them crashing down onto the windowsill. 'It won't do. We have to act or this war is going to be lost. We can move and feed our army very effectively, but all the energy we expend getting men to the frontline fit and healthy counts for nothing if they don't have the right equipment.'

Startled, Bauer, von Kirchberg and Gunter all sat up and looked at their colleague. Von Haueften never moved and slowly exhaled another smoke ring. With deliberate precision, he put the cigar down on the metal ashtray in front of him.

'My dear major ...' He paused for effect. 'I doubt that very much, and I suggest you are careful not to suggest that in your report to the Supreme Command or we could all find ourselves a trifle inconvenienced by a change in our circumstances.'

'Anyway,' interrupted Bauer, 'our heavy artillery is vastly superior to that of the British.'

'That may be true but what artillery also need is sufficient ammunition. There have been times in recent months when a shortage of shells has meant our guns have been reduced to firing only four or five shells a day.'

'Perhaps, however, you know fine well that this has been the same on both sides and our shelling is proving to be most effective. Preliminary reports from the recent battle at Neuve Chappelle suggest that the Allied causalities are higher than ours, with over 20,000 killed or injured compared to our 5,000.'

Nicolai sighed and ran the fingers of his left hand through his hair in frustration. 'I think the figures were actually closer to 12,000 and 8,000, but that's still a pretty high butcher's bill. It would appear they committed four divisions to the assault, around 40,000 men, so the casualty rate was about thirty per cent. However —'

Bauer cut him off in mid-sentence. 'My point exactly.'

His colleague's voice took on a sarcastic tone. 'However, they were only opposed by two divisions from our 6th Army. Around 20,000 men. Do the maths, Max. That's forty per cent losses on our side. We can't sustain that.'

'Don't be ridiculous. You know that Germany and the Central Powers can mobilise almost twice as many men as Britain and her allies. If anyone can't sustain things, it's the Allies.'

'But the British are taking steps to solve their armaments problem. Our agent in Scotland reports that a new Ministry of Munitions has been set up and tasked with increasing the supply of artillery shells to their Expeditionary Force. Existing sites are being expanded and new munitions factories are being set up across the country.'

'Come now, Nicolai. Can we really rely on this information? I can't imagine the British would openly discuss this kind of development.'

'You know Karl Lody as well as I do. He's been travelling around Britain for weeks using that American passport in the name of Charles Inglis. His cover as a tour guide for the Hamburg America Line means he's been able to move around the country unhindered, supposedly looking at potential sites for post-war visits. In reality he's been able to check on naval movements and coastal defences, and so far his information has always been accurate. He's also blackmailing a middle-ranking British diplomat after enticing him into an illegal sexual relationship with one of his paid low-life "associates". The man's petrified of being found out and has been extremely cooperative. He's told Lody that a decision to build a new cordite factory was recently taken as a response to Field Marshal Sir John French's recent tirade in the press about the acute shortage of munitions. It caused a public outrage against the government, who have apparently decided to establish a massive factory just north of the city of Carlisle on the Scottish border. It's to be the biggest of the new sites, producing 800 tonnes of cordite per year, more than all the other British factories combined. As yet it's top secret, but steps have already been taken to acquire the site: a contractor has been appointed and they are looking to start construction this summer. If that gets off the ground, we are in real trouble.'

Bauer spread his arms out wide and smiled. 'And who will work in these factories? Young boys and old men? Look, Walter, we don't have a remit to recommend strategy or actions. Our job is to oversee the gathering of intelligence and counter-intelligence, press and postal censorship, supervise our attaché service to those Allied and neutral countries stupid enough to let our agents remain in place and organise effective war propaganda. We need to stick to this. Besides, as Heinrich has pointed out, if we send a report to the Supreme Command suggesting that if they don't sort things out the war could be lost, we will either find ourselves not far from the frontline or ...' he paused, shrugged and gave a wry smile, 'missing in action in Berlin!'

'We cannot just ignore the problem. Given the unprecedented scale of the conflict, it is taking our armaments industry time to adjust and produce enough ammunition for the increasing needs at the front. The expansion of armament production is also limited because we do not have the necessary raw materials to make cordite, the vital propellant for bullets and shells. Our factories report that they are particularly short of cotton, camphor, pyrites and saltpetre. On top of that, the situation is made even worse by our lack of rail transport and infrastructure.'

'Walter — ' Bauer tried to cut in.

'No ... listen, Max. Now that we have a stalemate in the trenches with the trench line stretching 475 miles from Nieuport in Belgium to the Swiss border, artillery shells are needed in ever greater quantities. It's the only way for either side to force a breakthrough, but we cannot expand our production at the same rate as the British. Only 8.9 million shells were made this year, whereas the new munitions factories being built will supply the Allies with more than fifty million shells a year. Unless we do something the war is going to be lost, not in the trenches of Flanders but in the factories of Britain.'

'Walter ...' continued Bauer, '... there is nothing we can do.'

The room slipped into silence and people shuffled uncomfortably in their seats waiting for someone to break the spell and respond. After what seemed like an age a clear voice spoke from the back of the room.

'Well perhaps I might have a suggestion.'

The group turned to look at a young man who so far had sat quietly in the corner of the room and said nothing.

His name was also Heinrich … Heinrich Kohlmeir, and he was the only person in the room not in uniform and with no official position. Younger than the others, he was dressed like a tourist in a loose fitting light brown suit over a crisp white shirt. On his feet he wore a pair of well-polished brown brogue shoes. Officially he was a liaison officer in the Abteilung IIIb, but everyone was aware that this meant he worked as a spy wherever it was felt his 'special' skills could be of use to his country.

Kohlmeir had been born in southern Germany, but at the age of five his parents had sold up their failing wood carving business and emigrated to Canada, settling in a small town in French-speaking New Brunswick. There they had changed their name to Colman and purchased a run-down small holding. Despite having no previous experience looking after livestock or crops, they had thrived in their new home and been very happy. However, the rise of anti-German feeling immediately prior to the war had disrupted their idyllic life and persuaded Kohlmeir's father to sell up and bring his family back to Germany, where they had reverted to their original family name and bought a similar small farm in Bavaria. On returning to Germany, Heinrich had been conscripted into the army where the fact that he was fluent in English and French and held a Canadian passport had attracted the attention of the Intelligence Service. Able to move all round Europe as a neutral, 'Ricky' Colman had been able to collect valuable information to support the German war effort.

'What if we could slow down both shell production and the training and movement of troops within the United Kingdom?'

Nicolai moved to an empty seat at the table, sat down and looked directly at the young man. 'And how might we manage to do that?' he asked in a voice that reflected his obvious scepticism.

The younger German stood up, walked to the centre of the room and began to explain.

CHAPTER 3

Carlisle Town Centre

Late Evening, Monday 5th April 1915

He knew as soon as he ran into Dean Tait's Lane that he'd made a mistake. During the day the narrow passage between the historic West Walls and Paternoster Row adjacent to the cathedral was a welcome and busy short cut in and out of the city centre, but at night it was the haunt of muggers and thieves, a place to be avoided. However, having had to deal with a series of break-ins in Finkle Street, Inspector Jack Johnstone of Carlisle City Police was late for a meeting with Chief Constable Eric deSchmid, and his superior was not the kind of man to be kept waiting. Given the lateness of the appointment, the officer was particularly concerned about the reason why he had been asked to meet his senior colleague.

Despite his German sounding surname, deSchmid was Devonian and had moved up from the Exeter Force some two years previously, taking over from his cheerful predecessor

George Hill. Hill had been a 'hands-off' superior equally concerned with the force's 'outside' philanthropic work. His passion had been the police's prize-winning brass band and their concerts had brought in considerable monies for various local charities. He was happy to leave actual 'policing' to his junior colleagues and to tolerate Jack's sometimes unconventional but effective methods. This approach was well received by community groups but less so by the Police Watch Committee to whom he was responsible. Eventually it resulted in an enforced 'retirement' following allegations of inappropriate conduct. His successor was the exact opposite insisting on a more 'professional' approach and quickly upsetting his officers by selling the band's instruments and paying the money raised into the City Treasury rather than the force's widows and orphans fund. A stickler for rules, he appeared to have immediately taken against someone he saw as a maverick. Consequently, keen not to upset his senior officer, Jack had decided to take the shorter, direct route to the West Walls Police Station, up Castle Street and into Paternoster Row, rather than follow the ancient city walls on a long, semi-circular path past the 900-year-old Norman castle with its towering keep and impressive sandstone defences.

As he slowed to a walk, in the otherwise silent space, he was conscious of the 'clacking' sound his leather shoes made on the cobblestones. At night the ginnel was normally bathed in a yellow glow from three streetlights attached to the sandstone wall that separated the shortcut from the cathedral grounds on the south side. There was one at each end of the alleyway and another in the middle, but this evening only the latter gave out any illumination, and as he came to a stop underneath it, he twisted his head to the side to listen for any slight sound.

For moments all was silent, then, ahead of him, a voice came out of the shadows. 'Well, well, well. If it ain't my old friend "Smoking Joe" Johnstone, or, to be respectful, Detective

Inspector Jack Johnstone, the pride of the city police and friend to all and sundry. This is an opportune moment. I've been hoping to bump into you for a little chat.'

Seconds later a figure emerged out of a doorway in the warehouse that formed the north side of the alley. At first Jack could only make out the silhouette of a tall, thin man, his height accentuated by the top hat he wore at a slight angle. He noted that it was one of the shorter, more modern ones that people were now wearing instead of the high stove pipe hats popular ten or fifteen years ago. Never-the-less, it added to the man's stature, which was already significantly greater than Jack's five foot eight inches. As he moved further into the light, the shadowy figure became more distinct. Under the hat Jack could make out a weasel-looking face with a narrow nose and mouth, and two dark, unblinking eyes. He was dressed in a black wrinkled and well-worn suit that looked two sizes too small for him, so much so that you could clearly glimpse his hooped socks between his trouser bottoms and unpolished boots. Across his body he held a narrow walking stick with a silver handle.

'Hello, Dalton, you big streak of misery. I should have thought you would have had enough sense to keep out of my way and lie low after your recent difficulties. It just proves that you're more stupid than I thought.'

'But that's what I wanted to talk to you about, Jack. You've cost me a lot of money, you have, and I think that you owe me some compensation. One way or the other, I need to make sure that you pay it or I'll lose face with all my friends.'

'You mean no one will cough up protection money anymore,' replied Jack. 'I'm really sorry about that.'

'Oh I think you will be, Jack. I think you will be.'

Dowson Dalton had been a small-time crook stealing from those stupid enough to wander into quieter areas of the city at night on their own. The market day and weekend drunks provided him with a reasonable income until, on a visit to Durham to collect his younger brother Damian on his release from prison, he had wandered into a Gilesgate pub to wait for a delayed train. Looking for privacy, they had sat at a table in a quiet corner of the 'snug', a screened-off area attached to the bar. The pair had chosen it because they knew it was likely to be unoccupied and quiet mid-afternoon. It wasn't law, but the reigning social convention was that women didn't drink in the main bar. They were expected to do so in a slightly less conspicuous way, hence many pubs had a 'snug' at the rear of their premises. However, at that time of day they knew it was likely to be empty, and so it proved. So, when two other men had also entered this 'ladies' room', Dalton had looked up in surprise. One was a well-dressed individual of medium build, the other a bruiser with a huge frame, blotchy red face and squashed nose.

When, from behind the serving hatch, the landlord saw them, his face drained of colour and he approached the pair nervously. There was a whispered exchange which Dalton could not hear and then, with unexpected swiftness, the giant leant across, grabbed the barman's shirt and dragged him off his feet and part way through the hatch. 'Mr Hawkswell expects his money on the day agreed,' he growled at the terrified individual, but his partner gently touched his arm, shook his head and gestured towards the two visitors in the corner. Smiling, he spoke cheerfully to Dalton and his brother. 'Just a little misunderstanding, nothing to worry about.' He turned back to the man behind the bar. 'We'll return tomorrow and hopefully you'll be able to help us resolve our disagreement.' Touching his hand to his forehead in a salute, he beckoned to his accomplice, who released his captive, and the pair left.

'What was that about?' asked Damian.

'Protection money,' replied Dalton. 'The landlord must be late with his payment.' He paused as his mind raced and then, with a smile, he said, 'Why didn't I think of that?'

'Think of what?'

Dalton looked at his sibling and shook his head. 'No wonder you got nicked. You've got the brains of a sparrow. Listen ...' And he leant forwards to explain his idea to his younger brother, whose eyes lit up in pleasure.

Back in Carlisle, Dalton had immediately put his plan into action. Together with Patrick O'Malley, an ex-prize fighter from Ireland, he started to visit the public houses in the Caldewgate area of the city to 'negotiate' his fee for ensuring there were no 'disturbances' in their drinking establishments. Landlords not wishing to take up his offer found their hostelry become the subject of an increase in drunkenness and anti-social behaviour from the navvies working at the various new building sites in the area. With relatively high wages and a thirst to quench, they descended on the city each weekend and were happy to take a 'backhander' from Dalton to concentrate their 'social activities' on identified pubs. The result was inevitably broken chairs, tables and other fittings, and the owners found it cheaper to pay for the protection than the repairs. After hearing what had happened, Jack had managed to put a stop to the process by the simple expedient of getting each landlord to take on a temporary 'minder' at a wage less than the cost of the protection money being paid out. By themselves they were unable to prevent any damage, but the nine pubs in Caldewgate were all in close proximity to each other and, when trouble looked to be 'brewing', the minder would slip out and round up the others. Eight would return to the targeted pub to prevent trouble and the ninth would find the duty constable who would also hurry to help. Many navvies, having found themselves barred from every pub in the area, had turned on Dalton as a result of the hassle that supporting his little money-making scheme had caused them.

Jack was well aware that Dalton blamed him for the collapse of his short-lived 'enterprise' and guessed this confrontation was his attempt at retribution. He had no intention of allowing that to happen, but as he thought about how to deal with the situation, he heard a shuffling behind him. Turning to find the cause, he watched as a second man stepped out of the shadows behind him. The figure, who had obviously followed him into the alley from a hiding place on Abbey Street, was the opposite of Dalton. He was closer to Jack's height and wore a short grey jacket with matching waistcoat with a watch in one pocket and the attached chain across his stomach. The outfit was completed by a shirt with a 'wing collar' that stood up stiffly around his neck, baggy dark trousers and a bowler hat pulled down tight to his cauliflower ears. However, what made him stand out was the width of his shoulders. He looked as broad as he was tall, and his arms hung by his side like those of a giant ape.

'Inspector Johnstone, I am not sure that you know my friend and colleague, Patrick O'Malley, from across the Irish Sea. Patrick came across to help me with my little venture and now finds that his journey has unfortunately been wasted and that he is considerably out of pocket. He also felt that he needed to take this issue up with you,' said Dalton.

Jack turned back to Dalton but listened carefully to the man's feet as he approached slowly from behind. He had been a member of Carlisle Constabulary since first joining as a young officer in 1895 and was used to dealing with drunken fights on a Saturday night. Violence was a common event in his weekly life, but it was unusual to be faced with such a direct attack on his person.

Normally Jack wore a baggy, Harris Tweed suit, a gift from his parents on his twenty first birthday nearly twenty years ago. It had been a size too big for him, but his mother had insisted that he had plenty of 'filling out' to come and that eventually he would grow into it. It hadn't happened, and initially Jack had kept it 'for good', but after moving from uniform branch to become a detective he found it a useful item of clothing. He was able to hide the implements of his trade within its ample folds, including a vicious truncheon, slightly shorter than the standard one-foot-long 'Billy Club', which, as a consequence, he was able to keep in the upper left inside pocket of the jacket. The loose clothing meant that it was easy to be misled into thinking that Jack was frailer than he actually was. Under the mis-fitting wardrobe was a well-muscled frame. Jack's passion was Cumberland and Westmorland Wrestling, and for years he had trained regularly after work in the Peter Street Gym until both his technique and body were well-honed for the frequent local competitions.

Jack sensed the 'barn door' immediately behind him and felt a giant hand grab his left shoulder. In a flash he slipped his right hand into his pocket and grasped the truncheon handle. Swinging round in a single movement, he smashed it across the surprised Irishman's head. As O'Malley staggered back, he followed up with a savage kick to the groin and a second blow to the top of the man's head. With a grunt, the Irishman fell to the floor motionless. He turned back towards the slimmer man and took a step forwards, thinking to finish the encounter without further delay but he paused as Dalton unsheathed a rapier-like blade from his walking stick, the street lights glinting off its shiny surface. He slashed out, missing Jack's head by inches, but the swipe caused him to slip on the cobblestones. Jack took the opportunity to land a punch to the head, but his opponent proved surprisingly resilient and failed to go down. 'Not good enough, Jack. You'll need to do a little bit better than that,' he said, rubbing his jaw.

'Is that right, Dalton?' said a new voice from the shadows behind him. Before Dalton could turn, he felt two arms wrap around him in an iron-like grip. The more he struggled, the more the pressure increased. Unable to make use of his weapon, he was dragged sideways by his unknown assailant and his head was slammed against the sandstone wall of the cathedral. He dropped to the floor, unconscious, and his sword stick fell beside him.

Jack smiled. 'Hello Sergeant Gordon. You timed your arrival rather well.'

The man facing him smiled back. 'Aye well it wudna do if one of our officers was harmed during my watch, you know. Bad for the reputation and morale.'

Graham Gordon was the epitome of a regimental sergeant major, which was not surprising because that's what he had been before leaving the army to move back to his border homeland and joining the local police force. A giant of a man, he stood six foot four inches tall and was heavily built, with a handle bar moustache that was a throwback to the Boer War. However, those who made the mistake of thinking he was a lumbering giant quickly realised the error of their ways. Gordon was surprisingly light on his feet and quick with his hands if needed. He had been the undefeated regimental boxing champion throughout his time in the army, having learnt his trade on the rough streets of his home town of Dumfries, where he had run wild until his father packed him off to join the army.

'And why were you so daft as to wander into the ginnel at night on your own and why this wee toe rag was bothering you...? If you don't mind me asking, sir!'

Jack raised his eyebrows and sighed. He then explained why he was rushing and what had happened.

'Aye, well, you better get away then. I'll sort this little rat out and his sleeping friend,' said the sergeant pointing to Dalton's partner, who still lay unconscious on the cobblestones. Jack nodded and thanked him again before setting off towards the police station at a trot.

CHAPTER 4

Carlisle Police Headquarters

Mid-Morning, Tuesday 6th April 1915

Carlisle City Police Station was built into the city's medieval West Walls on two levels with the office space on the upper tier and the custody areas below. When it had opened in 1840 it had been one of the most modern in the country with purpose-built cells and a mortuary. Seventy-five years later the old red sandstone building was cold, damp and cramped for the increasing number of officers based there. It was rumoured that the force was to move into a new base in Rickergate on the north side of the city, but the war had put this, like everything else, on hold.

Having signed over Dalton and O'Malley to the custody officer, Graham Gordon had gone looking for Jack, but the duty officer said that he'd left shortly after the big sergeant had brought in the two bedraggled ruffians. Early the next morning he found him sitting in a leather captain's chair behind a little desk in his tiny office, lighting his pipe. The room, which was not big to start with, looked smaller courtesy of the dark wood panelling and a bookcase along one wall with shelves covered in files and loose papers. Even in daytime the leaded windows let in little light. In a shaded corner lay a large bag in which Jack kept his wrestling clothing. The sport was his passion outside of work. The overall impression was that of a large cluttered cupboard rather than a well-used office.

The sergeant stepped inside, closed the door and sniffed. 'I've always liked the smell of Condor slice. It's a sweet-smelling tobacco, although in this wee space it won't take long for yon pipe to form a lung-bursting cloud of smoke.' And, as if to emphasise the point, he waved his hand across the front of his face and coughed. 'What happened to you last night?'

Jack looked up, took the pipe out of his mouth and held it to the side before speaking. 'The chief sent down a message saying the meeting was postponed. I needn't have hurried after all. How are our two friends?'

'Happily locked up in the first-floor cells, where they will be held until their visit to the magistrates' court later this morning. I'll pop in to give evidence. Depending on who's dealing with it they'll be charged with either common assault or actual bodily harm. Either way they're both looking at twelve months at the very least. Given that they came off worst in the exchanges I doubt the matter will be passed on to the Crown Court.'

Jack nodded, took a long drag on his pipe and exhaled the smoke. 'How did they know?'

'How did who know what?'

'Dalton! How did Dalton and his thug know that I was going to be around Dean Tait's Lane at that exact time?'

The big man shook his head. 'He wouldn't. It was just coincidence. They'll have been waiting in the hope that any unsuspecting fool would cut through from the West Walls to the city. You just happened to be the fool!'

'I'm not sure Graham. My initial impression was that they were waiting for me. He used my name straightaway even though the alley was badly lit.'

'You were under one of the lights – he would see it was you. Anyway, no one else knew you would be in a hurry to get to headquarters and likely to cut through the alley.'

Jack paused, inhaled another lungful of tobacco and then replied, 'That's not quite true. One person knew I would be pushed for time to get to deSchmid's meeting after finishing my shift.'

'Who?'

Jack tapped his pipe out into the glass ashtray on his desk and popped the empty vessel into the top pocket of his jacket before replying. 'Chief Constable deSchmid himself.'

'Are ye mad, lad? Why would deSchmid want to do that?'

'I can think of one or two reasons. He made it clear that he was furious over my actions over the proposed shift changes and I think he would have been happy to have me demoted if he could have got away with it.'

Very soon after his arrival deSchmid had implemented enforced changes to the force's working conditions. The men were informed that they would be required to work 'split' shifts of two sets of four hours rather than an eight-hour continuous duty. The 'station' rose up against the enforced changes and Jack had organised a petition requesting that they be thrown out, but, under advice from the new chief constable, the Watch Committee had refused to entertain it. This left Jack and his superior on less-than-friendly terms.

'Perhaps,' said Gordon, 'but it would be a foolish man who decided to get rid of one of his most effective and well liked detectives over an argument about shift patterns. deSchmid is single-minded, but he's not stupid. If something like that came to light, his career would be finished and it would mean a long stint in the city goal. Even the Watch Committee wouldn't be able to save him.'

Jack shrugged his shoulders unconvinced. 'What if he had a finger in Dalton's little protection racket? It wouldn't be the first time an officer's been on the take, and by all accounts he isn't short of a bob or two. That house of his at the top of Stanwix will be costing a pretty penny. It would be easy to make sure Dalton had information on the foot-patrol routes and timings to ensure that there wasn't a constable anywhere near pubs he was going to target. Neither of them would be happy that I had stopped their money-making scheme. Letting our two thugs know that I would be coming along the West Walls for an evening meeting would have been relatively simple and it might have worked if you hadn't been around.'

'It's a bit of a stretch for the imagination, Jack, and anyway, how would they know you were going to take a short cut through Dean Tait's Lane?'

A knock at the door interrupted their conversation.

'Come in,' said Jack and a young constable poked his head round the door.

'Chief Constable deSchmid would like to see you in his office right away sir.'

Jack nodded and pushed back his chair.

'Well,' said Gordon. 'You might just be about to find out if there's anything in either idea. Let me know how you get on. I'll go and write some notes about yesterday evening's little event to share with the magistrate. Good luck.'

Following the sergeant out of his office, Jack turned right and took the stairs up to deSchmid's room on the second floor. Unlike his own door, the top half of which comprised of glass panels, his superiors was made of solid dark oak with a brass plate inscribed with the words 'Chief Constable' attached to it with matching screws. He gave a loud knock and was immediately rewarded with a loud, 'Enter.'

The room Jack entered was similar in décor to his own but four or five times bigger. To his left there was a large oak table with six chairs around it. To his right was a matching Victorian pedestal desk, behind which sat Eric deSchmid with his back to a large window that overlooked the Sallyport steps onto the West Walls. Jack smiled. The desk was well placed. Every officer had to use the steps to get into the city centre. The chief constable had a perfect view to watch his men and to see if they were late or early to their duties.

'What's so funny, Inspector?' asked deSchmid obviously not amused by Jack's entrance.

Jack stood to attention and replied, 'Nothing, sir. I was just admiring your office.'

deSchmid looked at him with a blank face, not sure if Jack was being sarcastic and disrespectful. He was well aware of the officer's occasionally outspoken views.

'Grab a chair, bring it over here and sit down,' he said in a brisk voice.

Jack did as instructed.

Eric deSchmid was only marginally taller than Jack, but he had a muscular frame and a broad chest. His blue uniform fitted him immaculately and even indoors he always wore his officer's peak cap. At thirty two he was one of the youngest chief constables in the country, but his square jaw, close-cropped dark brown hair, thick moustache and heavy eyebrows above grey-blue eyes made him look much older. He'd been appointed after the unfortunate enforced retirement of his predecessor, George Hill. Hill had been accused of victimisation after the Carlisle Motor Company had been prosecuted for leaving a motor vehicle on the road for longer than was necessary in contravention of the city bylaws. The company had alleged that this had only happened because they had declined to provide him with the free use of a motor car. The company's solicitor, a Mr Couch, had informed the Watch Committee that Hill had said that if he got the car, the prosecution would be dropped. The chief constable had vehemently denied the allegation, but the stress of the enquiry had left him unwell and unfit for duty. He was initially granted leave of absence and ordered complete rest, but it eventually became clear that he would be unable to return to his duties, and the committee had terminated his employment by payment of three months' salary in lieu of notice. It had been a harsh decision on a man who was only forty three years of age but the city council had endorsed the decision without comment and Hill had been removed from office. They had then appointed deSchmid, who came with a reputation for being a strict disciplinarian and a good organiser. At interview the Watch Committee had been impressed by his thorough knowledge of the law and, more importantly, his clear appreciation of the responsibilities of a chief constable.

'I hope you didn't mind that I put back the meeting until today. I thought you might like some time to recover yourself after the evening's little adventure with Dowson Dalton.'

Jack couldn't help but look surprised at deSchmid's comment. Having raced back to the station after the incident on Dean Tait's Lane, he had been waiting in his office for less than half an hour when a young constable had brought a message telling him to go home and that the chief constable would see him the next day.

deSchmid smiled. 'I wouldn't be much of a chief constable if I didn't know what was going on within my force, particularly when I am in the station when two individuals who had assaulted one of my officers are brought in. When I'm here the desk constable is under strict instructions to inform me immediately of any serious incidents and when I'm not he has a log to complete which I look at on arrival.'

Jack nodded in acknowledgement. *Definitely a different breed of fish to George Hill*, he thought.

'It was Dowson Dalton I wanted to talk to you about,' continued deSchmid. 'I was not happy about the way you dealt with his protection racket in Caldewgate. Not happy at all.'

Jack sat stony-faced at his senior's comments. They seemed to reinforce his view that he might indeed have had a finger in that particular pie, but deSchmid's next remark blew that idea out of the water.

'I need to be clear though Jack. It was not what you did, but how you did it. Dealing with Dalton on your own left you a target for the type of revenge attack he attempted tonight. If he had been successful I would have lost one of my most effective officers who, despite unorthodox ways, is fearless in carrying out his duties. "Smoking Joe" has the respect of the criminal element in the city and inspires confidence in his subordinates. Consequently my job is to ensure you don't do something totally stupid and get yourself injured or worse. This would diminish the effectiveness of my force and I don't want – or rather, I won't have – that. You should have cleared what you were going to do with me and we could have arranged a way to ensure that your plan was put into place without you being seen as the sole instigator. Am I making myself clear here, Inspector?'

Jack paused for a moment totally taken aback by deSchmid's comments. 'Ermm, yes, sir,' he finally replied.

'Good. I'm glad we see eye to eye. Now, I also need to offer you an apology, as I may have inadvertently been indirectly responsible for yesterday's attack.'

By this time his chief's comments had left Jack totally speechless and he just looked across the large desk, waiting for the next bombshell.

'You will recall that last November PC 43 Robert Brown was disciplined for being drunk on duty, assaulting a soldier and for punching his sergeant, PC Bone, in the face. He was reduced from first to third class constable with a reduction in pay and I cautioned him as to his future conduct.'

'Yes. It was me who pulled him off Bone and locked him in the cells to sober up.'

'Precisely. Well, yesterday lunchtime he was seen coming out of the Three Crowns Hotel in English Street in an unsteady state after his split shift break and I had cause to caution him again and fine him five shillings before sending him home. Unfortunately, before I dealt with him, I told the constable who escorted him to my office to get a message to you that I wanted to see you urgently when you had finished at Finkle Street. Obviously Brown overheard and it would seem he is not a man to forget a grudge. After leaving me, he went straight back to the Three Crowns and was seen through a window by PC Cranston chatting to our two friends. Cranston reported it to the desk constable when he came off duty who ...'

'Reported it to you,' finished Jack.

'Correct. But it wasn't until Sergeant Gordon brought in Dalton and O'Malley that we put two and two together. I intend to talk to all three miscreants tomorrow.'

'So that's how they knew I would be in a hurry and likely to cut through the ginnel. Never mind.' Jack smiled. 'No harm done. In fact, it proved a good opportunity to show the pair of them the full force of the law in its literal sense, although I doubt it will have knocked any "sense" into them.'

deSchmid's face took on a serious look as he said, 'Mmmm. You are aware Inspector, that I could never condone police brutality in any shape or form for any reason.'

'Of course not, sir.'

'Good. In that case you're dismissed.'

Jack stood to attention, turned smartly and quickly left. Outside the chief constable's room, he paused and permitted himself a wry smile and shake of the head before heading back to his own office.

CHAPTER 5

Tanyard Bay Near Parton in Cumberland

11.30pm, Sunday 11th April 1915

Heinrich looked down at the oily black water as it lapped against the grey hull of submarine *U24*. Through the darkness to his left he could just make out two young seamen holding onto the ropes of a small dinghy to prevent it being swept away. Looking out towards where land should be he could see the odd light twinkling in the distance but otherwise the overcast conditions meant it was almost impossible to separate the sea, land and sky.

Already he was beginning to regret his suggestion to the Intelligence Committee on the rainy day back in March. Dropping agents into mainland Britain with a view to sabotaging not only the existing or newly planned shell-producing sites but also the rail network had seemed like a good idea. The committee had agreed and decided on a trial run targeting the new munitions development in the remote border land rather than established places, like Coventry and Scotstoun near Glasgow, where they felt security would be much tighter. The west coast main railway line also ran through this area and was one of the routes enabling the Allies to bring both munitions and thousands of newly trained recruits down to the south coast, where they could quickly be moved across the English Channel. Destroying part of this line would have a catastrophic effect on Allied reinforcements to the front line, even though it might be short-lived. At the time he had felt honour-bound to volunteer for what had seemed to be a straightforward, albeit risky, solution to the armaments problem which, because of its audacity and multiple targets, held a significant chance of achieving at least partial, if not total, success. Now, facing the first of the many risks, the opposite seemed to be the case. A night-time drop on the west Cumberland coast had brought few concerns in the warm office at the Abteilung IIIb, but now even this first step seemed fraught with difficulties. The rubber dinghy was tiny and even in spring the ocean could be rough where the Solway Firth met the Irish Sea. Constantly changing winds and tidal conditions made it a dangerous seaway. He sighed and reassured himself that if he pulled it off he would probably be given a medal for propaganda purposes and, more importantly, gain a promotion allowing him to name his next posting.

Kapitänleutnant Rudolf Schneider looked down from the conning tower with growing impatience. He had made it abundantly clear that he was not happy manoeuvring his boat in these waters at night. Only a direct order from Admiral Alfred von Tirpitz, Secretary of State of the German Imperial Naval Office, had ensured that he complied with the requirements of the Intelligence Committee. He was not aware of Heinrich's mission, only that he was to be dropped off in secret and recovered several weeks later on 16th August. The date had been specified by Colonel Walter Nicolai of the Abteilung IIIb, who wanted his man back in Berlin to report to the High Command before autumn set in. It would involve an early-morning small boat pick-up since it was unlikely that either the submarine or agent would be able to find each other at night even if they were returning to the same general area as the drop-off. Schneider was to be on station between dawn and sunrise and look for Kohlmeir's signal. He'd also been told that once the pick-up was complete, or if he failed to show by the designated time, the need for secrecy would have passed and before leaving the area he should take the opportunity to shell the local chemical works where benzene and toluene were being extracted from coal. These were crucial ingredients in the production of TNT for use in the making of shells for the Allied war effort. However, at this moment all he wanted was to get rid of the 'intelligence officer' so that he could turn his boat round and head out into the safety of the Irish Sea.

'If you are ready perhaps you could get moving,' he shouted to Heinrich. 'Dietmar, get in the dinghy.'

One of the sailors stepped cautiously down to the tossing boat whilst the other tried to hold it steady against the submarine's hull. Heinrich had been holding on to the conning tower ladder with one hand but now he wrapped his arm and elbow around one of the uprights so that he could use both hands to carry out a final check of the canvas kitbag in which he carried the items he hoped would enable him to carry out his forthcoming challenge. Inside the bag were three smaller waterproof ersatz rubber sacks. In one were the papers to enable him to move freely around the countryside and a wedge of cash in various denominations. Although they were imperfect forgeries, including a new Canadian passport in the anglicised name of Richard Colman, he hoped that, being in the north of England and well away from the theatre of war, they would not be scrutinised too carefully. In the second was a change of clothes. His dark submarine jumper and trousers would be fine for general day wear, but he expected that there would be times when he might need something smarter. In the final sack was his fighting knife, a Luger P08 semi-automatic pistol with spare ammunition and a survival kit that included a torch, matches, a Morse code book, a metal water bottle and a lightweight canvas shelter. He reached in and felt the knife. It was American, obtained on his last visit to the States, and the built-in guard for individual fingers provided a much securer grip during a fight than the smooth-handled German version. It was kept in a leather holster that protected the blade and had a top loop that allowed it to be slid onto his belt. He hoped that he would have little need for either of his weapons.

He tightened the cord of the canvas bag and slung it over his right shoulder. When he reached land, he hoped it and the worn-out duffle coat he wore, would add to his disguise as a sailor who, having failed to find a berth on the fishing boats still plying their trade in the North Sea out of nearby Whitehaven Harbour, was now travelling to the nearby city of Carlisle to find work. He moved gingerly across the slippery submarine deck and stepped down into the dinghy. The waves that had seemed gentle ripples against the massive hull of the U-boat now seemed enormous and crashed over the bows of the tiny vessel soaking the coarse, thick, woollen material of his navy coat. He moved to the rear of the boat and sat on the wet floor before nodding at his companion, who took hold of two short oars and pulled in the general direction of the shore. In minutes the outline of the submarine was lost to view and both men were lost in the darkness of the ocean.

Heinrich looked at his companion, who was rowing with his back to the shore. The young sailor's face was ashen and he was clearly petrified of the situation he found himself in. In his right hand, as well as an oar, he gripped a chord which was attached to a canvas bag on his lap in which there was a compass, a map and a compact battery-operated spotlight. These were crucial to enable him to return to the submarine. Having dropped off Heinrich at the western-most point of the headland, he was to row back out to sea on a due west course and, after clearing the coastal breakers, switch his powerful spotlight on moving it in a semi-circular arc pointing out to sea. The submarine would stand off the headland and look for the signal before coming in to pick him up. It wasn't the greatest of arrangements, and the submarine's captain was concerned that if they missed each other, his crewman could be picked up by an Allied ship the following morning, leading to all kinds of awkward questions that might blow a hole in the clandestine mission bringing British warships searching for him in the narrow channel between Ireland and England. However, as a daytime drop was out of the question, it was the best they could come up with, although the idea sounded better in the warmth of Schneider's small cabin than the current reality.

The dinghy bobbed up and down over the waves as it made its way slowly towards the shore. As they got closer to their landing spot, more and more lights could be seen far to the south-east. *That must be the port of Whitehaven,* thought Heinrich. Unfortunately, as the waves rolled in towards the distant beach, the sea got much rougher. As one particularly large breaker hit them, the rear of the boat was lifted up and the front dropped into the trough of the wave in front. Heinrich watched in horror as the seaman fell backwards off his seat into the bottom of the dinghy. As he did so he jerked the chord he had been holding and the bag, to which it was attached, flew into the air and over the side into the sea. The young man panicked and as he clambered up after it, he slipped on the wet boards and followed the bag into the foaming waters. Heinrich jumped up and focused on where he thought the body had gone under, but without anyone at the oars the boat was spinning out of control and he was not sure if he was looking in the right place. He turned slowly round, hoping to see some movement, and eventually made out a dark shape in the water to his right. He grabbed the oars, intending to pull the boat over to it, but even as he did so the young sailor disappeared, weighed down by his heavy clothing and lack of a life jacket. The latter had been discarded to make it easier to row. He continued to watch as two arms reached up out of the sea and thrashed about in a final effort to stop their owner being dragged down to the depths before they slipped slowly under the surface, never to return.

Heinrich paused for a moment shocked at what he had just seen, then, as the dinghy lifted with another large wave, he grabbed the loose oars and manoeuvred himself onto the rowing seat. Despite the cold and the wet, he realised he was sweating. He settled and, after a couple of 'air' strokes, set into a steady rowing rhythm towards the shore. As the boat neared the beach the breakers grew even bigger and threatened to swamp the little vessel. With little alternative, he pulled even harder, wanting to be through the rough waters as quickly as possible. For what seemed like an age the foaming waters surged around him and then, with a startling suddenness, they subsided, and he found himself in the calm shallows at the edge of a narrow shingle beach which stretched north and south as far as he could see. A few metres inland, it gave way to a rocky shoreline, above which dark cliffs rose towards the overcast sky.

Aware that the water would be freezing cold, he used one of the oars to push the boat up the uneven shallows as far as he could get it. When it would go no further he jumped out, grabbed the front and, pulling it behind him, splashed inland until he reached a dry part of the beach. He stood shaking and wondered if this was caused by the cold or fear. Dietmar's drowning created several problems. First, he needed to try and let the submarine know what had happened or at least that he was alive. If no one returned it would be reasonable for Schneider to assume that both were drowned or captured. Either way it would relieve him of his duty to return to the area to pick him up. Given his reluctance to be involved in the first place it wouldn't take a lot to dissuade the skipper. His second problem was what to do with the dinghy. He might need it as an emergency back-up if there was a problem sending something out from the submarine on his return, so destroying it or simply setting it adrift weren't options. In either case, any one finding it would recognise the German markings and start asking questions. He needed to find a safe place to hide it away, but, looking around at the empty beach, there were no realistic options. Burying it was the obvious solution, but he wasn't sure he would be able to dig a trench deep enough, and without this a high tide might simply wash away the stones and carry it out to sea.

One thing at a time, he thought. He needed to send a signal before the submarine submerged and left the area. Opening his kitbag, he pulled out the sack containing his torch and signal code book. Flashing a message out to sea brought with it its own risks. The area between Ireland, England and Scotland was busy with marine traffic and there was a real risk that an Allied boat might see it. Dietmar's permanent signal would probably have been taken to be just another boat bobbing in the offshore waters and ignored, but, in a time of war, a series of flashes of different lengths would certainly not be, even this far north. Deciding he needed a high spot to send a message from, he walked up the beach, crossed the railway line that ran along the rocky base of the cliff, dropped his kitbag and scrambled up the cliffside to a point where he thought a signal might be seen from. Using his Morse code book, Heinrich flashed a message that he hoped would be understood despite its simplicity:

'Dietmar drowned. Am OK. Mission proceeding. Pick up dawn 16th. Will signal. HK.'

He stared out to sea trying to spot a reply, but there was nothing. After waiting a few minutes, he signalled again with a similar result. He sighed and a feeling of extreme loneliness descended on him. He wished he could simply grab the dinghy and row back out to the submarine. For a moment he thought it might be a possibility. It would be doubtful if anyone would criticise him after what had happened, particularly if he said that he'd been seen signalling and had used the boat to escape capture. Then reality sunk in. The submarine would be long gone by the time he got back onto the water, and even if it hadn't, they would be unlikely to respond to any signal light at sea after he had signalled that he was OK and going ahead with his mission. He needed to get moving; the dark sky was already getting brighter and with it a light rain began to fall. Dawn wasn't too far away and he didn't want to be messing about on the beach in daylight.

He moved to clamber down, and as he did so he noticed the shadowy outline of a small building on the side of the railway line some distance to the south. Once back down beside the track, he left his bag and jogged towards the outline. Running on the loose stones on which the rails were laid, it seemed to take an age to reach his objective, which proved to be a single-storey, small rectangular brick building, not much bigger than one of his father's storage sheds. It had a rusty corrugated roof, a window on each of the longer sides and a door on one of the others. The windows were painted white, so Heinrich could not see what was inside. The green door was locked shut, but the wood around the frame was rotten and splintered when Heinrich pushed against it hard with his shoulder. The inside was empty, except for an ancient-looking barrow with a broken wheel, a filthy canvas sheet and a large leather bag that contained a few dusty tools. He recognised one or two: a shunting pole, brake stick, pinch bar, pick, sledge hammer and two spades. It was clear from the state of both the building and the tools that neither had been used for some time, and as he stood looking at them, it dawned on him that this might be a possible hiding place.

He jogged back to where he had left his bag, picked it up and walked down to the dinghy. Pushing it back into the water so that it just floated, he set off, pulling it through the shallows towards the shed. When he was opposite his objective, he left the oars and his bag on the shingle, and dragged the boat across the beach and over the railway lines before tilting it on its side and pulling it into its hideaway. Getting through the door was a tight squeeze, and more of the rotten frame splintered, but in the end he managed. He wrapped the canvas sheet around it as best he could and then propped it up against one of the longer walls. Anyone entering the shed would soon see what was underneath, but someone looking through one of the many gaps in the door frame or areas where the paint had peeled off the windows might simply wonder what was under the covers.

By the end of his exertions he was breathing heavily, and his hands, face and coat were covered with dust. He walked down to the water's edge and washed. He then took his duffle off, shook it and, using his damp hands, brushed it as best he could. Putting the coat back on, he retrieved his kit bag and the oars before going back to the shed and pushing the latter under the canvas with the dinghy. Finally, he placed a thin piece of wood on the floor below the door and carefully pulled the door closed over it so that it jammed shut. He was aware that it would not deter someone determined to get into the shed, but he hoped that to anyone on a passing train the building would still appear to be locked. The drag marks on the sand and shingle would be washed away by the next high tide. Happy that it was the best he could manage in the circumstances, he turned and set off along the tracks in the direction of the coastal town of Whitehaven. If asked, his cover was to be that of a sailor fresh off one of the boats that arrived regularly to the thriving port.

*

Less than an hour later, Heinrich clambered up the north harbour wall, a great concrete barrier that circled a protective arm around the busy anchorage and sheltered it from the pounding of the sea. As he stepped onto its flat concourse, the rain passed and the morning brightened from the west. Fluffy white clouds were dotted against a clearing blue sky and his spirits lifted. Even the usually grey sea took on a bluish tint. There was a cool onshore wind, but Heinrich knew that as the day warmed up this would soon disappear. He walked along the wall towards the town and turned right, aiming for a vacant seat on the quayside. Leaning his kitbag against the end of a rusty metal bench, he sat down and stared out across the inner harbour to the sea beyond. He noticed the way the sun shimmered on the water's ripples and how the colour changed with the passing of the clouds above. At times the reflecting light off the water was almost blinding to look at, and for the first time in twenty-four hours, he closed his eyes and relaxed.

'Ist thoo alreet, marra?'

Heinrich started and for a second wondered where he was. As his thoughts cleared, he realised that he must have fallen asleep. Above him the sky was blacked out by a dark shadow that proved to be of a middle-aged man who spoke again in an accented voice.

'Ah sed, ist thoo alreet, marra?'

Coming to his senses, Heinrich sat up, holding his hand over his eyes to block out the sun and enable him to see who was speaking. Standing in front of him was a seaman of similar build and dress to himself. In fact, even his features were similar to his own, except that this individual looked about ten years older and his wool jacket and trousers were well worn.

'I ... I, mmm, I am sorry, I only speak English or a little French,' he eventually replied.

The stranger looked at him for a moment before his face broke into a broad smile and in a slower, clearer and much more understandable voice, he said, 'That was English, my colonial friend but perhaps not as you know it!'

'Pardon me!' Heinrich shook his head, baffled.

'It's dialect, matey. Good west Cumberland dialect as spoken by the proud people of Whitehaven and beyond, and by my own good self, although I'll be a bit more moderate for someone from across the pond... Samuel Armstrong, or Sam to my friends.' He stuck out his hand towards Heinrich who, after a second, took it, and the pair shook.

'Ricky ... Ricky Colman,' said Heinrich.

'What's a yank doing on Whitehaven Quayside, then?' asked Sam.

'I'm Canadian, actually, from New Brunswick, a coastal area on the eastern seaboard. Have you heard of it?'

'I'm a fisherman, lad. Which fisherman worth his salt wouldn't have heard of a place that builds some of the hardiest fishing boats in the world? How the hell did you end up in 'haven?'

'I was working on one of the few neutral merchant ships that crossed the Atlantic between America and Ireland. I thought it was an easy ticket, what with the States and the Shamrocks not being involved in the war, but the sinking of the *Lusitania* off the Irish coast last week changed all that. Nobody wants to risk another submarine attack. So I jumped ship at Queenstown, caught a lift on a fishing boat up to the Isle of Man and then on a coal boat to here. They dropped me off Friday gone and I've been sleeping in one of the quayside lodging houses over the weekend. I'd hoped to find some temporary work to build up my dwindling funds but nothing seems to be moving. Today I'm thinking I need to move on and look elsewhere, but it's as quiet as the grave.'

The lie came easily and he knew that the trawler man was hardly likely to check his story about arriving on Friday.

'Nay. You'll not find anything here, lad, at least not for a while yet,' said Sam shaking his head, his face turned grim.

'Why, what's happened?' asked Heinrich wondering if he was about to encounter an early problem to his plans.

Sam sat down next to him and launched into a tale that even Heinrich found shocking. All of the boats engaged in herring fishing out of Whitehaven had gone out as usual between 8.00 and 9.00pm the evening before last. They had headed north to drop their nets off the Mull of Galloway in South West Scotland. Just before midnight a tremendous squall caught them on the open ocean and the sea rose to a great height. Many of the late arrivals had not cast their nets and at once they headed for the nearest safe harbours along the Scottish coast. However, those that had cast them were in serious trouble and found it almost impossible to haul them in again. To avoid being dragged over, their only option was to cut them loose and in doing so many skippers had lost them, trading life over livelihood. However, for whatever the reason, the boat belonging to a man called John Crofts and his young crewman named Cassidy had failed to release their net and capsized. Both men had clung to the up-turned hull as long as they could, but eventually the cold had got to Cassidy and, unable to hold on any longer, he had been washed away by the stormy waters. At about 3.00am, as the squall abated and the sea had calmed down, Crofts was observed, still holding on to the boat, by a fisherman looking out across Luce Bay from his boat, the *Raven*, which had sheltered in the harbour at Drummore. He immediately roused the crew and they had rescued the exhausted man, who was delirious and clearly close to death. Later that day a dog walker had found the body of Cassidy washed up on the pebbly shore of Cairngarroch Bay, a mile to the south of the village. The local crown agent had been called and only late in the day, having spoken to Crofts and various other witnesses, allowed the *Raven* to set off back to Whitehaven with the body. They had arrived earlier that morning. Sam had been the rescue fishing boat's first mate.

'None of the boats will be going out until after the funeral in a week or so.'

Heinrich gave an involuntary shiver, which Sam mistakenly took as shock at the tragic events whereas in reality the German was reflecting on what could have happened had he tried to disembark from *U24* in the teeth of the storm. Given the events of the previous evening, he was under no illusion about what the outcome would have been.

'Your best bet is to take the train through to Carlisle and look for summat there. There's a big new munitions factory being built nearby and there's bound to be opportunities for labouring. It's supposed to be a secret, but they've recruited foremen to oversee the bringing in of navvies from Ireland. They'll do most of the labouring. Some come through here. After a few pints at the weekend, tongues soon wag. On top of that, more frequent troop trains mean the rail companies are also taking on more workers. C'mon, I have to catch the train home to Maryport, so I'll walk with you to the station.'

He picked up Heinrich's kitbag and threw it to him before turning and heading towards the town centre. The big German smiled: the suggestion to seek work in the munitions factory or on the railway fit his plans perfectly and added to his credibility should he be questioned at a later date. If that happened, he could confidently tell those concerned that the idea came from his new acquaintance Sam, who, if asked, would confirm this was the case.

CHAPTER 6

Carlisle Citadel Railway Station

Mid-Afternoon, Monday 12th April 1915

The railway journey from Whitehaven to Carlisle had been relatively uneventful. Heinrich had been nervous of checks on his papers at the railway station due to the war-time regulations. The Defence of the Realm Act had introduced curfews, censorship and, more importantly for his mission, severe restrictions on movement. In addition, the Aliens Restriction Act severely curtailed the civil liberties of non-British-born subjects, even naturalised citizens who had resided in the UK for decades. They were required to register, obtain permits if they intended to travel more than five miles, and were prohibited from entering certain areas. Virtually anyone could now be arrested for the slightest suspicion.

However, his worries came to nothing. He and Sam Armstrong had walked up the steep hill that was North Shore Road to the station, chatting cheerfully about the impact of war in the remote west Cumberland town before arriving at the ticket booth together. Heinrich learnt that although people were aware of the new restrictions, they had little impact on the day-to-day lives of the locals who saw the fighting as being in another far away world. They either ignored them or, as Sam put it, 'simply paid lip service' to them. 'Spy fever' hadn't really reached that far north. The main impact was on the increasing number of young men who were disappearing off to war. Children woke to find that their fathers had left for distant battlefields while they slept. As a result, women were taking over their jobs, although, as his new friend explained, this often did not go down well with some members of the community. They encountered hostility from many of the older men who still remained and were worried about competition and the upskilling of a female workforce that was paid around half their wage. Sam said that almost half the workforce in the nearby chemical works was now made up of young women.

'Cheap, y'see. A typical wage for male workers is about fifteen shillings a week, but women and children are paid much less. Women earn around seven shillings and kids even less, maybe three. So employers prefer to employ women and children. No wonder the blokes are angry.'

The ticket booth was in a small waiting room in which half a dozen people sat on the low, wooden benches along the sides of each wall. There was a gap for the entrance door, another for a door immediately opposite, leading onto the single platform, and finally one for a small window, above which a sign said 'Tickets'.

Sam banged on the window and shouted, 'Jacob, are you there? Jacob Bradshaw. Come on, you lazy good-for-nothing. Open up. Some of us want to get home today, not after the war has ended.'

Nothing happened for a movement and then the sliding window was pushed up and clipped open to reveal an aged, grey-haired man with long sideburns and a thick moustache. He wore a black waistcoat with silver buttons over a white collarless shirt, and as he spoke his face broke into a huge grin.

'Sam. How are you? I wasn't expecting you back for another day.' His smiling face then changed to a grimace and his manner took on a serious tone. 'I heard about Johnnie Croft's boat. Tragic. Tragic. They say he didn't cut his nets in the storm. Is that true? What was he thinking of?'

'Aye, he didn't release them. He was probably worrying about the cost of replacements, but in the end not cutting the cables cost him even more dearly. Young Cassidy's family will be fair grieving in the days ahead and sorely troubled when things settle down. He was the only breadwinner in the family. Croft won't be much better off. His boat wasn't insured so he's lost everything although at least he's alive.'

Bradshaw nodded and for a moment both men paused before he said in a more cheerful voice, 'And who might your friend be? He looks too well fed to have been working on your boat or, at least if he has, he brought his own victuals.'

Sam laughed. 'This is Ricky Colman. He was a Manx merchant man but signed off and came across on one of the coal shuttles to see if there was work on the mainland. There's nowt on so I suggested he go through to Carlisle to see if he can get something there. Best chance might be the munitions factory or railway, unless he wants to join the merry band of souls joining up.'

Heinrich listened, inwardly delighted, to Sam's shortened explanation. Unwittingly, it gave the impression that he had been a full-time merchant seaman which, because they were a protected occupation, would explain why he hadn't signed up to fight.

The railway man nodded and reached across the counter to shake Heinrich's hand. 'Pleased to meet you. Jacob Bradshaw.

Stationmaster, ticket seller, platform guard and general 'dogs body' while everyone's away to war. You'll be wanting a single to Carlisle, then.'

Heinrich smiled. 'I guess so.'

Having obtained a ticket and boarded the train without fuss, Heinrich was able to relax and enjoy the journey from Whitehaven to Carlisle. They found an empty compartment and, despite the hard, unpadded seats, within minutes of the train moving off Sam fell asleep. The warm sunshine streaming through the windows and his exertions of the previous few days took their toll on his weary body. The train travelled slowly and Heinrich forgot his worries as it passed through some of the most beautiful scenery he had ever seen. On his left a shimmering sea stretched to the distant hills of what he assumed was Scotland. To the right, a green swathe of fields and hedgerows extended to another set of much higher mountains, covered in what seemed to be a purple blanket.

It reminded him of long, sunny days spent walking in the New Brunswick countryside with his father. Not a man to show his emotions, his father rarely spent any significant time with his sons, leaving their upbringing mainly in the hands of their mother, so these were rare excursions, but Heinrich had relished them. His father was a keen naturalist and Heinrich loved to listen to him talk about the flora and fauna found in the woods and fields around his home. He vividly remembered one late July day when the sky was a cloudless blue and the heat made the air hazy. He had been about eight years old and after lunch, instead of returning to his work, his father had said, 'Come on,' and, grabbing the walking stick he always carried on these trips, he headed out the front door. His brother, who was nursing a swollen ankle, courtesy of tripping down the porch steps the day before, stayed with his mother to clear up, but Heinrich had paused for a second and then ran after him. Together they had walked across a flower-filled meadow thronged with bees and butterflies, through Parson's Wood and up onto Rowley Peak, a hill rather than a mountain, but the highest point in the area. Above them swallows raced back and forth, chasing the summer insect bounty. As they reached the top, they had heard the mewing call of a buzzard and, looking up, seen a male and female pair soaring above them. His father had stopped and lay down on the short summit grass with his hands behind his head and stared at them. Heinrich copied him and together they watched the birds as they glided on the warm air currents, wings held in a shallow 'V' and tails fanned. Both had dark wing tips and a finely barred tails but one, the smaller bird, was dark brown with areas of white underparts whilst the other was much paler all over. His father had said that this meant that the latter was a young female while the other was an older male. They had watched while the pair had ridden the thermals until they became just dots in the sky above them. Heinrich had not wanted the moment to end, but eventually the birds had drifted away to the north and his father had sat up and said, 'Well, this won't get the work done. Let's go, boy.' And, jumping up, he had set off back down the hill.

The train slipped past settlements in Parton, Harrington and Workington before arriving at Sam's stop in Maryport. Had Heinrich not been with him he would have slept through it, but the German had given him a nudge when the carriage stopped next to the station sign and Sam had jumped up and crashed out the door onto the platform, swearing profusely about the effects of growing older and muttering frantic goodbyes. Forty minutes later, having stopped at Aspatria, Wigton and Dalston, three more small settlements, the train shuddered to a final halt and Heinrich stepped out onto the west platform of Carlisle's Citadel Railway Station. This last part of the journey had been of interest to Heinrich for reasons other than the scenery. At regular points along the journey, the line split into two and looped off towards small grey hills of what looked like waste rock and mud. He had seen similar features in the industrial heartland of Germany and recognised them as the man-made mounds formed from the waste material or slag that was a by-product of coal mining. He made a mental note of the locations on the outside chance that this could be useful in the future.

Arriving in Carlisle late in the afternoon, Heinrich was taken aback by the grandeur of the station, which reminded him of a giant greenhouse. Under a glazed roof, supported on a series of hooped trusses, a central footbridge of crossed girders linked the island platform on which he stood with the main platform on the other side. The platform buildings were two storeys high, made of sandstone with windows in a mock-Tudor style and served a range of purposes, including offices, a large waiting area and a refreshment room. *Not bad*, he thought, *for a city in a far flung and isolated corner of the country.* Crossing the bridge, he exited the station through an entrance hall built under an octagonal clock tower and stopped to consider the bustling scene and bright sunshine that greeted him.

Both cars and horse-drawn carriages jostled to drop people off or pick them up from the open area in front of the station. Even this far north the signs of war were evident. Young soldiers in uniform kissed tearful sweethearts or hugged anxious-looking parents. On the far side of this open area a newspaper seller plied his trade from a small stall next to the entrance signpost for underground toilets. Beyond these and to his right people hurried in and out of shops along an elegant crescent-shaped street. To his left two immense and impressive crenulated red sandstone towers, which he guessed were at least sixty feet tall, dominated the southern entrance to the city and from each medieval walls disappeared off to the west or east. In front of them, small but beautifully looked after formal gardens were separated from the busy road by shiny black wrought-iron railings. It was a majestic sight and for a moment he simply stood and admired the view. Then, settling his bag more comfortably over his shoulder, he set off at a brisk pace along the footpath beside a narrow, cobbled road that followed the high wall separating the north-bound railway track from the city itself.

He did not have a map. It was thought this might look suspicious if a travelling itinerant was stopped, questioned and found to have one in his possession. However, he had memorised the route Sam had explained would take him to Caldewgate, an area to the north-west of the city, where there was a chance of finding a room for the night in one of the local inns. It was possible, Sam thought, that one of the other residents or an evening drinker might also be able to give him some information about work opportunities.

The road dipped down a hill and disappeared round a gentle curve. As he followed it, the city wall to his right and an equally high wall separating him from the railway tracks closed in around him, creating the impression that he was walking down a narrow gorge. The temperature dropped as he moved out of the sunshine into the shadow created by the two high structures, and he gave an involuntary shiver and wondered if this was due to the cold or his taught nerves. There were fewer people about here, which made him feel a little more confident, but ahead he could see a cluster of men congregating around what looked like dark patches in the railway wall. As he got closer he realised that they were a series of giant arches which ran under the railway line to a road on the other side of the tracks that ran parallel to the one he followed. The group was made up of about half a dozen individuals who were standing in a circle around a small, open fire on which a pot boiled. Some of the men were smoking, while others were drinking from metal cups, rather like the one he had been given with his military kit when he had joined the army. They were all shabbily dressed in baggy trousers, loose jackets, collar-less shirts and heavy boots. A couple wore cloth caps. Most had long, greasy hair with bushy sideburns and none had a moustache. It was an appearance that was in sharp contrast to the shorter, well-trimmed style preferred by most of the Englishmen he had observed since coming ashore. Behind them he could see other groups of men scattered around. Some were also standing, others sat on wooden crates and one or two were lying down in rough shelters made from cardboard boxes. They chatted, they drank, some from bottles of beer or spirits, or they slept. Heinrich recognised a 'doss' when he saw it. The arches were being used as free shelter by the homeless or tramps. He also knew that these were places to avoid. His path was on the opposite side of the road to the men, so he pulled up his collar, put his head down and increased his stride to a brisk pace, intending to pass by as quickly as possible. However, as he approached the gathering, three men detached themselves from the group, crossed the road and stood in front of him.

The tallest of the three spoke first. 'A few pence for food and drink, mate.'

Heinrich smiled. 'Sorry, lads, I have no change.' And he stepped to his left onto the road and made to walk round them. However, with surprising nimbleness, the leader skipped back and to his side to block the German's progress. The other two adjusted their positions on either side of him.

'That wasn't a request, mate,' he snarled. 'Just give us anything of value and you can be on your way unharmed.'

Heinrich looked at him. He was about the same height as himself but much older with a body that had gone to seed and a large belly held in his trousers by a rope belt. He was clearly out of condition and someone who could pose an initial threat but, if the first few punches didn't win him any fight, would struggle.

The other two were smaller, very thin and if they hadn't been wearing slightly different-coloured jackets would have been difficult to tell apart. Heinrich wondered if they might be twins or at the very least brothers. He had no doubt that he could deal with all three men if necessary; his Luger was still packed in his kitbag, but he had taken his knife out and slipped it onto his belt after Sam had left the train at Maryport. He could feel it on his left hip, hidden from sight beneath his duffle. Holding the other's stare, he put his kitbag down, unfastened the middle button of his coat with his left hand and slipped his right hand through the gap to grasp the knife handle. He was just about to pull it out when all three men moved their heads to one side and stared past him. They then looked at each other, turned, walked away without a word and rejoined their circle of friends. Heinrich released the grip on the knife handle, rebuttoned his coat and twisted his head to look back for a reason to explain the men's behaviour. Walking very slowly down the path about a hundred yards behind him was a policeman, but this was no ordinary officer. He was a giant of a man and his size was further exaggerated by the tall helmet he wore on his head. As he came closer, Heinrich could see sergeant's stripes on the man's arm and a black baton that was being swung in slow, graceful circles as he strolled along.

Heinrich had no wish to talk to anyone until he had a got a feel for the lie of the land, least of all a policeman, so he picked up his kitbag, slung it over his shoulder again and started to walk away.

'Wait!' came a booming voice that halted him in his tracks. 'I said wait a moment, sir, if you please.'

Heinrich dropped the kitbag and unbuttoned his coat again, then turned slowly round. He waited until the giant was standing in front of him and then asked, 'Officer! Is there a problem? Something I can help you with?'

'I rather think those questions are for you to answer, sir.'

Heinrich smiled and replied, 'No. I'm fine, thanks. No problems. I just stopped to ask those gentlemen directions and they were most helpful, so I'll be on my way.' He half turned to go but was stopped by another question.

'And where might you be on your way to, sir, might I ask?'

Heinrich could feel his heart start to beat more rapidly and, as he began his well-rehearsed explanation of who he was and what he was doing, he worried that his face might redden or voice falter, giving him away. Explanation finished, he slipped his hand through the opening in his duffle coat but instead of reaching for his knife he pulled out the forged papers and offered them to the officer.

For a moment the big policeman just stood there, looking at him and then slowly he shook his head and said, 'That won't be necessary, sir. If you are going up to the railway marshalling area they'll be thoroughly checked before they let you onto the site. Same with the munitions factory, if they've got anything.' He paused for a moment before continuing, 'I'm not clear, though, why you're walking down here, it's the wrong direction for the yard and Gretna's a good eight miles away. It'll be dark by the time you get to there and it would have been quicker to catch the train or bus.'

'Sorry, I've not made myself clear. I'm not going straight to either place. My friend Sam Armstrong from Maryport whose boat I was on said to look for lodgings on the edge of the city tonight and set off early in the morning. He suggested I try an inn in Caldewgate and I thought this was the way to get there.'

For the first time the policeman smiled. 'Aye, well. I'd probably do the same although you'll be hard pressed to find anywhere within the city. The pubs will be full with any labourers who haven't gone off to war. Everyone's hoping to cash in on the shortages created by the fact that most of our young men have joined up. Not everyone is happy employing women to replace them. It seems that every man for miles around who's not fit for service but fit to work is looking for employment, either on the railways or munitions building site, and they all need somewhere to stay. Your best bet will be the Globe Inn just over the bridge through the Irish Gate.'

'The Irish Gate? Sam said try Caldewgate.'

'They're one and the same. Irish Gate is the western gap in the city wallss but because the road out then goes over the River Caldew the locals call it the Caldewgate. The quickest way to get there is to go under the railway arches and follow the road that runs north beside the track, but I think that might not be the best idea. Your recent friends might not be so helpful if you ask them for another favour. If you come with me, we'll go onto the city's West Walls and I'll show you an "easier" way to get there even if it is a little longer.'

Heinrich looked across at the three men he had spoken to. They had returned to their position under the arches but continued to look over in his direction. Turning back to the policeman, he smiled and said, 'That'll be much appreciated.'

However, the giant officer hadn't waited for a reply. He was obviously used to his advice being taken and had set off striding down the pavement towards the distant sandstone barrier that formed the western boundary of the old medieval city. With a raise of his eyebrows he picked up his kit bag and set off after him, feeling rather like an errant little boy following his father.

CHAPTER 7

Carlisle West Walls

Early Evening, Wednesday 14th April 1915

It had been a long day with more trouble around Finkle Street, mainly involving groups of youths who congregated in the area to fight with each other or to break into unprotected property. Juvenile crime had risen significantly since large numbers of men had joined the army and gone off to war. Children were left without the controlling hand of their fathers and homes were vulnerable in the absence of husbands or sons. In the past months the juvenile court had dealt with increasing numbers of offences, from selling newspapers without a license to breaking into the local grammar school and causing damage. After this latest incident Jack had checked on various families to ensure they were safe and then left things in the secure hands of two constables who would patrol the area until daybreak the next morning. He was relieved that his shift was now finished and, having signed off for the day, he walked out of the front of the police station with his wrestling kitbag slung over his shoulder. Although the darkening sky was heavy and grey with the portent of rain to come, his mood was cheerful, and he skipped up the Sallyport steps onto the West Walls and headed for the Peter Street Gymnasium, located ten minutes' walk away opposite the city's covered market. The 'Academy', as it was known, was home to Carlisle Cumberland and Westmorland Wrestling Academy and Jack had been a member since he was a boy.

Jack had been brought up in the infamous Parhambeck area. Here houses were either side of the Newtown Road as it came into the west of the city past the Cumberland Infirmary. At the time it was acknowledged that those living on the south side of the road were generally peace-loving, law-abiding families who took a quiet pride in looking after their homes. In the tight pack of houses on the 'north side', things were very different. The city police were frequent visitors to the narrow lanes and hovels scattered along the canal bank railway line which ran through the area. In his early years Jack had been a lovely, well-mannered little boy and his parents' pride and joy. He was especially loved because, in a time of larger families, he was an only child, the result of his mother's difficulty giving birth. However, after he left the local school at the age of twelve things had begun to change. He had taken to playing with a group of young rogues from the 'banklands' who were constantly in trouble with the police. Smashing windows, damaging property, stealing from the local shops and out to all hours. The boys sought excitement in otherwise dull lives. His mother Bridget and father Len couldn't control him and were beside themselves about what to do. Eventually, one morning after coming in late from another overnight excursion, his father grabbed him, but, instead of the usual beating, he pulled him into the front room and told him to sit down on one of the four padded, flower-patterned chairs that surrounded an elegant dining table covered with a white lace tablecloth.

'Wait there and don't you dare bloody move until I come back,' he was told and his father left the room, closing the door behind him with a bang. Jack was shocked and a little taken aback. The front, or 'best', room was rarely used. In fact, he could only remember it ever being occupied when a 'special tea' had been provided after each of his grandparents' funerals. To be left in it seemed a bigger concern than the possibility of another thrashing.

After about twenty minutes the door opened and his father stepped back into the room accompanied by a short, stocky man who had jet-black hair and wore a matching black cassock. They looked at Jack for a moment and then their visitor said, 'Thank you Len. I can manage things from here. You go and have a cup of tea with Bridget while Jack and I have a wee chat.' His father had nodded and left the room without further comment whilst the priest turned to Jack and said, 'Now, young man, you and I are going to get to know each other and this is how we are going to do it.'

From then on Father Jeffrey had been a constant in Jack's young life. Every morning he arrived at 8.00am and escorted him to Holy Trinity, a great grey cathedral of a church on a low hill to the east of the estate. For two hours he spent the time improving his, and a small group of other youngsters', ability to read and write, which had never been well developed, before giving him a range of jobs, from cleaning to gardening. These kept him occupied until he was escorted home at 7.00pm. The tasks were hard, physical work and by the time he got home all Jack wanted to do was crawl into bed and sleep. On the odd occasion when Jack ran away during the day, two of Father Jeffrey's older 'helpers' would come looking for him and 'help' him back to his chores, although he often acquired a cut lip, bruised eye or another minor injury as he 'accidentally fell over' on the way back to church. Eventually he decided that it was better to stay put.

One afternoon at the end of his chores Father Jeffrey came to him and said, 'This evening we have something else to do before you go home, Jack. Grab your jacket and follow me.'

Jack groaned; he was tired, hungry and ready for home, but by now he knew better than to complain. In silence he followed the priest and together they walked down past the biscuit factory, which provided employment for the local residents, towards the city. They crossed over the huge sandstone bridge that spanned both the River Caldew and the mainline railway and eventually arrived at the Peter Street Gymnasium, where they were both greeted warmly by everyone present. For the rest of the evening they had watched one of the few indoor wrestling events that formed part of the Carlisle Wrestling 'Ring', a series of local competitions held throughout the year. Jack had marvelled at the man-against-man combat following a simple set of rules and using a subtle mix of strength, speed and agility allied to significant technical skill and determination. Further fascinated by the pride the men took in their traditional costume of long johns with an embroidered vest and centrepiece, he was hooked. He asked the priest if he could teach him, and Father Jeffrey had smiled and said, 'Of course, Jack, but it takes a lot of hard work and commitment to be a good wrestler. Are you really sure you want to make the effort?' Jack had looked around at the smiling faces of the wrestlers around him, both young and old, and nodded his head. It had been his passion ever since.

As time passed and Jack grew into adulthood he had become a regular participant in events around the county and a frequent victor. Eventually he had risen to become the academy's top wrestler and consequently, if a venue could be found and arrangements made, he was now hoping to wrestle against Douglas Clark, unofficial county champion, in an exhibition bout later that summer. Jack was much older than Clark, who'd been born at Ellenborough, near Maryport on the 2ⁿᵈ May 1891, but the policeman hoped that his intense training and greater experience would give him an edge over the younger man, who was currently serving on the front line with the Royal Signals Corps. He was also aware that there were other potential stumbling blocks to his ambitions. Apart from the difficulties posed by the war, only the 'Ring' champion could represent the academy against Clark, and Jack's nemesis, the infamous PC Brown, was also a member. Until Jack had taken over, he had been the number-one wrestler in the city. In a sport that prided itself on the sportsmanship of its competitors, the constable was an uncompromising wrestler who took his thuggish work behaviour into the ring. He was well known for 'accidentally' falling on opponents as they were thrown and driving a fist or elbow into a face, chest or arm. Broken bones were a rarity in most bouts but commonplace in those involving Brown. Bringing a competitor down was generally called 'throwing', but spectators named his aggressive approach as 'felling'. It was highly likely that Jack would have to resist a challenge from him before being allowed to take on the county champion.

Arriving at Peter Street, he pushed open the glossy black front door and entered into an outer hallway. The room had white painted walls with a black-and-white tiled floor. To his left was a long wooden table and chair. On top of the table was a large leather-bound book with a pencil lying beside it. Jack signed in, writing down the time, date and his name. Normally someone sat behind the table and checked people in and out to ensure that only members used the facility, but Wednesday evening was the Wigton mid-week 'meet', and he knew many of his fellow members would have taken the train through to the small market town to compete or watch. Both the number of meets and contestants taking part had been drastically reduced as a result of the war, but some events were still being held, although the majority of those taking part were in the youngest or older age ranges.

Today's work commitments had prevented Jack being with them. He smiled; at least it meant that someone else would have a chance of winning the evening's premier event – the 'All Weights' prize. Normally, separating fighters into weight groups helped to ensure fair fights. A wrestler weighing three stone more than a smaller opponent had a big advantage. However, any event's main prize was reserved for the winner of the 'All Weights' category, open to all comers regardless of height or weight, and this usually carried the biggest monetary prize which could run into several guineas at the bigger 'meets'. Jack was a lightweight in wrestling terms, but he had taken many a purse from 'All Weights' events and, when combined with his police salary, this meant he could count himself as reasonably well off.

He walked across the entrance area and pushed through two solid mahogany swing doors into a narrow corridor. To his right was another door with gold painted letters indicating that only seniors were allowed within. To the left was a similar layout with letters that spelled out the word juniors. On the wall facing him was a huge painting of two wrestlers struggling to throw each other with the Cumberland Mountains in the background. The painting was a copy of an eighteenth-century engraving by Thomas Bewick (1752-1828). The book showing the engraving had been published back in 1870. Most people were unaware of or had forgotten the name of the copying artist. Everyone in the academy simply referred to the picture as the Bewick and it had pride of place in the entrance.

Opening the door to the right, he entered a much bigger room with a number of low wooden benches arranged along the oak-panelled walls and series of numbered black-painted, cast-iron clothes hooks above them. The numbers started at eight, because on the remaining wall were seven cubicles, each about four feet square with an individual clothes hook and a small wooden stool. Every cubicle except one had an open wooden door with a brass key with a numbered fob matching the number painted in gold on the door. Jack crossed the black-and-white tiles to the one closed door. Number One. His locker. In recognition of the fact that at that moment, and for several years past, he was the number one wrestler in the academy. In fact, this had been the case for so long that below the figure one on the door someone had carefully painted a smoking pipe. His sign: 'Smoking Joe', a mistaken nick name that had stuck with him from his early days at the club. Jack reached into his jacket pocket and took out his own brass key and opened the door. Underneath the stool within was a small wooden box. Hanging his kit bag on the cubicle's hook, he bent down, lifted the lid and then carefully removed a pristine white costume with the initials 'JJ' embroidered on the front. As always, he looked at his competition costume with pride before re-folding it and placing it carefully back in the box. Five minutes later, fully changed into the training clothes from his kit bag, he entered the high-ceilinged main hall and, briefly acknowledging the greetings of the handful of other people in the room, crossed the white padded practice matts to the far corner, where an assortment of medicine balls, barbells and benches lay scattered about on an area of uncovered parquet floor. After some gentle stretches, he lifted one of the heavier medicine balls and carried it across to the edge of the padded area, where he sat down with his legs straight in front of him and the medicine ball on his right side. He twisted to face it, grabbed it with both hands and lifted it across his body to touch it down on his left side. 'One ...' he said, and he began to lift it back.

CHAPTER 8

The Globe Inn, Caldewgate, Carlisle

Evening, Monday 19th April 1915

Sitting at a corner table at the back of the room, Heinrich was able to observe everything going on in the bar. The big sergeant hadn't been wrong; the public house had been easy to find following his instructions. Leaving the German at the Caldewgate entrance through the city walls, he had told him to follow the northern side of the road out of town for about 400 yards and he'd find the building on his right.

'You can't miss it,' he said. 'It's got a large globe painted on the sign above the door.'

And so it proved. After crossing a bridge over a small river, he'd found the hostelry standing by itself on the corner of the main road and the aptly named Bridge Lane. Pushing open a swing door, he entered a room with a very utilitarian feel. A few tables and chairs were scattered in the space between him and a long bar counter was running almost the length of the opposite wall. The wooden floorboards had nothing covering them except the odd stain of spilt liquid which, he presumed from the smell, was beer. Four cloth-capped old men, who were playing dominoes at a table to his left, looked up for a moment before quickly returning to their game. Most of the furniture and fitments were of a dark wood – mahogany, perhaps – and the whole place would have been extremely dark and dingy were it not for the large frosted windows at the front of the building that let light stream in whilst protecting customers from the gaze of passers-by.

Given the warnings from Sam about the influx of workers into the city and surrounding area, particularly from Ireland, he'd been surprised to find that there were any vacant rooms. But in fact, the landlord had told him that he had two both on the first floor.

'There's a double room right over the front door, a bit noisy until we close up, and you'll be sharing with Jacob Porter, my odd-job man. Three shillings and six pence per week for bed and a light breakfast taken down here in the bar. The other is at the rear of the building. You'll be on your own, but its five shillings. Price includes laundry changed and the room cleaned once a month. If you want any weekly washing it's an extra six pence per week and a packed lunch is two pence per day. No guests allowed in rooms, particularly lady friends.'

Heinrich had opted for the single room, which was accessed through a door marked 'Private' at the back of the bar. This led to a flight of stairs, at the top of which was a narrow corridor running the length of the building. On either side were two rooms, each with their own lock. His was the last one on the left with a window that overlooked what proved to be the local brewery. Later he found out that the room next to his was another double occupied by the landlord and his wife. She proved to be much younger than her husband, no more than a girl, and Heinrich wondered from the way she was treated, more like a servant than a wife, if the two were indeed married or whether in fact she was a stray that the older man had simply taken in off the street as cheap labour. On the opposite side of the corridor in another single room was an ageing watch man, who provided night-time security at the local biscuit factory, and Porter's double room. The former slept most of the morning so was rarely seen, except on his day off on Sunday. Porter, it appeared, did whatever job he was asked, including acting as a 'bouncer' to unruly customers. He'd only been employed for just over a month apparently at the suggestion of the local police as part of a scheme being tried out in the local pubs to try and cut down incidents of drunken behaviour and the associated violence. Since he'd been employed, there had been little trouble, which surprised Heinrich. He couldn't imagine anyone being deterred by a fragile, ex-soldier with a decided limp. Porter told anyone who would listen that the injury to his right leg was courtesy of a Boer bullet at the Battle of Spion Kop in 1900, but when pressed he was always vague about the specifics of the encounter. *Perhaps,* he thought, *the peace might have more to do with people's initial reluctance to visit pubs in the scheme.* The Globe had certainly been relatively quiet over the past week.

The three days after his arrival had been uneventful. He'd spent the time wandering around the city becoming familiar with the layout and buildings, particularly the castle and railway station. Both were busy with groups of soldiers coming and going. On an evening he'd spent his time getting to know the 'regulars' who came into the pub most nights after work. None of them questioned Ricky Colman's generosity, he frequently bought a round of drinks, or his story about having worked on the merchant ships. He embellished his seafaring exploits by including himself as one of the crew working with his friend Sam Armstrong on the herring boats out of Whitehaven. He even included the tragic tale of John Crofts reluctantly allowing his listeners to coax him into revealing that he had been one of the heroic crewmen who had saved the man's life.

During these conversations he'd found out that the men who were labouring on the railway, or on the various building projects in the area, were living in so-called shanty towns mainly built close to where they were working. Huts were erected by employers, some of which could accommodate up to twenty men and the occupants paid one and a half pennies for a rough bed for the night. Those who were prepared to sleep on the floor paid even less. Five nights of floor sleeping cost one penny. Few were prepared to live away from their place of work or pay the much higher rates for more comfortable accommodation.

On the first Friday night after he arrived he was leaning against the bar talking to his landlord, trying to extract from him the whereabouts of the new munitions factory that Lody's initial intelligence reports indicated was to be built or, worse, was being built somewhere to the north of the city. Everyone in the pub knew of the 'secret' project, but as yet no one could provide him with any details. He hadn't pushed for information too hard in order not to raise suspicions, but he was conscious that his mission was time limited and that every day the factory could be getting closer to completion.

William 'Billy' Dixon, Landlord, was a middle-aged, fat man with greasy combed over hair and a beer gut that poked through the apron he constantly wore, whether working or not. He displayed the symptoms of a man who drank too much of his own beer. A bloated and puffy face was covered in spots and his body gave off a mild but constant smell of sweat and urine.

'You must have heard something, Billy. My savings are running out and I need a job. Somebody must have mentioned where this place is or who's taking on men and where. I've been going up to the hirings at the Market Place but there's nothing doing.'

This wasn't quite true. He'd gone up that morning to find eight other people waiting beside the Market Cross in the city centre. Five were young girls after domestic employment and the other three were late-middle-aged men hoping to get labouring work. None of them knew anything about the new factory and the only person offering work was a farmer from nearby Cumwhinton whose farm labourer had left him to join up. He'd looked at the men and walked straight over to Heinrich, said what the job was, and offered him a shilling of 'earnest money' to seal the appointment. The German, who didn't really want work, had held his gaze for a moment then pushed past and stalked off without comment, not even looking back when the man shouted a string of expletives at his back.

'I've told you. I don't know anything. Jobs is 'ard to come by and anybody with any information about one keeps it to themselves. You'll just have …' He broke off in mid-sentence, his attention taken by something over Heinrich's shoulder. 'Shit. We could do without this lot.'

The German didn't turn round but looked in the large mirror that hung on the wall behind the bar to see what had caught the barman's attention. He didn't like what he saw. Three familiar faces had entered the building accompanied by a fourth man he didn't recognise. His 'friends' from underneath the arches. Like the others, the unknown individual was untidily dressed. Medium build with brown hair, he had a pink birthmark running from just below his right ear, across the jaw and onto the top of his neck.

'You know them?' he asked.

'Not by name,' whispered Dixon. 'They're unemployed Irish navvies who came over to work on the railway a few months back but lost their jobs after they beat up their foreman when he docked their pay because they turned in late for work after a drunken "randy".

'Navvies? Randy?'

'Railway labourers. Navvies work hard and they drink hard. Their spending is welcome but more often than not they also bring trouble. A "randy" is a drinking spree that lasts a few days. Usually Friday night to Sunday night. The last time they were in here they smashed two tables in a fight with a couple of young recruits who took offence when they were laughed at for joining up.'

Heinrich knew that if they spotted him there would be trouble, but some instinct made him pause and, instead of going up to his room, he turned his body sideways so that his back was to the men and his face turned away as they approached the bar.

'I want no trouble from you lot this time,' said the landlord.

'Give us four beers then piss off, you fat lump of lard,' replied the tall man who had faced up to Heinrich near the railway station.

When the drinks came, the men moved across to the nearest table and sat down. They didn't try to keep their voices down and their conversation was loud and heated, with the 'leader's' single voice dominating the conversation. 'I still can't believe it. The bastard didn't even give us a chance. We'd walked all the way up there and he just shook his head and walked off. If there hadn't been a couple of guards on the gate I'd have "done him" for that and he'd have deserved it.'

The others nodded their heads in agreement and as the angry dialogue continued the German began to realise that this might be the break he had been looking for. It was obvious that these men had managed to find the location of the proposed munitions factory and gone there in search of work but been unsuccessful. From their unguarded exchanges he gathered it was just over the border into Scotland in the moss lands on the northern banks of the Solway Firth, wherever that was. Heinrich didn't know, but they'd managed to walk there and back in a day, so the distance wasn't excessive, which meant he could check it out without too much trouble. He realised his thoughts had drifted when his concentration was broken by an even louder exchange which caused him to re-focus on the mirror.

'This beer is flat. Give us another four pints.' It was the loud mouth again.

'They can't have been that bad, you've just about finished them,' Billy replied.

'I said, give us another round of drinks,' roared the other, and with that, he stood up and swept his hand across the table, sending the four glasses crashing to the floor. The handful of other customers in the room looked across at the incident and one or two got up and slowly edged out of the front door. Those who stayed bent their heads over and concentrated on their own drinks. At that point Jacob, who had been washing glasses at the sink below the bar mirror, stepped round the counter picking up a small cudgel from a shelf under one of the pumps.

'If you don't mind, I think it might be time to leave, gents,' he said in a nervous voice.

'Who the hell are you? No. I should say … what the hell are you?' The group laughed as their compatriot stood up and turned in a small circle with an exaggerated limp. As he did so, the others also got to their feet and moved to form a cordon around the now clearly worried ex-soldier. The man, who was unknown to Heinrich, moved behind Jacob and gave him a push in the back. As he stumbled forward, one of the pair that the German had come to think of as twins, stuck out his foot, causing the off-balance man to trip over. Unprepared and falling, he was unable to resist as the cudgel was pulled from his grip by the other twin and, with surprising speed, swung in an arc and brought down across the back of his head. He sunk to the ground groaning, partially stunned as his antagonists again started to laugh.

At this point Heinrich turned round and spoke. His voice was calm but firm. 'That's enough. Leave him alone and then get out.'

The men looked across at him and shifted their attention to face this new threat. As before, the taller individual took the lead.

'Oh yes, and who —.' He broke off in mid-sentence. 'I recognise you. You're that prat the copper saved beside the arches.' He paused. 'Well, there's no copper here now.' And with that he made a threatening step forward.

Heinrich didn't wait to see what the man had in mind. He knew that in a situation like this, where there was more than one adversary, it was best to take the fight to the enemy using surprise to counter numbers. He reached out and grasped his would-be assailant by the jacket lapels. Pulling him towards him with a rapid jolt, he smashed his forehead into the man's face and felt a crunch as the other's nose broke. When his opponent lifted his hands up in shock and jerked his face away from the impact, Heinrich brought his right knee up into the man's groin and, as he collapsed to the floor screaming, stepped rapidly on to the next person in line who happened to be the individual with the pink birthmark. Again he reached forward, this time using his left hand to take hold of and pull on the right lapel of the second rogue. The man was spun round so that he faced the bar and, before he could react, his hair had been grabbed and his face was crashed down onto the metal rail that ran along the front of the counter. The 'twins' looked on in horror and, as the second of their number dropped onto the wooden floorboards, they stepped back away from the man who, in seconds had left their mates in agony. At first, they worried that they might be next, but instead he looked at them and said, 'Pick up your companions and get out.'

They both nodded and, taking an individual each, headed for the door.

'Wait a minute,' said Heinrich, and as the men paused, he walked across to the ring leader and whispered in his ear, 'If I ever see you again, I'll kill you. Do you understand?'

The man slowly turned his head and looked into the piercing, emotionless eyes of the person threatening him. For once he was genuinely frightened and so he just nodded, and the group left. Turning back to the bar Heinrich watched as an amazed Billy Dixon stood shaking his head. Glancing around, he noticed that everyone else was also staring at him and knew he had to say something.

'At sea it doesn't pay to be a shrinking violet. If you have problems no one sorts them for you. You sink or swim.' He shrugged his shoulders. 'So you learn to look after yourself.'

'Well I'm glad you did. And you, you useless bag of ...' The owner walked over to Porter, who was now sitting up, rubbing the back of his head. 'You're fired. Pack up your things and get out!'

'But boss...'

'Never mind "but boss", you're paid to prevent things like this happening and if you can't do your job, you're not much use to me.'

'Where am I going to go at this time of night?'

'He's right, Billy.' Heinrich intervened. 'He won't find anywhere at this hour except a park bench.'

'OK. You've got until tomorrow morning, but I want you out before breakfast, and after that don't show your face around here again.' And with that, he turned and shouted out to everyone else in the pub. 'Sorry, folks. Let's be having you. Sup up and go home. It's nearly closing time, so we're shutting up a bit early to clear up the spilt blood and beer.' He grabbed Jacob by the arm and pulled him to his feet. 'And you're helping or you can get out now.'

The following morning Heinrich was sat eating his paltry breakfast of bread and cheese at a table in the corner of the bar where two windows, one on each wall, let in the watery spring sunshine. He'd just finished and was about to get up and go back to his room when his landlord came out from behind the bar, where he had been washing glasses left from the night before, and sat down on a chair opposite him.

At first he said nothing and appeared to be thinking whether to speak or not. Then, after a few seconds, he took a deep breath and spoke. 'I was thinking. You've been looking for a job. How'd you fancy taking over from Jacob?'

'I don't think so,' replied Heinrich.

'Eh! Why not? You're staying here. You're in the bar most nights. You can look after yourself and you need money.'

'But I'm not a pot washer or general dogsbody.'

'What if it was just to look after problems and serve the odd pint?'

'Twenty shillings a week.'

'You're kidding, right. No way. I can't afford that for part-time work.'

'If what I hear from some of the lads who come in here is right, that's a typical wage for the factories. It's certainly what I was getting on the boats.'

'I'll give you seven shillings and ten pence.'

Heinrich shook his head. 'That's not enough for me to risk getting my brains knocked about for.'

'Ten shillings. It's the best I can do.'

'No. It's twenty shillings or nothing.'

'Ten shillings and free board and lodgings.'

The German smiled. It wasn't a brilliant offer, but there were other benefits. He'd been given a significant amount of forged currency for his mission, but sooner or later it would either be spotted or run out, so the extra funds would be useful. It would also mean that he had even more of a 'history' if anyone asked.

'Done, but in my room, not Jacob's old one.'

'OK, but you still have to pay for cleaning and food, except for breakfast.'

And so the pair had reached out and shook hands, and Ricky Colman had a legitimate job and place of abode.

The following Monday night the pub was almost empty, everyone having spent their money over the weekend. Ensconced in a corner, Heinrich sat back and reflected on the past week and situation he now found himself in. Although the place had been busy, Saturday and Sunday had been relatively quiet and uneventful. The only slight disturbance had come the previous evening, when two old men had almost come to blows over alleged cheating during a dominoes match. His new boss said this wasn't uncommon if money was involved, even if the winner only picked up a couple of pence. However, the men had settled as soon as Heinrich had got up from the corner chair where he was now sitting, which, he had decided, would be his abode during working hours. Inwardly he smiled at the legitimacy his new position gave him if questioned and he was especially satisfied with the hours he was expected to work. After the outbreak of war, the UK Parliament had passed the Defence of the Realm Act, which covered a range of measures to support the Allied effort. A section of the Act looked specifically at the hours in which publicans could sell alcohol, as there were ongoing fears that over-indulgence with alcohol by factory and munition workers might cost Britain productivity and starve the army abroad of ammunition. Licensing hours, the time when public houses were permitted to sell alcohol, were restricted to midday to two thirty in the afternoon and then six thirty to nine thirty in the evening. Failure to observe these strict limits saw landlords lose their licenses and pubs forced to shut down. The gaps would leave him plenty of time to progress his other activities and, just to be sure' he had lied to Dixon that he might need a couple of afternoons off to fulfil promises he had made to help his friend Sam Armstrong on his fishing boat. His first task would be to investigate the castle where it appeared new recruits were housed and trained. The fact that it was just across the bridge from where he now sat made things significantly easier. He'd need to take a proper look inside, but, because he would pass it on any journey into the city, he could also observe it on a regular basis without drawing attention to himself. That would give him some idea of the regular comings and goings. Sitting up, he decided that the situation warranted a celebration and, rising to his feet, he pushed his chair back and walked over to the bar. *That's another perk of the job,* he thought, *free beer, even if it's considerably weaker and a strange colour compared to the stuff back home in Germany.*

CHAPTER 9

Carlisle Castle

Morning, Tuesday 27th April 1915 ·

Private Harold Roberts of the 11th Battalion Border Regiment – or the Lonsdales, as they were named locally – watched the stranger approach with only vague interest. He'd been on duty for nearly eight hours from 2.00am that morning and was tired and ready for a well-earned rest. Although there were two recruits on duty at any one time, one was constantly patrolling the castle walls and inner buildings, leaving his unfortunate colleague to stand guard on the sandstone bridge outside the gatehouse where the Castle Way entrance road crossed the moat. During the day you could at least watch the traffic and goings-on along the streets in front of the fortress, but at night the duty was tedious and time dragged. Having signed up to fight the Hun, he'd expected to be sent out to France sooner rather than later. Instead he had ended up at the castle for training, which at the moment consisted mainly of route marches carrying full packs and night exercises in moving quietly. Time should also have been spent on shooting practice on the rifle range at nearby Cummersdale, but a shortage of firearms meant this had been postponed for the moment. An appeal had been published in the local papers for the loan of small rifles and air guns so that training for those men who had never handled weapons could go ahead, but although the army had promised to return the items in a good, clean condition, the response had been poor. Instead the battalion had been put through a rigorous programme of physical training in Bitts Park just behind the castle, an event that drew an enthusiastic audience of spectators keen to cheer their 'local heroes'. It would have been even worse had recruitment not remained slow. In the last month only thirty men a day had presented themselves at the castle to sign up, and the newly built huts in the outer bailey which could accommodate 1,000 men remained almost empty. After an initial race to sign up, the process had been affected by the first trainloads of returning wounded who had arrived in Carlisle in March. Although the date and time of the trains was supposed to be kept secret, they invariably leaked out and the large crowds that gathered to welcome the men back had been shocked by their injuries. Not surprisingly, this led to many young men's reluctance to take up arms.

He was particularly annoyed, because this was the second day running he had been singled out for the unwanted chore. During another night route march three days previously he'd been unwise enough to voice his discontent about the situation to his mate Sandy Lowther and unfortunately his drill sergeant had overheard.

'So you don't like our little evening walks, Roberts,' he'd said. 'Well, I've just the alternative for you.'

The alternative had been five consecutive early mornings on guard duty with a clear warning that if he was found to be asleep he could expect a field punishment. This consisted of being placed in fetters and handcuffs or similar restraints and attached to a fixed object, such as a gun wheel or a fence post, for up to two hours per day. It was an archaic practice and not something Roberts found appealing.

The man continued his approach and as Harold stepped out in front of him he stopped and smiled. 'Hi. Am I in the right place? My name is Ricky Colman and I'm thinking of signing up.'

'But you're a yank. Yanks aren't part of this war.'

'Canadian, actually,' replied Heinrich. 'And after spending the last few months serving on your merchant ships and watching as some of my friends' ships were blown out of the water by German U-boats, I've decided I want the chance to hit back. Personal revenge rather than patriotism, but I guess that in war your reason for fighting doesn't much matter.'

Harold looked at the man in front of him. He was tempted to tell him to clear off and come to his senses, but he was clearly fit and healthy, and during a briefing a couple of weeks previously the recruiting officer had made it very clear that those on guard duty were to ensure that anyone who looked like he could fight should be directed to his office on the far side of the barracks.

'OK. Come with me and I'll show you where to go.'

Turning, he led Heinrich through the gatehouse, with its crenulated towers passing beyond the heavy wooden gates and under the ancient portcullis. Pausing on the other side, he pointed across a wide tarmac drill space to a row of two-storey brick buildings set on the far side below the castle's north wall.

'You want the building in the north-east corner. The one with the door open and a private stood outside. Tell him what you want to do and he'll sort you out.'

'Thanks. Much appreciated,' said the German, and with a nod he set off slowly across the tarmac in the direction given.

However, after a few steps, instead of continuing he turned to watch the young soldier who now had his back to him and was returning to his guard post. He waited for a few minutes and then hurried across to a recess on the inside of the gatehouse where he was almost hidden from view.

His hiding space offered him the opportunity to study the castle layout in detail. It was an impressive building. The curtain walls enclosed a large outer ward centred on the tarmac-covered parade ground. Along the north and west walls several more recently built buildings were clearly currently being used by the army for accommodation or offices. Scattered between them were a number of smaller storage facilities. To his right an inner ditch and half-moon battery provided a second line of defence between the outer ward and the entrance to an inner ward, which was dominated by a huge sandstone keep.

The castle's capacity to house a large garrison was immediately obvious, but so was the difficulty of destroying that garrison, one of his three objectives. The war in mainland Europe had turned into one of attrition. Effectively both sides were attempting to wear down the other to a point of collapse through continuous losses in personnel and materials. The war would be won by the side with greater such resources. In real terms this meant the side that could reinforce the huge frontline casualties with more men and ensure that they had enough weapons and ammunition to continue fighting. At the meeting at Abteilung IIIb headquarters, it had become clear that the Allies were winning this race to reinforce, and his mission was to try and disrupt the supply of both. The problem was that much of the Allied preparation for war was located in places far from the coastal south which you could easily reach simply by slipping across the English Channel at night-time to land on an isolated beach. Information on what was happening further north was sporadic, limited in detail and often inaccurate. In reality he was working blind and was going to have to come up with his own plans to achieve his objectives.

Well, he thought, *I'm here now and there's no going back.* He needed more information, and however dangerous this was, it meant having a better look round. Deciding that in this case bravado was a better strategy than stealth, he stepped out from his hiding spot and strode confidently across the parade ground in the direction he'd been sent heading towards what appeared to be an administration building. As he walked he noted several barracks blocks to his left with numerous stores in between and what looked like a munitions store between them and the building he was aiming for. However, as he moved to take a closer look he was halted by a loud shout behind him.

'Hey, you. Stay where you are!'

Heinrich stopped and turned, to be confronted by a tall sergeant with a swagger stick tucked under his arm.

'What are you doing? This place isn't open to civilians.' The tall serviceman walked over and stood directly in front of him with a frown on his face, waiting for an explanation.

'I'm here to ask about joining up. The solider on the gate sent me over here, but I'm not sure which of the buildings that he pointed to is the recruiting office.'

Sighing, and with a shake of the head, the man looked over towards the gatehouse. 'That bloody idiot. He can't do anything right. I'm sorry, sir, but the recruiting office has moved. It was here until last week, but it's been moved to the Citizen's League building in Devonshire Street. You need to go back into the centre of town. If you go up Castle Street until you reach the Old Town Hall I'm sure someone will be able to point you in the right direction.'

Heinrich faked a look of frustration and thanked the officer for his help. 'What time does it shut?' he asked.

'It's open all day. I shouldn't say it, but recruitment's slow, so there'll be people there until early evening. They don't want to chance missing anyone who turns up.'

He nodded and set off back across the tarmac towards the gatehouse. Half way he stopped and looked back to find, somewhat disconcertingly, that the non-commissioned officer was still watching him.

CHAPTER 10

Castle Street

Morning, Tuesday 27th April 1915

Finkle Street again, thought Jack as he hurried down Castle Street. The sky was clear, but it was an unusually cold spring day and he shivered despite the brisk pace. It hadn't been possible to leave two constables on duty all day every day, so he wasn't surprised that once they had been removed trouble had started again. A young boy of around ten years old had arrived at the West Walls Police Station, out of breath and breathing hard. He'd reported that a group of youths had been terrorising residents. Bricks had been thrown through windows and fires started outside front doors, presumably because they had had the nerve to inform the police of recent incidents. Really a constable should have been sent to the disturbance, but, having dealt with the families previously, Jack had volunteered to go back and look into this latest incident. He wondered what it would take to bring a halt to the rising crime rate amongst the city's juveniles.

It wasn't even half way through the year yet, but over a hundred youngsters had already been brought before the courts and eight had been ordered to be whipped.

His thoughts were momentarily interrupted by a burst of bells from the city's cathedral and he looked at the imposing sandstone building on his left. He smiled to himself despite his grim mood. Jack was a keen student of his city's history and was aware that the cathedral had been founded as a priory by King Henry I in 1122. For the umpteenth time in his life he stared at the magnificent east window, which was over fifty feet high and depicted the life of Christ. He wasn't really a religious man, but the site always left him feeling uplifted.

As he paused, a movement caught his eye and he looked down towards the castle at the end of the street. Above the adjacent houses, wisps of black smoke spiralled into the air. He felt a sickly feeling rise in his stomach and he began to run towards them. As he approached the road junction where Finkle Street, Annetwell Street and Castle Street all met, he could see that the end terrace house on the corner of Annetwell Street and Castle Way was on fire. A group of people stood on the opposite side of the road, some of whom were holding a female who was struggling and screaming to be let go. She was in her late twenties or early thirties and, despite her shabby dress and unkempt hair, Jack noticed she had a pretty face.

'Police!' he shouted. 'Has anyone sent for the fire brigade?'

'Silus Walker's just gone off to fetch them,' said one of the men holding the woman. 'But by the time he gets to Spring Garden Lane and they come back with him it'll be too late for the building and her boy.' And he nodded towards her. 'The lad's still in there but the place is well alight. If we're lucky, the best we can hope for is that they can stop it spreading next door.'

Jack stood for a moment, then stepped in front of the young

mother and looked her straight in the eyes. 'Where is he?' he asked her quietly.

'Upstairs,' she cried. 'Jimmy was upstairs taking a nap after being up early for his paper round.'

Almost without thinking, Jack turned to face the building, took a deep breath then pulled his jacket up over his head and plunged through the front door into the waiting conflagration. Smoke billowed through the open space and stung his eyes. The heat was so intense that it made him catch his breath and the flames flickering around him singed the hair on the back of his hands and scorched his skin. Instantly he started to cough and tears flowed, creating black streaks down his cheeks and onto his white shirt. Around him the flames were unimaginably bright. The smell of burning was overpowering and the roar of the inferno as it consumed the building seemed to fill his head. It was a small one-up, one-down terrace house, and Jack knew the stairs would be straight ahead. Retaining a hold on his jacket, he pulled his elbows in front of his face to shade his eyes from the heat, and ran forward, taking the steps two at a time. Reaching the top landing, he turned to his right and pushed open the paint-bubbled bedroom door but was immediately forced back by an initial blast of heat and flames. He paused for a moment to recover his composure and stepped into the small room.

'Jimmy,' he roared. 'Are you there? Jimmy! Jimmy!'

At first there was no response and in the black, lung-bursting smoke, he couldn't see anything. Then, with an almighty crash, the street-facing window exploded and the heat sent hot shards of glass flying outwards, but for a second the wind cleared the smoke. In the corner he saw a small, immobile figure, lying curled up on a mattress on the floor. Dodging the flames that were now flickering through the floorboards as well as climbing the walls, he quickly crossed the room and lifted the boy over his shoulder. Retracing his steps towards the stairs, he was almost at the bedroom door when there was slow rumble before the house shook with an almighty crash as the stairs gave way and with it their way out disappeared. Jack slowly retraced his steps backwards towards the window, but the disappearance of his route to safety seemed to drain the strength from his body and, as the smoke thickened, he felt like his lungs themselves were on fire, and he sank to the floor on one knee. He knew the window was only a couple of feet away and if he could only get back up, he could drop the boy down to someone below. But while his mind was willing, his body simply wouldn't move and, as he found it almost impossible to breathe, he realised with a startling clarity that he was choking to death.

*

At the castle gatehouse Heinrich saw that the young soldier was still on duty. He nodded at the German and asked, 'Did you find what you wanted?'

'Not really. Apparently the recruiting office has moved into town.'

The man's face dropped. 'Oh, shit. So it has. We were told about the move, but this is the first time since then that I've been asked and I forgot. Sorry, mate.'

'Don't worry, but I think your sergeant might have something to say about your loss of memory. Unfortunately he was the one who showed me the error of my ways.'

'Bloody hell.' He scrunched his face up and shook his head. 'What's the bet that that means another period of extended duty? Bugger!'

Heinrich smiled, but before he could reply the conversation was cut short by a distant scream from the direction of the city. Hurrying through the gates onto the moat bridge, the two men looked down Castle Way to observe a terrace house on the corner with Annetwell Street, from which plumes of dark smoke were escaping through the door and roof. Standing in front of a small crowd outside the building was a young woman who was screaming incoherently at the top of her voice. The pair raced down the cobbled road until they reached the front of the burning house. The woman was still hysterical, and the German grabbed her arms and shouted at her. At first she just froze and looked at him, so he repeated his question.

'Is someone in there?'

The woman broke down into tears and sobbed an answer. 'My son, Jimmy. Jimmy's still in there. He was asleep in the front bedroom. A plain-clothed copper went in after him, but neither of them have come out.'

Dropping his bag onto the cobblestones, Heinrich made to enter the front door, but as he did so there was a loud bang and a wall of flame shot out into the street. The air smelt of burning and the accompanying smoke choked his lungs, making it difficult to swallow. He turned to ask if there was another way in, but his voice was reduced to a croak and he had to wave his arms and mime to get the woman to understand.

'There's a back door into the yard from the kitchen, but if you managed to get in you would still have to come through to the stairs to get anywhere and they've collapsed.'

Looking at the upstairs window it was clear that this was the only possible way into the building, but without a ladder he could see no way of getting up there. He cast his eyes around for an alternative but could see nothing until an idea slowly formed in his mind.

Just along the street the soldier he had been talking too had run past him and stopped the traffic on the road coming down Annetwell Street from Caldewgate. At the front of the queue of vehicles, with its engine still running, was a black-panelled bus with white trim and the initials 'WMSC' along the side. It had five rows of bench seats capable of taking four people, but only the front row was occupied by a driver in a smart blue uniform and matching peak cap. Although a single-decker vehicle with open sides and no windows, Heinrich noted that it had a solid roof shade supported by four metal pillars on each side. It was an old machine and the pantheon-style radiator grille at the front of the bonnet was inscribed with the name 'Arrol Johnston' and above the driver hung a sign saying 'AO1636 Lady Favourite'. It was just perfect for what he intended to try. He ran over to the driver and told him what he wanted to do.

'You must be crazy. No way!' he replied. 'This bus has a tank full of petrol under the wooden floorboards. If that goes up it'll be completely destroyed, and me with it.'

'And if you don't ...' Heinrich started to explain but thought better of it. Time was of the essence, so he simply reached up, grabbed the driver by the lapels of his jacket, and yanked him out of the bus. As the startled man fell sprawling onto the road, he climbed up into driving seat, put the bus into gear and drove it towards the house. The startled young soldier who was controlling the traffic at first stepped out in front of him and raised both his arms in an attempt to stop the mad individual who seemed to be stealing the vehicle, but he quickly realised that this wasn't what was happening and jumped out of the way. Bumping up onto the pavement, he brought the bus to a stop under the burning building's front window just as it blew outwards with a loud crash, raining a potentially damaging shower of glass onto the top. Knocking the engine off and putting the handbrake on, he crawled past the steering wheel through the open space in front of him and onto the bonnet. Turning back to face the way he had come, he used the dashboard as a step and, reaching up, grabbed on to the low rails that allowed luggage to be stored on top of the bus. With an almighty heave, he hauled himself onto the roof, ignoring the cuts to his hands from the scattered shards.

As he stood up, a voice behind him shouted, 'Wait! Take this.' An elderly man in a striped suit and straw boater, realising what was going on, grabbed an old tartan blanket from the second row of seats in the bus, dunked it in the shallow water left in an old horse trough by the side of the road, draped it over his walking stick and pushed it up to the would-be rescuer. Heinrich grabbed the woollen rug, swept it over his head and, gripping it as if it were a cloak of invulnerability, stepped over the windowsill into the burning building.

The heat was intense and even through the blanket it felt like his skin was burning. At first the thick, black smoke made it impossible to see anything and the noise of the fire blanketed out any other sounds. However, as he knelt down to avoid the flames that were now devouring the room's low ceiling, he found he could see a few feet in front of him to two shadowy figures kneeling on the floor; the larger individual was using his body as a shield around the other. He crawled across to them and realised that one was an adult who had his arms wrapped round a smaller figure who he presumed was the missing Jimmy. Neither was moving, so Heinrich grabbed the man's shoulder and shook it. There was no response, so he tried again but much harder. This time the hunched figure shuddered and uttered a raking cough. *At least one of them is alive,* he thought, and he dragged part of his blanket over their shoulders so that all three were cocooned in its damp shelter. He leant over until he was next to the man's ear. 'We have to get out of here,' he screamed at the top of his voice. 'Now!'

The presence of a rescuer and temporary protection of the blanket seemed to give the man renewed strength, and with the tall German's help, he dragged himself to his feet and between them they lifted the boy from the floor, one carrying his legs, the other his head and shoulders. Like drunken men on their way home, they staggered across the room to the window. Leaving the tartan shawl around the older man, Heinrich stepped out onto the bus roof, first pulling the boy's torso with him until finally his legs slipped over the windowsill onto the litter-strewn canopy. Laying him carefully down, he then reached back to help the other soot-covered figure follow them into the sunlight. Safe at last, the man released his grip on the blanket and as it fell to the ground Heinrich looked down at what was left of the beautifully woven yellow, green and blue tartan. It was now stretched out of shape and charred out of all recognition, but it had done its job, they were out and, amazingly, they were alive.

As the two of them dropped to their knees and tried to cough to clear their smoke-filled lungs, the bus shuddered and the canopy shook as the vehicle pulled away from the house into the middle of the road. It stopped and seconds later the grinning face of the young soldier appeared over the rail at the front of the bus.

'Wow. That was touch and go. Are you OK? You must be mad. Both of you could have been killed.'

The German lifted his head, nodded gently and then leaned forward and threw up.

CHAPTER 11

Territorial Army Rifle Drill Hall on Strand Road, Carlisle

Early Evening, Friday 7th May 1915

'We should do it and now we know we can do it. Of course we can do it. It will show that our city as a whole wants to support those brave young men who are leaving their homes to fight in this unhappy war. Carlisle will not allow them to go short of ammunition. We'll do our bit.'

Theodore Carr, patriarch of the local biscuit factory, addressed the hastily convened committee of businessmen and local union representatives in a room at the recently vacated Territorial Army Drill Hall on Strand Road. Approaching his fiftieth birthday, he was an elegantly dressed man, of medium build with a thick head of greying hair and a neat, well-trimmed matching moustache. After attending university in Manchester, he had entered the family firm, eventually rising to become chairman of directors.

The group had first met on 22nd March in the St Nicholas View house of local MP Richard Denman to explore how to provide better support to the British Expeditionary Force sent to confront Germany on the Western Front. Although Denman was much younger than Carr, the pair got on well. Both were Liberals with strong views about the need to support the troops. Denman had gone so far as to become a member of the Union of Democratic Control, a pressure group of Liberal and Labour politicians who were critical of the government's war policies. After the acute shortage of artillery ammunition at Neuve Chappelle, it had become apparent that victory on the battlefield depended as much on the strength of the country's manufacturing base as it did on the strength of the men on the frontline. Millions of shells were needed to feed the voracious appetite of the artillery and it was clear existing production couldn't meet demand. Early discussions had focused on how Carlisle could make a greater contribution to munitions manufacture. Denman had appealed to the engineering companies and trades unions attending to cooperate in cutting through local and national red tape to set up a local munitions factory. It wouldn't be a large enterprise but it would demonstrate what a community could do when they put their mind to it. There had been unanimous support for the venture and Carr had been elected as chairman of a newly constituted 'Munitions Committee'. Henry Campbell, a stock and insurance broker who was also a city councillor, was elected as his 'second-in-command' and committee secretary.

From the committee's first meeting, things had progressed at a rapid pace and much faster than everyone had thought possible, prompted by the British Commander-in-Chief Field Marshall Sir John French's interview to *The Times* on 27th March calling for more ammunition. The city was fortunate in already having a large manufacturing base and, now that the group had come together, there was the political will to harness it. An appeal was sent out for lathes and machinery suitable for making munitions and also for anyone with the expertise to train a workforce who, given the circumstances, was anticipated as being mainly female. Three members and the secretary visited the Woolwich Arsenal in London to meet with representatives from the Ministry of Munitions to see what had to be done and how.

The committee's original plan to take over one of the local engineering works had fallen through, but the War Office had agreed to the use of the Drill Hall, in which they were meeting, rent-free for the course of the war together with the nearby Territorial Force Association Hall. They'd also taken possession of a neighbouring terrace house as an administrative base and a nearby mission hall was being adapted for a canteen. The city council was providing electric generators at no charge and the East Cumberland Shell Company was almost ready to start production.

'Gentlemen, our vision is now almost a reality. I can now confirm that the factory will be administered by a Board of Management, acting in association with our Munitions Committee and a government approved engineer. The board will include members of this committee and I can report that we have signed an initial agreement to produce 1,500 eighteen-pounder shells weekly. Despite our makeshift facilities, our aim is to increase this to 2,000 shells once the site is fully operational. The intention is to start initial shell-making training in late July or early August. Due to the limited availability of male workers, most of the trainees will be women. When sufficient people are in place, production will start, hopefully before the end of the September. Once operational, newly trained staff will be assisted by volunteers with engineering experience.'

Carr paused and the thirteen men in the room clapped enthusiastically. Jack wondered for a moment if their vigour was encouraged by the fact that, despite the time of year, the room was freezing cold. After a week of pretty mild weather, temperatures had dropped as a warm wind from the south had swung round to bring more icy blasts from the north-east. The drill hall had little heating, and a host of internal and external doors meant drafts whistled through the building like water through a sieve. *Typical spring uncertainty,* he thought, and he pulled up the collar on his jacket in response to a cold draft across his neck. It would be a chilly place to work until summer arrived.

Beside him Chief Constable deSchmid waited for the clapping to stop before he coughed and stood up. 'Like everyone here, I am delighted with the developments and also with the speed that you've been able to respond to what is a clearly a national priority. The possibility that this factory could be up and running in a matter of months is fantastic, but it also raises the question of security. As chief constable it falls to me to ensure that the city is safe, and I wondered what steps you – or should I say, we – are putting into place to safeguard the site. The building may be suitable for a munitions factory, but the fact that the site is in the centre of town and in a terrace of other properties presents certain security issues.'

Jack and deSchmid were on the back row of chairs set out for the meeting. Technically he wasn't back at work yet after his short stay in hospital, but his boss had asked him to attend because he had a feeling that decisions taken at the meeting might affect the overall organisation of policing in the city and he wanted another senior officer there to witness things. He hadn't been wrong and in response to his senior's voice, the audience shuffled in their seats and turned round to look at the two officers. For a moment no one said anything, then Richard Denman stood up. Unlike Carr, he was dressed in a modern, grey, pinstripe, three-piece suit, with a dark blue tie with yellow dots and what could only be described as a brilliant white shirt.

He was a rising star in Westminster, having been appointed parliamentary private secretary to Sydney Buxton, president of the Board of Trade, in February 1910, at the relatively young age of thirty-four. Few people stood in the young politician's way when he set his mind to something, so deScmidt was expecting a response, but he was somewhat taken aback by the nature of the response.

'As the local MP, I have raised this with the War Office and our Watch Committee have been directed to assist in ensuring the security of the building for the duration. It has been agreed that a small force of police officers will be allocated to protect the building around the clock. This group will be seconded from the city police and come under the jurisdiction of the military. In effect they will become military rather than civilian policemen.'

Jack sensed his superior officer tense up.

'With respect, that's totally impractical. The force is already losing officers to the colours on a daily basis and finding suitable replacements is a real problem. More and more of our young men are going off to war, creating a local workforce shortage. That shortage has meant high rates of wages prevailing in the district, making it almost impossible to get men over military age to take up appointments as constables. Poor recruitment results in rising rates of crime, particularly juvenile crime. Taking more officers off the streets will make it even harder to deal with this situation. I would suggest that the security of a military building should be the responsibility of the military, and that means it should be guarded by soldiers.'

Without even a blink of an eye, Denman's response was instantaneous and directed around the disconcerted audience. 'The chief constable is right. Protection of military establishments should be the responsibility of the military. However, as has already been stated, this will be a facility provided by the local community with a civilian board of management that is made up of members of this group advised by the Munitions Committee for East Cumberland. It is a community enterprise, and as such the War Office has agreed that it is down to the community to make sure it is secure, and it has been made clear to the Watch Committee that this responsibility falls to them. I am afraid this is not open to debate.'

deSchmid stood for a moment, looking at the local MP, and then, with a shake of his head, he sat back down.

However, Denham wasn't finished. 'For those of you who may have some quiet concerns about the site, can I give you some further reassurance. Let us be clear that this is a factory for the production of shell cases. The factory will not be handling the explosives that go in them. Instead the shells will be sent south by rail, initially to the Royal Arsenal at Woolwich near London, but I believe that new national filling centres are to be established around the country, including one at White Lund near Morecambe. I am not certain, but it is possible that our shells, together with those from the national projectile factory in Lancaster, may end up there. If so, it will show the government that we in the north of England take our responsibilities to support the war effort very seriously.'

'Aye, and as the man behind it, it won't do your parliamentary ambitions any harm,' whispered deSchmid to no one in particular.

Jack was just about to respond when the door at the rear of the hall opened with a loud bang and a woman backed her way into the room, pushing the door with her backside. She entered in this way because hanging on to one arm and trying to pull her back was a man of similar age who, from his non-aggressive body language, Jack took to be a friend or relative.

'No, Martha! Come away,' the man shouted. 'You'll get both of us into trouble. Please come away.'

The plea fell on deaf ears and with an almighty pull the woman broke free and turned to face the others in the room, who looked in amazement at the new comer. As soon as she turned Jack recognised her. Martha McNaughton was in her late thirties and a prominent voice in the city, speaking out against the war even before its outbreak. Once hostilities had commenced, together with a small group of friends, she had made public her anger at the rising death toll on the frontline and the impact of war on personal liberties and food prices at home. He assumed that the man with her was her husband, Daniel McNaughton. He wasn't surprised that Daniel was trying frantically to stop his wife from disrupting the meeting. He worked for Hudson Scott and Sons in James Street, who produced boxes for Carr's Biscuits, and, with the owners of both companies attending the meeting, he was in a very vulnerable position if either took offence.

'Richard Denman you should be ashamed of yourself. Truly ashamed. You profess to be a member of the Union of Democratic Control, which advocates diplomacy over military action and international cooperation rather than war to ensure peace. Yet here you are at the centre of a group seeking to support the government's war effort. It's disgraceful. And you others, you're as bad. Young men are already dying in their thousands and you are proposing something that will only help to increase the number of dead and injured. You should be pressurising the government to seek international cooperation rather than to escalate hostilities.'

She paused for breath, but as she started to speak again, a late-middle-aged man in a heavy wool overcoat and black homburg hat shouted her down. 'Madame, I understand your concern, but you don't appreciate the realities of the situation. We men have been tasked with responding to a national emergency and it would be wrong of us not to respond. Men have to stand up and be counted in times of war.'

Jack gave a wry smile. He didn't know the respondent, but his put-down was quite clear. The inference was that, as a

95

woman, Martha McNaughton did not grasp what they were trying to do and should not interfere. However, to her credit, she wasn't deterred.

'Oh, I don't appreciate the realities of the situation, do I not? Well, I appreciate that the Cumberland Infirmary is filling up with young men who went away to war in response to a nation that implied that fighting would be a "jolly" adventure and have come back with injuries that will leave them crippled for life. I understand that Maggie Graham has a telegram that says her son died of his wounds when what really happened was that he was blown to bits by a shell barrage, together with thousands of other young men on both sides. And I understand that you intend to produce even more shells to kill even more soldiers rather than lobby the government to negotiate a peaceful solution to the conflict. I understand all that. Do you?'

The final words came out with a sob and with that, she collapsed, crying, to the floor. The room was stunned to silence and after a moment Jack pushed his chair back and walked over to the prostrate woman. Dropping onto one knee, he put his hands softly on her shoulders. 'Come on, Martha. Let's get you home. This is one battle you're not going to win.'

He gently helped her back onto her feet and, putting his arm around her shoulder, he walked her back to the door she had entered with such a flourish only moments before. Her husband followed sheepishly behind them, pausing only to look back at the still-silent room and mutter, 'Sorry'.

Outside, Jack turned to the impassioned woman and her husband. 'You know, Martha, have you ever thought that you're fighting the pacifist battle in the wrong place and in the wrong way?'

He paused. It was the first time he had articulated his thoughts about what was being termed the Great War, and he surprised himself with the clarity of his own views.

'The whole country is being mobilised on a national level in response to the prompting of our government. It will only be stopped in one of two ways. If one side sweeps the other away in battle, and that is what the men in that room are trying to achieve. The other is if the peace organisations also mobilise on a national level, change public opinion and force the government to explore a negotiated end to the conflict. Local communities will never deviate from the national approach because they would run the risk of being accused of a lack of patriotism.'

Martha looked at him and smiled. 'You seem to have a fine grasp of the political situation at local and national level. Why don't you encourage your political friends to explore the alternative?'

'They're not my political friends. I'm only a policeman tasked with keeping the peace in a time of escalating turmoil at home and you're not helping.'

'A policeman! I thought ...' Her response faded as her face betrayed the surprise at Jack's revelation. 'I didn't know the city police had such a fine grasp of the politics. Constable ...?'

'Inspector. Inspector Jack Johnstone. I'm not sure that's the case, but I do know that any sane man would want an end to the atrocities currently taking place across the channel.'

'And sane woman, Inspector. And sane woman! But sanity seems to be in short supply in our government, rather like the ammunition they crave.'

Jack's voice took on a sardonic tone, yet his eyes held a glint of humour. 'I couldn't possibly comment on that, Martha. Now, can you please go home? I've had a long day and until that meeting is ended, it is isn't finished.'

For the first time, the woman smiled. 'OK, Inspector. Just for you I'll go home, but I can't guarantee that we won't meet again in similar circumstances. We do need to lobby nationally, but we also need our local politicians to support our movement and that means encouraging them to change their minds. Not an easy task, as you can see.'

With that, she turned on her heels and walked off, beckoning her husband to follow. Jack watched her go and wondered how long it would be before their paths crossed again. Then, with a shrug, he went back into the drill hall, hoping that the meeting might have drawn to a close in his absence so that he could at last go home.

Inside, things were winding up. deSchmid walked over to him and raised his eyebrows. 'I don't believe it. It's hard enough staying on top of things with the men we've got. How are we to be expected to manage if we lose some to the military? Should anything serious arise we may well not be able to cope. It'll only take one major incident and we'll have anarchy on our hands. Bloody politicians. Oh, by the way, how's the woman? She's lucky one of them didn't insist we arrest her, although I suppose that might not have gone down well in the press.'

'Fine sir. Just a bit upset. I'm sure she'll be alright once she gets home and calms down but you're right. Here's hoping we don't have anything out of the ordinary to deal with or we're buggered. If you'll "pardon my French" sir.'

'Apt in the circumstances, Jack. Very apt.' And with that he headed for the exit.

CHAPTER 12

Carlisle Castle

Midnight, Sunday 9th May 1915

Heinrich waited until what he thought would be the darkest hour of a cloudy, overcast night before he slipped out of the pub and headed for the castle. Dressed in a dark jumper and trousers, he carried two boxes of matches in his pocket and his knife in the scabbard attached to his belt. It was almost two weeks after the incident with the burning house and, following a short but uncomfortable walk back to the Globe, he had spent several days laying low in his room. On the first night Billy Dixon had banged on his door to ask why he hadn't been down to start his shift, but he'd simply wrapped a blanket round his body like a shawl to hide his injuries, opened the door and croaked a response to say that he was down with a sickness bug and would have to miss a few evenings.

Billy had stepped back nervously and said, 'You sound awful. Whatever it is, keep it to yourself. I'll have some food sent up each morning and early evening. If you get up, stay out of the bar until you've recovered.' And with that, he'd turned on his heels and hurried away.

The soreness in his throat had not had to be faked. Looking at the mirror in his room, there was little in the reflection to indicate outwardly his brush with death. Once the initial redness calmed down, the skin peeling off his forehead, hands and nose might easily be mistaken as the effects of sunburn or a mild skin disorder. Although uncomfortable, the pain was bearable, and he knew he had been lucky not to sustain more serious injuries. The old man's blanket had provided better protection for his body than might have been expected. Unfortunately it was ineffective against the smoke and fumes, leaving him with a rasping cough and the feeling that someone was drawing a cutthroat razor across his throat each time he breathed in or out. He knew that the key to a quick recovery was plenty of fluids and so, despite the discomfort, he drank as much water as he could. He also left a message outside his room asking the landlord to leave him porridge and soup rather than solid food for his two promised meals. He had been surprised by how much of the first few days he had spent sleeping. *Clearly,* he thought, *I've been more affected by the trauma than I was aware.*

After a week passed, he had felt stronger and risked evening excursions using the pub's back door to escape notice. The initial worry that an onlooker at the fire might have recognised him and sought him out at the Globe receded as time passed. On several occasions he had walked up to and around the castle to reconnoitre the area in preparation for carrying out the plan that had formed in his head during his enforced rest. Eventually he felt ready to put it into operation. His short time in the city had already given him time to reflect, and it was clear that disrupting the flow of troops to the front would be his first and easier task. As yet he had little more detailed information about the possible munitions factory than he had when he'd overheard the Irishmen's conversation. He'd thought of two possibilities, and tonight he hoped to carry out one of them.

Reaching the Caldewgate, he stepped into the shadow of the west walls where the road passed through them into the city. Behind a row of terraced houses, broken stonework provided simple handholds for anyone wanting to climb up onto the walkway. Checking that he was not observed, he scrambled up and followed the wall towards the south-west corner of the castle itself. He was nervous about the task ahead but also felt incredibly alive. *At least,* he thought, *I'm now doing something other than waiting and planning.* Relief mixed with fear, but he reassured himself that if things went well he would be back in his bed before anyone really realised what had happened.

Heinrich was prepared to kill anyone who got in the way, but he was counting on it not coming to that. From what he'd seen security was pretty lax and although he was uncertain how many sentries there were, he hoped that, like daytime, it would only be two. It was strange, he reflected, how he felt unsettled by the thought of killing someone in cold blood but would have no concerns about maiming or destroying large numbers of soldiers in an act of large-scale sabotage. That was the way of war. Hand-to-hand fighting was a frightening thing, but a mass bombardment depersonalised things to the point where it didn't seem like killing at all, just some strange game of chess, and the winner was the side with most pieces left on the board. In this case he hoped the destruction of two barrack blocks and the men within them would bring Germany a step closer to checkmate.

Reaching the junction of the city and castle walls, he dropped over the ramparts onto the parapet that ran around the latter's outer ward. Pausing to listen for any sounds of alarm, he was relieved to hear only the low hoot of a night owl in some nearby trees and the pounding of blood in his head as his heart beat fast with both the exertion of climbing and the fear of setting off the alarm. Shapes and distance were impossible to judge in the dark, but he knew from his daytime investigations that he had to skirt along the battlements to the north-west corner, where he noticed that it was possible to jump down onto some single-storey storage buildings and from there drop to the floor. The area was protected from open view by the barracks buildings built parallel to the outer ward wall. In the darkness the walkway in front of him was hard to make out and he was conscious that on his right the parapet was not protected by rails of any kind so that if he fell he would not survive the thirty-foot drop to the yard below. He also had to negotiate a number of twenty-four-pound cannons installed in the mid-sixteenth century when Scottish invasion remained a possibility and left guarding walls from a now non-existent enemy. As he crept slowly forwards he started to relax, but this was a short-lived experience. About thirty feet ahead there was a burst of flame and in the light Heinrich observed a young sentry turn his back to the castle buildings and light up a cigarette. For a moment his youthful face was lit by the match as he put his gun on the floor and sat down with his back to the wall behind one of the twenty-four pounders. Heinrich slowly exhaled and closed his eyes with momentary relief. The guard was hiding from view whilst he smoked his gasper and as luck would have it he was on the far side of the cannon, so the two of them were hidden from each other's view. *At least,* he thought, *the sentry's presence on the wall seemed to confirm the same two-man guard duty as during the day.*

Creeping silently forwards using the wall as a hand guide, the German moved stealthily towards the ancient gun and slipped his knife from its scabbard as a precaution. He stopped as he reached the opposite side from the smoker and wondered what to do next, but his thoughts were disrupted as a hand appeared on the top of the cannon and the soldier started to lever himself back to his feet. Heinrich reacted instinctively, he stepped round the gun and shoved him back down. As the man stumbled backwards, he muttered, 'What ...' but the rest of the sentence was cut off as Heinrich brought the hilt of the knife down on the front of the man's head. With a grunt, he slithered down to lie prostrate across the sandstone paving. Blood gushed from a nasty cut and for a moment the German thought he might have killed him, but, placing his hand on the boy's chest, he could still feel him breathing. Replacing his knife in its scabbard, he took the sling off the soldier's gun and bound his feet before using his belt to tie his hands behind his back. A gag from a hanky in his pocket completed the process. He was pretty sure that a determined individual would eventually be able to wriggle out of his confinement but at least it should give him some time to complete his task.

Five minutes later he dropped down from the ramparts and was standing beside a small storage shed. Located between the castle wall and the largest barracks block, it was out of sight from open view. Painted on each of the double doors was a sign warning:

DANGER.
No Admission.
Authorised Personnel Only.

Heinrich had wondered how, without explosives, he hoped to destroy the building and the soldiers within it, but the fuel store he'd observed on his first visit had given him an idea. Petrol was strictly limited to the war's 'key workers' and 'tickets' were issued, allowing small amounts for ordinary motorists, but there were no such limitations on the military, where stocks were built up to aid troop movement using trucks. The use of motorised vehicles had first been introduced in France and Belgium.

Before that soldiers arriving at the train station nearest to their final destination had to walk to the combat zone carrying all their military equipment. Trucks were now being used by both sides to transport troops between the railway and the front. He knew that the British were also starting to use them to shuffle units around during training where marching or train travel proved inadequate. Consequently most 'home bases' had access to a number of trucks which in turn required fuel and fuel had to be stored.

The store was so close to the large barracks that he was certain that any explosion was bound to do serious damage to the accommodation and the individuals within. The lockless door was secured with a single padlocked hasp and staple under the doorknob. This was easily prised off using his knife as a lever. The snap of it breaking sounded loud in the silence of the night but there was no reaction from either the barracks themselves or from the entrance gateway on the other side of the parade ground. His idea was a simple one. He intended to open one or two of the fuel cans, pour the petrol over the remaining ones, throw in a lighted match, wait for the explosion and escape in the confusion. If the explosion didn't destroy the barracks, he expected that the ensuing fire would. As an added guarantee he had wanted to pour fuel across the two entrances to the building, front and rear, to delay or stop anyone from escaping the developing inferno. However, he'd realised that this second step introduced another level of unpredictability and danger to the process. It would take time to do and there was an increased chance that he would be seen as he poured the fuel across the entrances. Instead he'd decided to try an idea he'd thought about during Abteilung IIIb training. There had been a common theory among recruits that the new petrol engine vehicles would blow up if the fuel tank was shot. This had been tried and quickly proved to be incorrect. Five bullets had been shot into an old infantry support vehicle, and to everyone's disappointment there had been no explosion and no fire. The more perceptive in the group had suggested that ignition required both heat and oxygen, and that while the bullet was heated by the explosion that propelled it, the bullet itself wouldn't be hot enough to ignite the petrol. Also, if there wasn't enough air in the tank, an explosion wouldn't be possible. It had made Heinrich think about how you could cause the vehicle to explode and he had eventually come up with the idea of pushing one end of a rag into the fuel filler neck and lighting the other. This had proved to be a spectacular success. So much so that several sceptical recruits who'd got too close to his demonstration had needed to be taken to hospital with severe burns. Since then he'd experimented with various ways of using petrol as an incendiary device and eventually come up with the idea of a crude portable bomb consisting of an open petrol can containing the fuel and an improvised cloth wick that was ignited just before the can was thrown at the target. It wasn't one hundred percent reliable, but he thought it less risky than the alternative.

Slipping into the store, he realised that he hadn't planned for how dark it would be inside. Moving around would be difficult in the darkness of an unlit building. He doubted it would have a light switch, and even if it did, he was reluctant to use it for fear of being seen. The alternative was to use one of his matches but the thought of lighting up in a petrol store was not one he wanted to contemplate.

The problem was solved when the door of a second adjacent barracks opened and someone stepped outside. It was the young private who had been on duty during the day. The boy sat on the step to read a letter that he took out of his shirt pocket and light from inside the building spilt across the yard to the store. Although some way off, with the door of the fuel shed left slightly ajar, it provided sufficient illumination to see the contents within. Hiding in the shadows of the room, Heinrich at first thought that the broken lock and open entry would be seen, but the reader was so engrossed in his message that he didn't look up. Focusing his attention back on his task, he noticed for the first time the overwhelming stink of the petrol. In front of him were dozens and dozens of two-gallon cans. All were pale grey with plain sides and 'Petroleum Spirit, Highly Inflammable' embossed on the top. He picked one up for closer inspection and noted that it was date stamped with a broad arrow marked on the handle. The construction was incredibly flimsy and when he ran his hand along the side he noted that it was wet. A quick sniff told him that it had leaked, and when he looked at the floor he could see it was damp due to escapes from other cans. Realisation dawned on him that he needn't risk the potentially noisy dispersal of petrol over the stored contents, instead he could simply throw in a burning match and the exposed fuel would ignite. There was one flaw in the idea. He'd really need to be in the building to drop the match, and if he was inside he might not have time to get out.

After a short pause to think, he decided that an adaption of the cloth wick idea would work. Picking up one of the cans, he unscrewed the top. Taking one of the rags he had brought with him out of his pocket, he soaked it in petrol and stuffed one end into the open hole. Placing the finished article down just outside the store, he repeated his actions with a second can. When it was ready, he stepped back inside close to the exit away from the main contents of the storeroom and set it down by his feet before carefully lighting a match. Picking it up by the handle, he lit the fuel-soaked material and in the same instance flung it into the centre of the room. Feeling his hand singe as he let go, he quickly backed out the door, slamming it shut behind him and grabbing the other can as he ran. As it clicked shut, Heinrich heard his projectile land and the reaction was instantaneous. There was a whoosh as the leaked petrol ignited and then the store erupted into a massive fireball and a series of explosions lifted the roof off, sending flames soaring into the night sky. A huge plume of sparks and smoke billowed above the castle walls. The German was knocked to the floor, but the closed door, although blown open, protected him from the worst of the discharge. It ended up hanging on one hinge, burning with the rest of the construction. As he rose to his feet, he checked himself for injuries, but incredibly, beyond a few cuts and scratches, plus a ringing in his ears, he seemed fine. The blast had shaken the nearby buildings and several windows had shattered, but to his dismay there seemed to be no major damage, even to those closest to the conflagration. Most of the force of the blast appeared to have gone upwards rather than outwards.

A few yards away the startled serviceman stood his mouth wide open and his hands on his head in amazement. At first the shock of seeing Heinrich seemed to throw him and instead of raising the alarm he simply pointed at him and muttered, 'You. The Canadian. What are you doing here?'

His eyes then dropped to Heinrich's hands and as his nose picked up the strong smell of petrol, he noted the open can in one and watched the other pull a knife from behinds the man's back. His face changed from one of puzzlement to horror. Stepping back, he shouted at the top of his voice, 'Help! Sound the alarm! We're being attacked.'

They were the last words he uttered. Heinrich stepped forwards and slashed backwards with his blade across the man's throat. As the soldier slipped to the ground blood spurted from the cut, splattering onto the floor and across the front of the German's clothes and face. The rusty metallic salt-like taste in his mouth made him gag and he spat a couple of times in an effort to get rid of it. Looking up, he could see several people already coming out of the other nearby barracks and glancing nervously around. Fortunately for him they didn't seem to appreciate what was going on and for a moment Heinrich realised he had a choice to make. He could light the petrol bomb still gripped in his hand and throw it through the nearest window in the hope that it would cause at least some of the building to catch light, but that would inevitably draw attention to himself and increase the odds of being caught to a virtual certainty. The alternative was for him to slip back behind the untouched building, leave the incendiary device somewhere out of sight and try to escape quietly. Had the destruction of the barracks been his only sabotage objective, the first course of action would have been the only honourable option, but with other targets still possible, he chose the second.

Keeping hold of his knife, he ducked behind the barracks, kept to the shadows and was glad not to be observed before he slipped into the dry moat in front of the castle keep's half-moon battery. He emptied the can of its contents and threw it away before bending low to ensure that he could not be seen by anyone above and sprinted along to where the moat ended below the main gatehouse. Dropping onto his stomach, he then crawled up to the edge of the ditch and looked out just in time to see two entrance guards run back into the castle, holding their rifles in front of them. Fleetingly he realised that he'd been wrong in his assumption about the number of guards patrolling at night.

'What's going on?' one yelled in the direction of the now considerable group of people milling around the burning building. When no reply was forthcoming, he turned to the other and said, 'Come on, we need to find out.' Both men shouldered their guns and set off at a run across the parade ground. Heinrich let them get half way before he stood up, slipped his knife into its scabbard and, with cold sweat running into his eyes, walked quickly out of the open and unguarded main gate. Twenty minutes later, he collapsed, fully clothed onto his bed and, with his tired body getting the better of his racing thoughts, was asleep within minutes.

CHAPTER 13

Carlisle Police Headquarters

9.00am, Monday 10th May 1915

It had been an eventful couple of weeks, reflected Jack, as he hurried up the stairs towards the chief constable's office. If the meeting at the drill hall was counted, this was only his second full day back at work, although he had regularly popped in and out of the station since being discharged from hospital. His hair had almost grown back, and he wore a new green and brown wool suit. The tailor had been reluctant to agree to Jack's request that this be made slightly bigger than necessary, complaining that if anyone asked where he had got it they would never visit the shop of someone making such an ill-fitting garment. But the officer had been insistent and eventually got his way. His lungs and airway were still a little swollen and irritated from the smoke inhalation, meaning that breathing remained slightly uncomfortable, but at least he was alive and the doctor at the hospital had said that things would eventually settle down and return to normal. After the rescue Jack and young Jimmy had been taken to the Cumberland Infirmary. An off-duty nurse had watched them being pulled out and insisted that the driver of the bus turn round and take them up to the hospital, where they had been treated in the new Lonsdale Wing. As it turned out, the ward that she worked on was the same one in which Jack had been cared for and the two had become good friends, although she had been at pains to ensure that this did not get in the way of his recuperation. She made sure Jack strictly adhered to the ward doctor's recovery programme, which included plenty of rest and sleep, four hourly doses of a foul-tasting medicine and no smoking. After she had found Jack's pipe in a cabinet beside his bed following a visit from Sergeant Gordon, she had taken to checking his possessions after anyone visited. She had also given the officer a severe tongue-lashing when he had returned a few days later.

'I suppose you're happy to extend your friend's recovery period?' she said sarcastically. 'Or perhaps you don't want him to recover so that you can have his job. Have you no sense, man? He nearly died of smoke inhalation and you want to let him inhale some more. Idiot!'

Jack had never seen the big policeman cowed by anything, but he was clearly taken aback by the nurse's outburst and muttered sincere apologies before backing out of her way as she fussed around the bedridden detective.

'Out! Out!' she cried. 'If you want to bring something useful next time, get him some cough drops or hard candy that he can suck on to soothe his sore throat.'

Elizabeth 'Lizzie' Alexander was in her late thirties. She had left home to live in London with her Aunt Mary after the death of her parents in a typhoid outbreak in 1894. Her wealthy aunt, who had never married, was happy to pay for her favourite niece to train as a nurse at the Royal London Hospital in Whitechapel.

After successfully completing her training, Lizzie had worked in the capital for several years, but after her aunt had passed away and left her a considerable amount of money, she had moved back to Carlisle and obtained a job at the community hospital. Slim, with brown hair and matching eyes that twinkled with mischief, she lived in one of the smaller Stanwix town houses on Eden Street not far from Jack. For company she rented her two spare bedrooms out to nurses, both of whom worked with her at the infirmary.

During his time in hospital, her conversations with Jack had become more relaxed and longer. She was able to tell him that Jimmy was recovering well and that when he got out of hospital he and his mum were going to move back in with her parents. Sadly her life had been dealt a double blow as just a few days after the fire she had been informed that her husband had been killed in action in France. Unfortunately this was becoming a more and more common event in the city. After the local *Carlisle Journal* of 16th April had published a list of nearly sixty men of the 2nd Border Regiment who had been killed at the Battle of Neuve Chappelle in late March, the casualty list had been steadily growing. Relatives now dreaded the arrival of a brown envelope through the letterbox informing them of the death, injury or unknown whereabouts of their loved ones.

By a minor miracle the fire itself had been contained. The fire brigade had arrived just after Jack had been pulled from the building and although they had not been able to save the house or the one next to it, which was fortunately empty, they had been able to prevent it spreading further. Normally there was no dividing wall between the loft spaces in rows of terrace houses and there could be a continuous space across several houses, through which fire could spread rapidly once it caught hold. However, in this case the empty house had once been used as a temporary storeroom and the owner had built two single-brick partition walls in the loft to prevent anyone from the adjacent properties gaining access. The fire in the end terrace had managed to break through the first of these but not the second.

Amazingly, Jack's other injuries had been relatively minor. He had burns to the back of his hands and singed eyebrows, but his heavy wool suit had protected him from the worst of the blaze, although it had been totally destroyed. His hair was burnt and scalp scalded, but slowly this was growing back, covering the worst of the scars. Jenny had informed him that the barber on the corner of Castle Street, opposite the burning house, had offered him a free haircut when he was recovered as a reward for his heroics. Similarly, the tailor on Abbey Street had offered to replace his ruined suit with cloth from stock that he had found difficult to sell. She joked about what kind of material this might be, but, never one to worry about fashion, Jack didn't really care as long as it was not too outrageous.

Of the man who had pulled Jack out of the building there was no sign. Lizzie had checked him over and left him sitting on the kerbside while she had talked to the bus driver, then supervised the loading of Jimmy and Jack onto the bus. However, when she returned to get him, the man had disappeared and no one could recall seeing him leave. Although concerned about his health, she had put this down to him being a reluctant hero. Jack was a little more sceptical. He understood why a man might not want to be the centre of attention – not everyone wanted to be in the papers, and the fire and rescue would certainly get a mention; one of the local journalists had even come to see him in hospital – but why would he want to avoid medical attention?

'What do you remember about him?' he asked her when the two of them were chatting on the morning of the day he was due to go home.

'Not much. He was tall, but his face was black with soot. I think his hair was blond or light brown. His clothes weren't as badly burnt as yours. I think he might have had something wrapped round him when he entered the house.'

'Voice?'

'Pardon?' Lizzie gave him a questioning look. 'I'm not one of your suspects down at the police station, you know.'

Jack smiled apologetically. 'Sorry. Force of habit. Was there anything you noticed about his voice?'

'Not really. The only thing he said was thanks when I sat him down. I told him I'd be back in a minute and then went to sort the transport to the hospital out. When I got back he was gone.' She paused for a moment before continuing. 'It might be my imagination, but I think my initial reaction was that he sounded American, but on one word, who knows? He could have been from Devon. It definitely wasn't a northern accent, though. Anyway ... does it matter? If he doesn't want to be bothered, why should we worry? After what he did, he deserves a bit of privacy, if that's what he wants.'

'Mmmm. I suppose so,' said Jack. 'Now, about tomorrow. I was thinking you might like to come and check on your patient and accompany him for a walk round Victoria Park. At this time of the year the flowerbeds have been newly planted and the colours will be beautiful to look at.'

'Oh were you now?' Lizzie raised her eyebrows. 'Were you now? We'll have to see about that.'

*

When Jack arrived, deSchmid and two army officers were standing around the large table in the chief constable's office. It was a warm morning and the windows of the room had been flung wide open, letting in the bright sunshine and a view of the West Walls beyond. The voices of people using the Sallyport steps to access the city carried from below and the ever-present gulls screeched above. As Jack entered they looked up from the papers they had been shuffling through.

'Ah! Inspector Johnstone, glad you're here. May I introduce Major Binning. William is acting second-in-command of the Lonsdales and this is Lieutenant Colonel Percy Machell who is in charge of the training battalion at Blackhall Racecourse.'

Jack crossed the room and shook the proffered hands. Machell was a well-known figure in the neighbouring county of Westmorland. He had spent much of his military career in Egypt, having served in the Nile Expeditionary Force, the Egyptian Army and Egyptian Coastguard, among others. He had retired to his substantial retreat at Crackenthorpe Hall, near Appleby, from where he lived the life of a country gent. Middle-aged with a stocky build but slight paunch, Jack had come across him at the county show when he had presented prizes to the winners of the various wrestling contests including Jack himself. He had been surprised that he had been prepared to shake the foundations of his quiet country life with a return to the military. However, the young soldiers who took their leave in town and visited the local drinking holes spoke well of him. He pushed the men hard in training and was a firm disciplinarian, but they respected a man who, despite being CO, was constantly on parade with them, training and smartening up both officers and men, drawing up programmes of work and seeing they were carried out, plus ensuring the welfare of his men.

Binning was the epitome of the officer class. Tall with broad shoulders and light brown hair, he had a handlebar moustache that could have been the model for Kitchener's recruitment poster.

'Pleased to meet you, Johnstone. Eric tells me that if anyone can get to the bottom of this mystery, you can. Obviously it happened on a military base and we need to be kept informed, but I just don't have the manpower or, for that matter, anyone with the skills to investigate it.'

Jack looked from Binning to deSchmid puzzled. 'Thank you, sir. I appreciate your confidence in me but …' He hesitated. 'What mystery would that be?'

Binning put his hands on his hip before almost shouting his reply. 'Murder, that's what! Murder and sabotage! The slaughter of one of my men right outside one of the castle barracks. Inside the castle, mark you! A place that's supposed to be secure. Whoever did it also blew up one of the fuel depots and caused a hell of a lot of damage to the adjacent buildings. It's a miracle no one else was killed.'

CHAPTER 14

Carlisle Magistrates Court, Town Hall Buildings

Afternoon, Wednesday 19th May 1915

'My colleagues and I have considered the evidence carefully and have come to the conclusion that the case against the defendants is not sufficiently strong to convict them. They have admitted owning the cocks and fitting them with spurs, but they weren't actually caught fighting the birds, and the police have been unable to demonstrate that any cruelty has taken place. On the contrary, the birds themselves seem to have been in excellent health. Convicting the accused on the assumption that they intended to fight the birds would not be sound. Neither would a conviction on the basis that they were responsible for setting up a cock fighting event. The police found the four on their own in the barn at Etterby Farm. Despite suggestions that this had recently been vacated by a large crowd, no members of that crowd have been presented to support either of the allegations which the men have vehemently denied. I can do no more than warn them as to their possible future conduct and dismiss the case.'

With that he nodded towards the clerk sitting at a small desk in front of the bench, who got to his feet and turned towards the body of the court. 'All rise.'

As everyone stood up, the three magistrates also rose and shuffled along the bench to leave by a door at the rear of the room. After they'd departed, there were wild whoops from the accused and much back-slapping of the lawyer who had represented them. Jack shook his head in frustration and taking his pipe from the inside pocket of his suit, thrust it between clenched teeth. He stood and watched as the four men hurried out of the room, no doubt heading for a local hostelry to celebrate their good fortune. He felt no malice towards them; they were ordinary farm labourers and he knew that they would have been well paid to organise an event by others with deep-enough pockets to get someone else to do their dirty work. The same men who paid for a lawyer experienced in dealing with such cases to travel up from Lancashire to defend them. Of course, it also helped to have a sympathetic magistrate hearing your case.

James McGee, the chair of the bench, was a retired major and strong-willed individual, well used to expecting and getting his own way, both in his previous career and now in public life. His forceful, many would say bullying, approach meant those sitting beside him on the magistrates' bench rarely succeeded in presenting opinions contrary to his own. Dissenting views were quickly and often loudly quashed. Once a well-built, good-looking man with a fine head of hair, age had not been kind to him. Muscle had turned to fat, leaving him with a large belly hanging over a bursting trouser line. Wavy golden locks had been replaced by a fringe of grey-white hair around a balding, mottled scalp. His cheeks and nose had a red tinge, which together with the expanding waistline was testimony to his love for fine wine and vintage port. He lived at Harker Manor on the north side of the River Eden, less than half a mile from the isolated farm where the men had been caught, and, although Jack had no evidence, he strongly suspected that behind the wealthy land owner's eminently respectable front, he was someone with a high standing in the banned sport. A lot of the practice was to be found in the rural community, and if a farm had a lot of game birds then it was likely that cock-fighting was going on. Many respectable citizens including magistrates attended cock fights and there was evidence of some police officers colluding with the organisers.

Previous chief constables had tended to turn a blind eye to the 'sport', but this one was different and, much to the annoyance of one or two local dignitaries, had pursued the practice with some vigour. However, catching and prosecuting those involved was difficult. They increasingly met in out-of-the-way locations, of which there are plenty in the Carlisle area. Meetings frequently took place early in the early morning, before anyone else was up and about, or late afternoon, when most folk were at work.

Jack had hoped that the two supporting magistrates, one a retired grocer and the other a part-time teacher at the local grammer school, would sway McGee, but he'd hardly consulted with either before announcing his judgement and they in turn had spoken few words throughout the proceedings. He wasn't really surprised. Once he'd become aware that McGee was to preside and that the court case would take place less than ten days after the arrest, he knew the chances of conviction were low, despite the strength of the evidence and the clarity of the law. The Act for the more effective Prevention of Cruelty to Animals 1849 clearly stated that it was illegal for anyone to keep, use and manage a place for the purpose of animal-fighting, including cockerels, or to encourage, aid or assist in the fighting or baiting of an animal. The penalty for these offences was set at not less than five pounds but no more than ten.

The afternoon raid on Etterby Farm had been well organised. A justice of the peace could authorise in writing for the police to enter a place that was being used or suspected of being used for cock-fighting and take into custody anyone suspected of breaking the law. A warrant had been duly obtained and Jack plus Sergeant Gordon had entered the farm's barn, where they thought the meet was taking place, leaving four constables outside to catch anyone who tried to avoid arrest, one on each side of the building. However, except for the four accused who were caught in the act of trying to remove the razor-sharp spurs from the bird's legs, the building was empty. Jack was disappointed but not surprised. At meets, lookouts were deployed and men scattered via planned escape routes as soon as the police were seen or heard. In addition, he suspected that one of the constables sympathetic to the sport had leaked information about a raid to the organisers. The 'Paddy Wagon' had been brought up and the men had been paired with a constable and loaded onto the bench seats that ran along each side of the secure rear compartment.

'Will you take them back to the station and charge them, Graham?' Jack had asked the big sergeant. 'I'm going to call it a day and walk home. The walk might help me relax and get rid of the annoyance at our birds fleeing the coup this afternoon. Can you sign me off at the front desk?'

The sergeant had pulled a sympathetic face, nodded and pulled himself into the driver's seat in the front section of the black vehicle. Making himself comfortable, he'd started the engine and drove away. Jack strolled slowly after them. The warm afternoon sun was relaxing and, lighting his pipe, he'd puffed gently on the rich tobacco and his thoughts had turned to whether the afternoon, and the time taken up planning the raid, had been an effective use of police time.

As he left the dark corridors of the town hall and moved into the bright sunshine outside, he was approached by Robert Jardine from the local paper and knew that this same question was about to be posed by the journalist. Tall and well turned out, with bright eyes and a ready smile, Jardine often reported on the local wrestling events and Jack counted him as a friend. However, he also covered countryside sports and the two disagreed about cock-fighting and whether it was a barbaric, illegal act or legitimate activity. The number of incidents and prosecutions had declined significantly since the turn of the century, but the practice still existed and local opinion was divided. For many it was still seen as an acceptable part of rural life and some papers tended to reinforce this view by taking a light-hearted view of the offence. Jack recalled the furore caused when the local journal had reported that:

'The North Cumberland Cock-Fighting Club had a successful meet last Saturday. The event was well attended. Unfortunately your correspondent was not in a position to publish the names of the hardened law breakers who took part in this disgraceful affair.'

There was frequently criticism of police attempts to stop cock-fighting and they were repeatedly derided for interfering in a 'traditional' field sport.

'Hello, Jack. Another few days of wasted police time. I bet the local burglars are delighted to see Carlisle's finest focused on animal welfare rather than them.'

'It's a crime, Robert, just like burglary, and it needs to be stopped. The baiting or fighting of any animal is cruel and has no place in civilised society.'

'Be reasonable, Jack. The idea that it's cruel to cockerels is laughable. It's no different to fox and deer hunting or culling badgers with dogs or even two birds fighting in the farmyard.'

'I don't hold with hunting deer or foxes either, but at least in those situations the animals have a chance to escape. In a yard an ordinary cockerel can also run away after a sharp peck, but the game bird is ringed in and won't or can't give up until it drops down dead. That's not sport as I understand it.'

'Alright, alright. I understand you're upset about the court case. Why don't we adjourn to the Kings Head and we can talk about something else over a pint?'

Jack was inclined to say no to Jardine's olive branch, but he realised that this might be seen as surly and ungrateful, so instead he smiled and said, 'Fine, but you're buying.'

Five minutes later, they were sitting in a wooden booth under the front window of the Kings Head each with a pint for company. The hostelry was located in Fisher Street, behind the town hall and next to the Guildhall. The seventeenth-century, split level building had a stone floor and low wooden beams, that could give a careless customer a fearsome crack on the head, supporting a yellow, nicotine-stained ceiling. The lunchtime rush had abated and the early-evening crowd was yet to come, but there was still a friendly, bustling atmosphere.

At first, neither man spoke, each taking a first sip of their beer and gazing out onto the busy road, where a healthy trade in fish, meat and game was taking place in the shops lining the busy thoroughfare. Jack was not a big drinker. Contrary to popular opinion within his academy, he was convinced excessive drinking would affect his ability to wrestle, particularly if he drank the day before a meet. However, he did like an occasional drop of stout. The dark liquid had a rich, creamy head, and was flavoured and coloured with barley so wasn't as sweet as some other beers.

Jardine took another sip and smiled contentedly. 'Not bad, eh, Jack! Not bad at all. The first of the day is always the best.'

Jack said nothing but gently nodded his assent.

'So what did you make of the court case?' the journalist continued.

'You couldn't print what I really think,' replied the inspector, 'and if you did I'd be out of a job.'

'Ah. So I can report that the arresting officer was disappointed with the court verdict but vowed to continue the fight against this cruel injustice to animals.'

'You can report what you bloody like, but keep me out of it.'

'Come on. The public are always interested in both sides of a story.'

But Jack wasn't listening. His attention had been taken by a scruffily dressed individual who walked unsteadily across the room and then elbowed two men standing at the bar out of the way. One of them, a tidily dressed workman with a flat cap, turned angrily towards him.

'Hey mate steady on. I was here first.'

Time seemed to stand still as the drunk stood for a moment, looking at flat cap. Then he shook his head, either to clear it and make sense of the response or in amazement that someone had dared to challenge him. He looked at the other, sizing him up, and Jack knew immediately what was going to happen. Getting to his feet, he moved quickly over to the bar, stepping in between the two men and facing the trouble maker.

'I know you. Weren't you in here at the weekend? Saturday night, I think.' Jack gambled that this was the man's regular haunt and that, given his state on a mid-week afternoon he'd probably not remember much about a weekend binge. 'Yeah. It was you. You don't look too happy. I think it's my round. So let me buy you a beer to cheer you up.'

The man grabbed Jack by the lapels of his jacket and pulled him close up to his face. The policeman could smell the alcohol on his breath. For a moment the pub went quiet as the customers waited to see what was going to happen. Glasses paused, half way to mouths, and heads turned.

'Now, gents. No trouble, please,' said the landlord from behind the safety of the bar.

'Either you let me buy you that drink or we'll move on. Time's passing and I'm still sober,' said Jack calmly, and he tilted his head, waiting for a response. He could tell that this time the man was sizing him up and wondered if he was thinking about something other than beer. Then, with a low growl, the other's face broke into a glassy, drunken smile

'Aye, I remember. The drinks on you,' he joked. 'Get me that beer, and a shot of whiskey while you're at it.' And, letting go of the suit, he looked around the bar, laughing at his perceived clever banter. The barman served the drinks and the drunkard knocked back the short in one gulp, belched and with a muttered, 'Thanks,' shuffled off to his seat at the rear of the room, slopping beer from his pint glass onto the floor as he went. Jack watched him until he sat back down, then turned to walk back to his own seat.

'Hey. Who's paying for the beer and the whiskey?' the barman asked.

'You are,' said Jack with his back to the man. 'I reckon you got off lightly. A couple of drinks is the least you could expect to pay compared to the cost of repairing a damaged bar.'

'Well,' said Jardine as the other man slid back into the booth. 'That was fortunate. What would have happened if he'd refused your offer?'

'Well, you'd be cobbling together an article on either police brutality to a helpless man during a pub brawl, and the need for greater sympathy when dealing with the public, or brutality towards a policeman, and the need to put more officers on the street to curb the rise in drunkenness in the city. I don't suppose you'd be bothered which one. A story is a story. You get paid either way.'

'That's a rather cynical way of looking at things don't you think?'

'But it's what you would do.'

Jardine thought for a moment and then smiled. 'True. I can't deny it. One has to make a living. Changing the subject slightly. On the matter of violence, what's all this about a soldier being killed at the castle? Apart from confirming a private died, the army are saying virtually nothing about the circumstances of the death. Killed in an accidental explosion is the official line. Anything you can tell me about what happened? The rumour is that it wasn't an accident but murder.'

Jack looked at the young reporter and shook his head. 'Even if I knew something, you know I couldn't talk to you about an incident currently under investigation.'

'So if it's under investigation, it's true, there is something fishy about the situation. Come on, there must be something you can tell me.'

'All I can say is that, as you seem to be aware, there was a death at the castle barracks which the army are currently looking into.'

Surely it's the police's job to look into an unusual death, accidental or otherwise?'

'Perhaps, but it happened on army property, and in this instance we are working together to look into the matter. Now, I really can't tell you any more than that.'

'Can't or won't? Look, Jack, maybe I have a little bit of information that would help the investigation, but I want something in return. That's reasonable, isn't it?'

'What's reasonable is that if you have information about the attack it's your duty to inform the police, and without any pre-conditions or you could find yourself arrested for withholding evidence.'

Jardine shook his head. 'I thought we were friends, Jack. Friends don't threaten each other.'

'Perhaps not, but then neither do they keep secrets from each other. Look, tell me what you know and I'll make sure that anything that can be released to the press gets to you first. That's the best I can do.'

For a few seconds the two men looked at each other, each wondering if the deal would work before the reporter nodded and spoke. 'The rumour going round on the street is that it was murder. Drink loosens young soldiers' lips, particularly when it's free. By all accounts it was a particularly violent attack just outside one of the barracks blocks. A cut throat and lots of blood, plus significant fire damage to the building itself. Am I right?'

Jack said nothing. It didn't surprise him that news of the attack was common knowledge, even though the 'powers that be' had tried to keep it quiet for fear of creating panic within both the military and civil communities.

'I'll take your silence as a "yes". Well, the word is that the attack wasn't carried out by anyone local. The criminal elements in our fair city are not averse to making money out of certain aspects of this war, there's a healthy trade in some shortage items, but they draw the line at attacks on young men, who in a few weeks will be off to fight for their country with a strong possibility that they won't be coming back.'

Jack raised a questioning eyebrow. 'Honour among thieves, eh, Robert?'

'Something like that, but Grandfather is adamant it's not someone from round here.'

'He's certain of that?'

'He has no doubt and if he says that it was an outsider then it was an outsider.'

Whilst Jardine and his iron monger father Samuel had been law-abiding men all their lives, the same could not be said about Robert's grandfather Abraham. In the last decades of the nineteenth century he had been at the heart of the criminal fraternity in the city, particularly illegal gambling. In the mid-1800s, anti-gambling sentiment had grown due to the establishment of several powerful anti-gambling groups, including a loud religious voice that argued passionately against the immoral and corrupting nature of the activity. Following a number of high-profile betting frauds, the government had decided to step in and passed the Gaming Act of 1845 and the Betting Act of 1853. Except for on-course betting at horse-racing tracks, which working class men could rarely afford, the practice was outlawed. As a result, gambling went underground and onto the streets. Abraham Jardine had seized the opportunity and quickly established an illegal betting network. He set up 'unofficial' bookmakers in the licensed drinking tents at sporting events such as wrestling meets, fell races or athletic events. Initially he attended the events himself, but as his business grew he employed 'bookies' who got the odds on an event from 'the boss' and whose job was simply to collect cash from the gamblers and make payments depending on the outcome of the bet. At the bigger events the 'bookie' was accompanied by a 'minder' for security. Prohibition notices were ignored by the punters and the police were happy to turn a blind eye, unless the combination of drinking and gambling led to a disorderly incident. Consequently, he quickly developed a lively trade and profits were good, allowing him to expand into licensesd premises within the city. Landlords were paid a 'back hander' to allow betting to take place in their hostelry and, if they were caught and prosecuted, Jardine paid the fine on their behalf or, in some instances, bribed magistrates who owed him money through their own illicit gambling activities. By the turn of the century his influence was everywhere throughout the city and what 'Abe' Jardine didn't know wasn't worth knowing. Then, at the height of his powers, he'd decide to retire. He set his son up in a thriving ironmonger's store in the town centre and bought a large manor house and surrounding land on the western outskirts of the city, where he took on the role of country squire. To all intents and purposes, he presented the façade of a retired gentleman, but despite his denials very little went on that he wasn't aware of. If he said it was an outsider who carried out the attack, then an outsider it was. The question was, who was he and where did he come from?

'Did he say anything else? Was he able to gather any other information that would help us find out who did it?'

'Information, no! But he did say to tell my bloody copper friend that if it wasn't a local crime then it has to be someone from outside the city, and in time of war, even this far away from the conflict, that might suggest *sabotage and a saboteur.*'

The two men spoke the final four words together and Jack realised that, if true, his troubles might be bigger than he'd imagined and were likely to get even bigger.

CHAPTER 15

Quintinshill Near Gretna Green

5.00am, Saturday 22nd May 1915

Heinrich had laid low after his attack on the barracks, expecting a reaction but there had been nothing in the papers about sabotage and no heightened police or military action. He'd continued his pub job but avoided going out and about as much as possible. Now, several weeks after the incident, he thought it was safe to resume his clandestine activities and the priority was to find the mythical proposed munitions work. He'd told Billy Dixon that he needed a few days off to take care of some personal business and, although not pleased, the landlord had grudgingly agreed when Heinrich had said the alternative was for him to quit. So he'd arranged to have Wednesday after lunchtime closing, plus Friday and Saturday mornings, but to be back for his shift on each night. The landlord had asked the obvious questions about where he going and why but had been met with a simple, 'It's private.'

His aim was to explore the mainline north, aware from the pub gossip that the munitions factory was somewhere just over the border in Scotland. However, despite the constant generalisations, no one seemed to know the specific location. At some point he hoped to find a place where a track branched off to the proposed site. Much of the building materials would be brought in by locomotive, so it seemed probable that rails would have been laid to accommodate this. His initial idea was to use the train to travel up to Gretna and the other border stations, then explore the locality on foot but, after initially checking out train times and destinations, he'd changed his mind. There might be travel restrictions and even if there weren't it might look strange if he was found to be travelling regularly without any real purpose. On top of that, he'd no real idea where to look and without transport a search could take forever. So he'd decided that a bike would suit his purpose, provided he utilised an early start and stuck to weekends when the countryside was likely to be quieter.

He'd begun his search the previous Saturday, leaving the pub early before anyone was awake, taking a bicycle from the back yard. He didn't worry about it being missed, as it had stood unmoved from the day he'd started work, almost unseen and probably forgotten, behind a pile of empty wooden crates and various items of junk. Although apparently left uncared for, the black enamelled Raleigh, with a wicker basket attached to the handle bars, was in surprisingly good condition and, once the Dunlop tyres had been blown up with the brass inflator that had been left screwed to the main frame, he'd peddled it to nearby Bitts Park on a trial run and was pleased to find that it performed as good as new.

Taking the road across the River Eden to Stanwix and

Kingstown and then out of the city, he loosely followed the train tracks north. Although the wind off the Solway blew strongly into his face, making his eyes water, the route was pretty flat so he managed to maintain a good pace, and eight miles into his journey, as a pale sun broke through a cloudy sky, he crossed the River Esk into Scotland. A couple of miles further on the tracks split, one heading west while the other continued north. He'd opted for the former and followed the road and trainline into the small hamlet of Gretna. As he rode through the village, he'd noticed some new building work on the south-western edge. It was small scale, only a few houses, but he had intended to investigate this further.

However, as he reached his initial destination of the railway station, the weather changed, and dark clouds blew in across the vast waters of the Solway Firth that separated Cumberland from Dumfriesshire. The sun disappeared behind grey skies and spots of rain fell from the sky. At the same time a slim man, in the uniform of what he assumed was the stationmaster, had come out of a small wooden building on the platform and asked him what he wanted and if he needed any help. Heinrich wasn't really expecting to meet anyone at this time of day and hadn't really thought through how he might respond if someone did approach him. Unusually flustered, the best that he could think of at short notice was that he was out for a weekend cycle and had ridden up from Carlisle intending to get the train back. As soon as he said it he realised that, in a thick coat and trousers plus the heavy boots that he was wearing in case he needed to leave the bike and explore, he wasn't really dressed for a day out cycling, but it was too late to change his tale.

The man looked at him as if he was dealing with a simpleton and then smiled, shook his head and responded in a broad Scottish accent. 'Nae chance this morning, lad. You should hae checked the train times. There's nowt coming through here 'til this afternoon. You're welcome to come in oot 'o the rain and shelter in the waiting room, but it'll be a few hours before the local train stops.'

As he finished, a second man in shirt sleeves, dark blue trousers and a white shirt with rolled up sleeves and black braces came round the side of the building. For a second the German's heart skipped a beat as he noted that perched on his head was a policeman's helmet.

'If you len a hand and help us move a few storage boxes Constable Mackay and I might even share a spot of lunch with ye.'

Not wanting to waste time sat in a waiting room or having to speak to two inquisitive locals, he'd nervously thanked the men for their kind offer but said he needed to be back in Carlisle around lunchtime and would just cycle back.

'Aye, well. Please yersel, but you're gonna get richt wet if ye peddle back noo!'

Heinrich had made an excuse about it being his own fault for not checking the train times and, with a wave, had set off back the way he'd come. Where a side road headed west towards the construction work, he paused, thinking he would take a look at the new buildings, but when he looked back he could see in the distance that the two men were still watching him and reluctantly decided it would be prudent to continue his journey home.

Today he'd decided to follow the northern line and, skirting east of Gretna, he'd passed through the smaller hamlet of Springfield and then, as the tracks had gently curved away from the main road, he'd turned on to a narrow lane that he hoped would bring him alongside them again. This time wearing lighter clothing, he rode through flat, rich farmland where cattle and sheep grazed on grass that seemed unnaturally green. It was a bright summer morning with the sun already high in a cloudless blue sky and, although there was still an early-morning chill in the air from the light breeze sweeping across the road from nearby fields, the horrors of war seemed totally unreal. Eventually he arrived at a bridge which passed over what he knew must be the north-and-south bound main lines. On one side the word 'Blacksike' had been painted on a piece of wood nailed to a fence post. As he bent over the parapet and looked down onto the tracks, an outrageous idea popped into his head. He was aware from briefings back home that soldiers were often moved by sea embarking from various ports up and down the country, but he also knew, again from incautious bar-room chatter, that troops recruited in Scotland were frequently brought south by trains using both the east and west coast mainlines. If the bridge was destroyed then there would be significant disruption and all train movements up or down the west coast would be halted. Given the remoteness of the location, repairs could take some considerable time.

Slipping down the grass bank on the north side of the bridge, he paused beside the tracks and looked up at the sandstone structure. He then followed the tracks underneath, examining its construction, but as he passed through to the other side, his initial excitement drained away. The bridge looked impressively sturdy. The abutment and buttresses supporting it were in good condition, as was the archway between. Even the wing walls which extended beyond the structure showed no sign of cracks from the pressure of retaining the earth behind the abutment. With a sinking feeling, he realised that to succeed would take significant amounts of explosives and the specialist knowledge of where to place the charges, neither of which he possessed. He might be able to get his hands on the former, but he had only a limited idea of how to use it and certainly not enough to bring down such a solid structure. He scrambled back up to the road and stood for a moment looking south. *It's a shame,* he thought, *it's an excellent, albeit impractical, idea.*

As he looked towards the Cumberland Hills, he noticed for the first time the layout of the tracks to the south. To the north the lines simply disappeared into the distance, but to the south there was what looked like a small marshalling area. Here the railway company had installed two overtaking loops, one each for the north-and-south-bound tracks. He'd seen similar layouts back home in Germany and knew that it meant that a slower goods or passenger train could be shunted into either of these lay-bys, allowing a faster express to pass through on the mainline and overtake it. There was also a short piece of track connecting the two mainlines, which he guessed was to allow trains to cross from one track to another, and a two-storey signal box to his left, on the outside of the up loop. The north-bound overtaking loop was currently occupied by a small goods train, the absence of any steam escaping from the stack on top of the boiler indicating that it had been there for some time.

Slipping his binoculars from the bicycle's wicker basket, he focused them on the upper floor of the signal box and made out a man moving around inside. Presumably this was the signalman who controlled the tracks in front of him. The sign on the side of the building read 'Quintinshill', which he took to be the name of the marshalling area. He stared at the set-up for a long time and then made a decision. It was still possible to salvage something out of the morning's travels if he could find out something about troop or equipment movements which might later prove useful. The best way to do this was to talk with the signalman and, if he posed as a lost labourer, he might even find out something about the location of the mysterious munitions work. Should the railway man get too curious, then the place was isolated enough for him to have an unobserved accident. Returning the binoculars to the basket, he lifted the bike up, carried it down the bank and leant it against the wall under the bridge. Here it was out of sight from anyone, except those on a passing train.

He then walked along the side of the track towards the signal box.

Heinrich had been in a signal box during an Abteilung IIIb visit to the Berlin Marshalling Yards the year before. Senior army officers had been annoyed at what they thought was the far too slow movement of freight in and out of the city and had visited the yard to pressurise the superintendent in charge. He in turn had responded by explaining the time-consuming process of coordinating train movements in and out of the station, and the limitations of the track availability and signalling system to achieve this. As he approached he could see that the Quintinshill box was very much like the one he had visited then, although much smaller. The two-storey building was rectangular in shape with its longer sides running parallel to the train lines. A red brick lower floor supported an upstairs operating room, with floor-to-ceiling windows on three sides giving views directly out onto the tracks and up and down the lines. Access to the upper area was gained by external timber steps up one side of the building, leading to a small landing outside the main entrance. Moving quietly up these stairs, he reached the already-open door and peered hesitantly into the room. The signalman was looking out of the south-facing window and therefore had his back to him, so for a moment he was able to glance around the box. It was much as he had expected. On the long, solid wall furthest away from the tracks hung two clocks and a number of diagrams and warning notices. Beneath them the levers controlling the points and signals were to be found, and he knew that these would be linked to the lower part of the lever frame housed in the locking room below. Whilst the levers in the frame on the operating floor allowed the signalman to move points through rodding and to operate signals through wires, it was the equipment in the locking room that prevented the signalman from accidentally setting up conflicting movements.

Locking was the mechanism in the frame by which the levers were prevented from being moved until other levers were in the appropriate place.

Eventually the man turned round and Heinrich took in an individual in his early thirties, of slim build but quite tall. He wore a flat cap that seemed much too big for a head with narrow features and a prominent nose under which grew a thick, dark moustache. He was smartly dressed in a dark waistcoat and trousers over a white shirt with a narrow tie knotted loosely at the neck. For a moment the two men looked at each other before the signalman spoke. 'Sorry, mate, you can't come in here. Just wait outside.' He stepped quickly across the room until he stood in the doorway, blocking access to the room. 'What is it you want?'

Sticking with the story he had prepared, Heinrich said, 'I think I've got myself a bit lost and wondered if you could help. I'm supposed to start a labouring job this morning with a gang laying side tracks to the new munitions factory somewhere round here. I cycled up from Carlisle and I've followed the directions I was given but I don't see any evidence of track-laying, so I've no idea if I'm in the right place or if I've made a wrong turn somewhere. I left my bike by the bridge and nipped along here to ask.'

'Aye, well, I know nowt about any new munitions factory and you shouldn't be walking along the mainline tracks, and you definitely shouldn't be in this signal box. It's illegal for civilians to trespass on railway lines or bridges, so I suggest you cycle back down the road to Gretna and ask someone there. Now, I'm expecting a train any moment now, so if you'll excuse me, I'm busy ...' And with that, the man closed the door in Heinrich's face and went back across the room to resume his vigil at the window.

For a moment, the German thought about what to do next, but there seemed little to be gained from taking the matter further and the man posed no obvious threat, so in the end he decided to do as he had been asked. He descended the stairs, but as he reached the bottom step he felt the ground shudder, and ahead of him what appeared to be a goods train trundled into sight from the south and slowed as it approached the north-facing lay-by. There were a series of loud clangs, the cross-over rails vibrated and re-aligned, and the lumbering giant was shunted off the main line onto the side loop. In a swirl of steam, it came to a screeching halt just a few yards in front of him. He had no idea why, but he was curious as to what would happen next, so he took up a position underneath the stairway where he was partially hidden from sight. Glancing at his watch, he noted the time, 6.14am. Minutes later, a stocky man in a loose-fitting blue jacket and matching trousers jumped down from the brake van at the back of the train. He walked along beside the track, briefly inspecting each freight wagon before crossing the two main lines and empty south-bound lay-by and skipping up the steps into the signal box. From his actions, Heinrich guessed that he was the train's brakeman. Standing directly below the open control-room door, he could hear the men's voices clearly. After a brief greeting, the visitor asked about two late-running London to Glasgow express trains and how long he would have to wait in the siding to allow each to pass through. He caught the signalman's response that they were imminent before his attention was distracted by the arrival of another train from the south.

At first, he thought it was one of the main line expresses, but instead of roaring through, it gradually slowed down and came to a halt on the north-bound track a hundred yards or so past the goods train standing in the parallel lay-by. From the size of the engine and the number of carriages, it was clear that this was no express train. It was more likely to be some regional service, although he wondered why it had stopped. As if in answer to his unspoken question, a man jumped down from the engine cab and made his way across the two unoccupied sets of tracks to the signal box. In looks and clothing he was not dissimilar to the signalman in the control room, although slightly shorter and with a stockier build. Slung over his shoulder was a small canvas bag, from which poked a rolled-up newspaper. Once again Heinrich caught the conversation in the box, although this time only in fragments because of the engine noises still coming from the stationary locomotive.

From what he could gather, the new arrival was the relief signalman, who, having overslept, had caught the local train as it passed through his home in Gretna, knowing it was due to stop at the signal box. His colleague informed him about the position of the other trains on their section of the line and approaching their box, including the need to move the one he had arrived in before the expresses arrived. Heinrich wondered how this would be managed, but the second man came back out onto the landing at the top of the stairs and, after some frenetic signalling and shouting across to the driver's cab, the engine started to move again. Slowly it reverse shunted from the north-bound track across the bridging rails to face the wrong way on the south-bound line. At this point the fireman jumped down and walked towards the signal box. As he crossed the track a third train came into sight, this time from the north, travelling on the south-bound mainline. At first it looked like the new arrival, an empty coal wagon, would plough straight into the local train facing the wrong way on the same line. However, like the freight wagon, it slowed down as it approached and was shunted into the south-bound lay-by directly in front of the signal box leaving only the north-bound main line empty.

In another fractured burst of conversation, the first signalman reminded his relief to up-date the train book with information that should have been written in, had he started on time at 6.00am and, as the local's fireman entered the box, he was told to make sure he logged the 6.30am arrival time and details of his train.

'Right! It's 6.35am. The trains are all sorted. Expresses should be through soon. I'm off duty, but before I head off home, I'm going to have ten minutes with a cup of tea reading the paper to find out what the latest war news is. I'd be happy if you left me out of your conversations.'

With that final comment, the signal box went quiet, except for the sound of footsteps on the wooden floor. However, the silence was short-lived as a young man appeared from the back of the coal wagon and shouted up the stairs, 'Hi gentlemen. Any idea how long we're going to be kept in the loop?' Not receiving any reply, he ran up the stairs, taking them two at a time, and bumped into the rail men from the other trains as they exited the control room.

'Give him a minute, young 'un. Signalman's just up-dating the train book. I think we'll all get to go when the two late-running London to Glasgow trains pass through. Shouldn't be too long.'

As he waited a whistle screeched from the south and the first of the late-running north-bound expresses ran past. The men waved cheerfully and the youngster from the coal wagon pulled out his pocket watch and said, 'Well that's one gone. 6.38am. Let's hope the other's not too far behind.'

At that point the calm, easy-going atmosphere of the signal box changed. From the north came a series of short whistle blasts and as everyone looked up the line, another locomotive came hurtling under the Blacksike Bridge tunnel down the south-bound mainline heading directly for the local train still facing the wrong way on the same track. Although directly in front of the signal box, the stationary train was partially obscured by the other trains on the tracks outside. It was clear that, because of this, the signalman had forgotten it was there. His view blocked by the bridge, the driver of the approaching locomotive only saw the local at the last minute, but with only 200 yards to react, he had no time to apply the brakes and with a crash that shook the earth, hundreds of tons of wood and metal ploughed into the smaller, lighter static train. It's engine was driven back along its tracks and, although it did not overturn, both its tender and the carriage behind were shattered and, couples broken, pushed across the north-bound line. The other train fared even worse. Like an iron horse, it rode up over the smaller locomotive and came crashing down on its side, further blocking the north-bound line while its tender fell sideways onto the other track. With the force of the impact, the wooden carriages concertinaed into each other and broke apart, scattering debris everywhere.

Over the sound of the crash, Heinrich heard a voice above him shout, 'Whatever have you done, Jimmy?' and then seconds later the same voice screamed out, 'Where's the 6.05 express?'

The railway men must have figured out at the same time that another disaster was imminent, because they all rushed down the steps and raced along the side of the north-bound line, frantically waving their arms in the direction of the yet unseen train. Seconds later the second express came from the direction of Carlisle, but the driver's sightline was affected by the long left-handed curve as he approached the signal box and, although he jammed on his brakes as soon as he saw the waving arms, the breaking distance was again too short to stop a train of that weight travelling at around seventy miles per hour. As a result, at 6.50am, only fifty-three seconds after the first collision, the 600-ton Scottish express ploughed into the first crash, smashing the wreckage lying on the tracks. It also mowed down many of the survivors who had dragged themselves out of the damaged carriages or who were trying to rescue those still alive but trapped under the debris. Only when it hit the engine of the train lying across the rails did it come to a sudden and juddering stop.

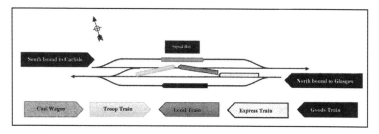

Diagram of the Quintinshill crash

Heinrich was scarcely able to grasp the horror of it all. The spectacle was one of utter destruction. For a second or two a dreadful quietness seemed to hang over the place, then the screaming began and he saw figures crawling from the debris. Others staggered out, shaken but seemingly unharmed. He stepped out from his hiding place with the initial intention of offering help, but then he noticed that nearly all those emerging from the wreckage were soldiers and it dawned on him that the train which had run into the stationary local was a troop carrier, presumably transporting its load south to embark on ships that would eventually take them to the battlefields across the channel. Although the crash itself would ensure that many of the men would never reach mainland Europe, he wondered if there was some opportunity for him to increase the casualty list. He ran over to the devastated trucks as if to give assistance, but then paused and looked around. The engine and carriages of the troop train were so damaged as to be virtually unrecognisable. The wooden rolling stock was obviously old and had simply broken up on impact. As he watched, what remained of the front carriage burst into flames, ignited by hot coals from the overturned tender. Train crews from the express and coal train ran over and tried desperately to extinguish the flames with water, also from the tender, but there was little left and their efforts came to nothing. They stepped back just in time to avoid an almighty explosion as gas from the carriage's damaged lighting system came into contact with the fire.

As the initial blast died back, one of the men shouted at Heinrich, 'Come on, mate, we need to get well away from here. These old wooden coaches are lit with gas lamps from cylinders stored underneath the floor. If the flames spread any further and more of them go up, then there'll be one helluva blast.'

With that, he and his colleagues hurried off down the tracks to focus their help elsewhere. But Heinrich didn't move. Instead he stood gazing into the conflagration, mesmerised by the dancing flames, an idea slowly forming in his head. It was dangerous; he could be seen or even worse blown up, but it might work. He jerked back into action, looking around for something to help him execute his idea. Beside the track, presumably thrown clear by the impact, was a dirty black bucket and a few yards further on pair of grubby, heavy duty leather gloves with the initial 'CRR' stamped on the back. Pulling the gloves on, he picked up the bucket and returned to the fire, where he began to shovel burning embers and glowing coal into the container. He then walked down the side of the damaged trains, keeping well back from the wreckage itself but close enough for him the identify the round, grey containers that he sought. He saw his first only a few yards from the first explosion and nervously clambered through the debris until he reached it. He was sweating profusely and wondered whether this was from the heat or fear. Using some of the smouldering remains from his bucket and smaller wooden pieces from the shattered carriages, he stoked a fire under it then scrambled clear. Hurrying along the side of the tracks, he could see that in some places fire had already taken hold, but on three more occasions he repeated the process. Within minutes of the flames taking hold, the undamaged gas cylinders began to explode creating an almighty inferno, driving the rescuers back and engulfing those who had not already been dragged clear of the remains.

Amazingly, the rescuers around him were so intent on moving the confused and injured away from the remains that they failed to register what he was doing. There was one exception. At the final fire he'd heard a voice from within the rubble and turned to see a young soldier crawling out from underneath what looked like a carriage door. He was using a bayonet with a broken tip to help clear the rubble blocking his way. Somehow the wooden structure had protected him from the carnage of the crash and explosions. His clothes were covered in dust and blood ran down his face from a nasty cut along his forehead, but he was able to push himself up onto his feet and glared at the German.

'What are you doing?' he said in an almost hysterical voice.

'Looking for survivors and trying to put out the fires. Are you OK?'

'No you're not, you were starting them,' the private shouted back. 'Who the hell are you? Get away from here. Get away.' And with a tired action he threw the broken weapon at German's head. It missed, and Heinrich stared back at the man before bending round to pick it up. He turned back, intending to silence his accuser with a thrust of the damaged blade, but when he looked up all he could see was an outline disappearing into the smoke and steam that swirled around the whole site. His heart skipped a beat in momentary panic, but then he calmed himself. In the circumstances he doubted that anyone would have the time to listen to the boy's panicked tale, and even if they did, would someone half crazed with shock be believed? A satisfied smile slowly spread across his face. Rescue would now be replaced by recovery. *A job well done*, he thought as he turned and walked away towards the bridge and his waiting bicycle. Behind him several hundred people lay dead, dying or injured, most of them soldiers who would no longer be able to reinforce their comrades on the Allied front line, many who might have survived had it not been for the German's actions.

CHAPTER 16

Chief Constable's Office, Carlisle Police Headquarters

6.30am, Monday 24th May 1915

The stranger's interrogation of deSchmid was brisk.

'Are you sure?'

'Yes!'

'And the signalman Meakin saw the same man?'

'Yes!'

'And all three gave the same description?'

'Not enough to be certain, but Meakin and the soldiers' descriptions are identical. At the barracks he was wearing different clothes, but the build, height and looks were similar. Tall and well built with short, cropped, light brown hair. Both thought his age was early-to mid-thirties.'

'Where are the two soldiers now?'

'One's still at the barracks, but he's unaware of the potential link between the two events. The other was sent back up to Edinburgh to be checked over at Craigleith Hospital before him and the other uninjured survivors parade at the city's Rosebank Cemetery for the funeral of their comrades this afternoon. From tomorrow they all have two weeks' leave before they're due to re-join the battalion as reinforcements in Gallipoli.'

'And the officer the lad spoke to?'

'Also at the funeral.'

'Good. Where are Meakin and the other signalman Tinsley now?'

'At home, I presume. They've not been charged with anything yet. The Board of Trade's Enquiry into the incident starts this afternoon at the County Hotel. It's being conducted by Lieutenant Colonel Druitt of the Railway Inspectorate, and I believe he wants to interview both men later this morning prior to the enquiry. The inquest also starts today, but the coroner's certain to adjourn it until Druitt reports. If they're found to be responsible, it's likely both of them will be arrested, although we're not sure how this might be carried out. The accident was in Scotland, but many of the men died in England, so we're dealing with the investigation. They could be charged in England or Scotland. If the Scots go ahead, the charge is likely to be culpable homicide, whereas I can't see anything other than a manslaughter charge on this side of the border.'

Jack was back in deSchmid's office with the same group of people who had met together after the attack on the barracks. This time no one was seated. Instead they milled around the room, looking anxious. The chief constable, Major Binning and Lieutenant Colonel Machell were all present, together with one notable addition. Also present was a middle-aged, clean-shaven man with neat features and wearing a long, dark coat. When everyone had arrived, he'd shown a letter to deSchmid and Binning before introducing himself as a Home Office civil servant sent north by the government to find out about the attack on the barracks and the accident at Quintinshill. He'd given his name as Smith, which Jack assumed was false, and made it abundantly clear that the missive was confirmation that he had the responsibility and authority to take whatever action he deemed necessary with regard to either incident. He'd listened to the two army officer's descriptions of what had happened at the castle and then to deSchmid's harrowing tale of the train crash. As chief constable he was also head of the local emergency services and, having been telephoned at home, had arrived at the site at 10.00am to take over coordination of the rescue activities. Smith had listened carefully to the gruesome account before picking up on the report of a stranger who was alleged to have been seen twice at the crash site and possibly at the castle. He'd questioned deSchmid in detail. The others were uncertain why.

'Look, what's this about?' an exasperated Machell asked the enigmatic government official.

'In recent months His Majesty's government has become aware of one or two individuals around the country who are working against the best interests of our sovereign state.'

'What do you mean, "working against"? Would you like to put that in plain English?'

'Spies, saboteurs, secret agents! That's what the man's talking about, Percy. He means we've got someone working up here in Cumberland doing all they can to damage the war effort,' said Binning.

'But that's ridiculous. The train crash was obviously an accident caused by the two signalmen's lax behaviour and failure to abide by the rules. The murder and fire at the barracks was no doubt perpetrated by someone who belongs to one of those socialist, anarchist or Marxist groups opposed to the war.'

Smith shook his head. 'If Meakin and the private's story are to be believed, by accident or design, this man was present at

Quintinshill before the trains collided. In the aftermath he took the opportunity presented in the ensuing chaos to massacre many of the initial survivors by deliberately setting fire to the gas cylinders stored under the carriages, causing a series of explosions. He may have been trying to do something similar at the barracks, this time to the petrol cans stored on site.'

So Robert Jardine could be right, thought Jack, and he interrupted the exchange to tell everyone about his conversation with the journalist. 'To be honest,' he said, 'I've kept his remarks in mind, but there's been no firm evidence to suggest he was right, so our investigation hasn't specifically looked into the possibility.'

'Alright then,' continued Binning. 'Assuming this is true, we need to get a message out to the public, warning them of the danger.'

The civil servant shook his head for a second time. 'No. We need to do exactly the opposite. I need to see Meakin and probably Tinsley as well, to make sure that this individual is never mentioned in any of their testimonies.'

'But why? People need to know he's out there in order to protect themselves.'

'On the contrary. We are better served saying nothing. Can you imagine what would happen if people thought that we had a German spy in our midst or that the government can't protect them on their own shores? There'd be large scale civil unrest. Every stranger would be a suspect. Angry mobs might take things into their own hands and do something we all later regret. On top of that, our suspect would be warned and could either go to ground or leave the area. No. Predators that can been seen by their prey are rarely successful. We need to stay calm and use secrecy to our advantage. That means making sure that our signalmen stay quiet.'

'And how do you propose to guarantee that?' asked Binning.

'Well. It's possible that their cooperation could lead to a lighter sentence in the more-than-likely event that they are found guilty of manslaughter. It's even possible that they could be re-employed by the railway after a suitable period of absence, although, to avoid a public backlash, I think that it would have to be in a lower-grade non-signalling job. I'm having lunch at the County Hotel with representatives of the Caledonian Railway Company to discuss the failings in their procedures which contributed to the accident. I'm sure that in the circumstances they will be amenable to my suggestions.'

'So, if they agree to keep things quiet, how do we go about finding this agent? Search every house in the city and surrounding area for someone who speaks English with a German accent? Something of a daunting task don't you think?'

'He's not going to have an accent, Major. We're looking for someone who is English or comes from an English-speaking country,' interrupted deScmidt. 'No one who has reported contact with this man has mentioned anything about him speaking in broken English or a foreign accent. Nor did he have a Scottish, Irish or Welsh lilt, and it's one of the first things they would have noticed. We're looking for someone with German sympathies who's been here all the time or, more likely, was brought up in an English environment and has recently slipped into the UK un-noticed. I think we focus on the latter and start a low-key search initially in and between Carlisle and Greta to see if we can find anyone matching his characteristics and description. We start with the pubs, hotels and boarding houses. It's possible that he's living rough in the countryside, but, given the length of time between the two attacks, I think this is unlikely. I think he's living more comfortably, hiding in plain sight.'

'I'm not sure I understand your meaning?' said Machell.

Jack coughed and spoke for the first time. 'What the chief constable is saying Colonel, is that this man isn't hiding. He's living and working in the area right under our noses as one of us. The minute he gets wind that we're looking for him, he can simply stop any clandestine activities and go about his normal, day-to-day activities until things calm down. Our best chance is if he's a recent arrival from overseas. The Aliens Restriction Act requires everyone from a foreign country who stays at a hotel or lodging house to sign a register and the owner has to ensure that register is maintained. The person is also supposed to register with the police. If we're lucky, we might catch him before he realises that we're on to him. The problem is that registration isn't taken that seriously this far north and some landlords don't always keep their registers up to date. Neither is it likely that a spy will have regsistered voluntarily with the police. It's also possible that he's British with German sympathies and so has no need to register. So finding him could be much harder than we might initially think, and if he goes to ground or runs, then in true Cumberland fashion, the hunt will be in full cry as the hounds try to bring their quarry to book. I assume from my presence here that I'm to be master of the hounds.'

*

A week later Jack was again in deSchmid's office, this time sat in the chair he had occupied during their last face-to-face discussion. The chief constable sat opposite him, hands behind his head in a relaxed pose. More details about what the papers were calling the Quintinshill Disaster had slowly emerged in the days following the accident. Figures issued by the Board of Trade indicated that 226 people had died and another 246 were injured, but there was speculation that the final death toll could be even higher, as the flames had been so intense that bodies had simply been obliterated by the fire. Most of the dead were soldiers belonging to the Royal Scots, but others had also lost their lives including the driver and fireman of the troop train, together with a railway attendant and a number of civilian passengers. Horrific stories had emerged of doctors having to amputate limbs in order to release people from the wreckage and mercy killings, with trapped and injured men begging rescuers to shoot them to end their pain. Survivors told of incredible acts of bravery, including a private who, seeing another soldier lying injured beneath a burning tender, had risked his life to crawl undereneath and pull him out. Both men's clothes had been so singed and smouldering with the heat that nearby rescuers had to throw water over them to prevent them bursting into flames. In another instance, a Royal Army Medical Corps colonel, having survived the crash, had picked up nearby track tools and gone back into the blazing remains to break up the coaches and pull men from the debris. Eventually the fire brigade had arrived from Carlisle at 10.00am and poured gallons of water onto what was left of the trains, but with little initial effect. The fire was so intense that it had taken until the next day to dampen it down. The repercussions from the tragedy had been as expected. Prior to the start of the Board of Trade's inquiry Lieutenant Colonel Druitt had spent time visiting the accident site and interviewing witnesses, including Meakin and Tinsley. Both men had apparently been honest about their slack behaviour and failure to follow the rules and procedures required, and although the enquiry was ongoing, it was clear that the outcome was going to lay the blame squarely at their feet. The inquest had also opened on the 25th but been immediately adjourned until the 23rd June to allow Druitt to finish his investigation. However, in a somewhat surprising development, the Scottish authorities had not waited on the findings and charged Tinsley with culpable homicide on the 29th May.

'That was a rather unforeseen development at the weekend, Jack. I thought that the authorities in Scotland would have waited for Druitt's findings before pressing charges. The Home Office has instructed the coroner to go ahead with the inquest on our side of the border and it's possible that he could also face a manslaughter charge based on the same evidence. It makes no sense at all to have two trials. What happens if they come to two different verdicts? One would hope that there will be discussions between the law officers of England and Scotland and a decision made to proceed in only one country. Anyway, that's for others to decide. What about our investigations? Anything positive to report?'

'Not really, sir. Mackay, the constable at Gretna, visited likely places in the village and spoke with the locals. He kept it low-key saying that we were looking for an unaccounted-for stranger seen leaving the crash site. Most assumed that he meant someone who'd received some kind of injury and had wandered off confused, so he didn't contradict them. I sent Graham Gordon up to help the acting sergeant in Longtown. I thought he might need a bit of help as the only time the Grahams and the Armstrong's aren't feuding is when they unite against a visit from the police. However, a meeting was called at the Graham Arms Hotel, which was well attended and for once they were comparatively helpful. Annie Graham was there and she'd watched the cars taking wounded soldiers along Swan Street to the Claremont Hospital. She made it very clear to the menfolk that differences had to be set aside to help in this case. However, she's not stupid, and I think she had an idea that we were looking for this man for reasons other than to ensure he wasn't hurt.'

'Had anyone seen or heard about anyone?'

'No, and the thing is that these are tight-knit communities. Everyone knows what everyone else is doing and what's going on, whether it's legal or not. They would know if there was a stranger in their midst.'

'What about if he was living wild in the countryside?'

'The local poachers know exactly who's out and about on an evening, friend or enemy. If they didn't, the gamekeepers would have a lot more success stopping them. No. The more I think about it, the more I feel our man is living somewhere in Carlisle. The population is bigger, so everyone doesn't know everybody else and strangers are less likely to stand out. If he's still in the area, then he's here. We just have to find him. I've got Sergeant Gordon and two of our more diligent constables working round the city. They'll visit pubs and hostels, but they're also going to do door-to-door. It's time-consuming but gives us a better chance of success. Graham will do over the river and the other two will visit the east and south sides of the city. I've told them to be particularly vigilant in the hostelries around St Nicholas. There's quite a bit of coming and going in the engineering workforce at Cowan's Sheldon, the crane makers. It would be easy for someone to go unnoticed. While they're doing that, I'll ask around Denton Home, Caldewgate and the area to the west of the centre.'

'Have you any idea how long it will take to get round everywhere?'

'Well, I've made it very clear that it needs to be a very thorough check. So it's going to take time, I think at least ten days, perhaps as much as a fortnight. It's a big area for four men. That's assuming that we don't have to pull them off and use them for something else. The only alternative is to flood each area with bobbies, and our man couldn't fail to notice that and run or go to ground.'

'Alright. Keep me informed of any developments.' If you need extra men I can spare a couple although having to guard the shell factory has left us very short.

CHAPTER 17

Methodist Central Hall

Evening, Tuesday 15ᵗʰ June 1915

Jack looked around the hall and sighed. It had now been over three weeks since they'd started their hunt for the unknown saboteur without the sniff of a lead. The search was taking much longer than he'd expected. The door-to-door had been a particular challenge. Officers had needed to return to some houses again and again before they were able to talk to the householder. The men were away to war and as a result the women were often out at work. Although they had found one or two newcomers to the area, all had legitimate reasons to be in the city mostly to do with work on the railways, the new shell factory or other local engineering projects. With only Caldewgate and the western approach roads into the city left, it was looking less and less likely that anything was going to turn up. In the circumstances, he could have done without having to attend tonight's event, but the chief constable had been insistent.

Recruitment had been slow and this talk by an officer who was not only active on the frontline but was developing a reputation for heroics – he'd suffered a number of physical injuries from bomb-blast shrapnel – was aimed at encouraging young men to 'sign up'. The problem was that he'd also upset many people by being fiercely critical of those who failed to do so. Major William Athol Murray, or Bill to his friends, was an outspoken critic of some groups of so-called 'working men', who, he suggested, spent their time 'loafing about and spending free time drinking and going to football matches', while men on the front line were being mown down. He believed that it was outrageous that after the war these 'loafers' might benefit from having everything their own way because all the decent men would have been wiped out. He'd even gone so far as to express the opinion that the whole lot ought to be put under martial law, and every man who shirked his 'duty' should be shot, as they were in France. This was emotive language which had upset a lot of people in certain quarters.

He was back in the city for a short period of leave and the evening's talk was to a scout group run by his sister Claudine. Whilst no explicit threat had been made to the event, it was felt that the presence of the local constabulary might deter any troublemakers, particularly those from the growing pacifist movement who believed that violence, even in self-defence, was unjustifiable under any conditions and that negotiation was preferable to war as a means of solving the dispute with Germany and her allies. Although small in number, they were becoming increasingly vociferous and, despite their beliefs, were not averse to physically disrupting recruitment events. On top of that, there was the chance of hecklers from within the group of men he had accused of shirking their 'military responsibilities'.

The invited audience was made up of the members, friends and family of the 6th Carlisle Troop, and as far as Jack could make out, none of them looked likely to cause any trouble. People sat on chairs and benches facing towards a low stage at the front of the room. The atmosphere was calm but the conversation animated in anticipation. When Claudine Murray came out of a side room and stepped onto the front platform the hall settled, people stopped talking and listened intently as she introduced her brother with the minimum of fuss. She was an attractive woman and, although it was clear that she was still in her late twenties, she came across as someone full of confidence and used to dealing with groups of people. Her brown hair was arranged in a neat bun and she wore a long, cream dress of the type that was all the fashion among the better-off classes. It had a low collar and around her neck there was a pretty diamond necklace that sparkled in the stage lights.

'Good evening, everyone, and welcome to this evening's talk to be given by Major William Murray of the Warwickshire Battery of the Royal Horse Artillery.' Pausing for a moment, she smiled before continuing. 'Otherwise known as my brother Bill.' The audience laughed, and she waited for this to die down before adding, 'Bill is currently serving in France but is home on leave and has agreed to give this talk before returning to active service in a couple of days' time.'

She turned and nodded to the partially open door of the side room and immediately it was opened and her brother strode out to join her on the stage. William Murray was a tall, well-built man with a neat moustache and intense brown eyes. He wore the uniform of an army major, including, even though he was indoors, an officer's peak cap which covered his short, brown hair. Jack guessed that he was in his late thirties or early forties. He was a sight to impress any young boy, which presumably was the point of the meeting, but that impression was somewhat diluted by the fact that walking along beside him was a scruffy little terrier dog with a coat that was predominately white, except for a black face. Although a chair had been left at the side of the stage, Murray remained standing and began his talk with a loud, booming voice that resonated around the room.

'Hello, everyone. It's lovely to be here today and to be able to talk to you about the little disagreement that's taking place across the channel and the sterling work of our men on the front line.'

As if scripted, the audience duly laughed and applauded the predictably light-hearted opening remark.

'I should start by introducing you all to the friend who has accompanied me. This little rascal is Morty. He accompanied me to France in 1914 and has been with me throughout my time at the front. He'll also be going back with me in a few days' time to resume his absolutely essential duties in the trenches. Morty is our top rat-catcher and keeps the men's living quarters free from being overrun by the horrible little monsters. Without him, the rats creep all over our sleeping soldiers while they are trying to get some rest and can spread disease, causing debilitating fevers that can last for days and which, if not treated, require a recovery period of two to three months when the man is out of action. Every man out of action means one less to fight. At the moment a third of the causalities are a result of disease, so Morty has a very, very important job.'

He bent over and ruffled the little dog's ears, and another ripple of applause went round the audience. The rest of the talk was much as might be expected, with little contentious content. Murray said he had always been interested in the scout troop and enjoyed reading about their exploits in his sister's letters. He spoke about how proud he was of the old members who had joined the army and offered his congratulations to everyone concerned. When he'd come across men who had been scouts, they stood out among the other soldiers because of their hard work, willingness to 'get things done' and devotion to duty. This, he suggested, was entirely due to their scout training and consequently he was always delighted to have one join his battery.

Jack wondered if this was entirely true. Looking around the room, he was sure he recognised one or two young faces from his frequent visits to Finkle Street, but he couldn't be certain, and after a moment's reflection, he thought perhaps that he was mistaken. As he got older, young people seemed to dress and look the same. A bit like the young constables who joined the force.

The major brought his talk to a close by telling the scouts that what they were doing now was the best preparation anyone could have who was going to take part in the Great War. Reliability was the most important trait in a soldier's character, as a man who could be relied on to do his best was of the greatest worth to his fellow men. This was what they were developing in the scouts and it was a lesson worth its weight in gold. He wished them every success and hoped that their turn would come so that they would get the chance to show what they were made of.

At these final words, the audience stood to applaud the speaker and he nodded in acknowledgement before moving across to the lone chair and sitting down.

At this point Claudine addressed the audience. 'Thank you, everyone, for your kind applause. I am sure they are much appreciated by Major Murray.' She looked across at her brother, who nodded again, before turning back to the audience. 'Now if you'd all like to be seated again, Bill will be happy to answer some of your questions if he can.'

Jack was surprised by this. Normally soldiers returning from the front were reluctant to talk about their experiences, to the point where some had even been drawn into arguments in the city's pubs when unsympathetic individuals had interpreted this unwillingness as an indication that they'd never really been in action. However, the cheerful, positive young recruits who marched off, raring to give the Hun 'what for' often came back changed men. Most said very little about the things that they had come across and the few that did simply limited their comments to vague generalisations.

However, it soon became obvious that this wasn't really an open session. The scouts raising their hands read out carefully prepared questions written on small prompt cards, to which Major Murray gave encouraging replies.

'What's it like to be at the front line?'

'Well, I've had a great many exciting experiences. Enough to last a lifetime. Where my battery is situated, we have German shells and bullets flying over us every few minutes, but our guns keep firing giving as good as they get.'

'Do you ever get frightened?'

'Sometimes. I once had to go to the infantry trenches to see if our guns were firing at the right place. It was a very alarming business, as, to get to our own trenches, I had to cross an open field about 200 metres from the German trenches. I felt rather like a rabbit in a farmer's shotgun sights.'

'Have you met any Germans and spoken to them?'

'Yes. We sometimes come into contact with those who have been taken prisoner. Frequently they're young boys, badly equipped and often very thin. When asked they say they have been miserably clothed and fed. It would be easy to feel sorry for them if they weren't the enemy.'

And so the questions continued until, after about twenty minutes, his sister announced that she thought that Major Murray had answered enough and it was time to bring the talk to a conclusion. She thanked her brother again and also the audience for coming. They in turn clapped enthusiastically for a final time before everyone rose and made their way out through the exit at the rear of the building. Claudine hurried past them so that she could shake their hand as they left.

Murray remained seated and as the hall emptied Jack walked across to him.

'Inspector Johnstone, sir, from Carlisle City Police. May I say that was a very interesting talk, Major, and thankfully it went off without a hitch?'

The soldier looked up and replied in a voice that was almost a whisper. 'Yes, an impressive performance was it not, Inspector. Just the right tone to encourage them to volunteer and join up as soon as they're able to. It wouldn't do to put them off, would it, or with the current rate of casualties on the front line we'd lose the war through lack of manpower.'

The puzzled look on Jack's face prompted him to continue.

'I'm sorry. That was very cynical, and I didn't mean to dump my frustrations on you. Excuse me, but I don't know your first name.'

'Jack, Major. It's Jack Johnstone.'

'Well, Jack, I'm Bill,' he replied, holding out his hand towards the confused officer. Jack took it and was shocked at the gentleness of the grip.

Murray noticed the surprise. 'Ahh … no manly grip, I'm afraid. You don't have time for more than a tentative slap as you shake the hands of large numbers of men about to put their lives on the line when the whistle's gone and they're about to go over the top. Sad, isn't it? A cursory acknowledgement for men, many of whom will not return.'

Jack didn't know what to say and just stared at Murray, who gave a sad smile and asked, 'Fancy a cup of tea before you go off duty, Inspector?'

Jack nodded and was led down the hall and into the room from which the Major had first emerged. It was a small kitchen and, while his new friend proceeded to make two teas on the small gas cooker in the corner of the room, he was directed to an old wooden table with two chairs and sat down to wait.

'No milk or sugar, I'm afraid, so black will have to do. Is that OK?'

'Fine. As long as it's warm and wet, I'm happy to drink it,' replied Jack.

When the pair were settled opposite each other with their drinks cupped between their hands, the major looked at Jack and, after a long pause, he shook his head and spoke. 'This is a horrible war, Jack. More horrible than anyone back home can imagine. If they knew what was really going on, there'd be no rush to join up. As it is, people are starting to hear things from soldiers who are returning home injured. Fortunately, most just want to forget about their experiences rather than re-live things by talking about what they've been through.

'Do you read the papers, Jack? If you do, then you'd get the impression that the Germans are taking a huge beating. In March the broad sheets detailed that our infantry had given the Bosch a real shake up at Neuve Chapelle. 6,000 dead and 2,000 prisoners. They went on to report that the 7th Indian Division's charge at the first German trench was inspiring to watch. What they didn't say was that during the attack that single division suffered 2,353 casualties.

'In April my battery moved to a place the Tommie's call by a name that reminds one of napkins – Ypres. I've never seen anything like it. The Germans seem to have masses of guns, and firing is continuous. Every house is knocked down, every field is a mass of shell-holes and, apart from the mud-filled trenches and odd ruin, there is no shelter. There are hundreds of dead horses and cows lying everywhere. Everyone is on edge and fearful for their life. Officers as well as the men. Death is no respecter of rank. Shortly after our move there, the major in the next battery to mine was killed, shot by a sniper while observing fire for his guns. He was a splendid fellow and well liked. The same day our brigadier was badly wounded.'

Murray stopped for a moment, rested his elbows on the table and put his head in his hands. Jack thought for a second that his depressing tale was finished and was considering what to say or do next, but, just as he came to the conclusion that a quiet departure might be in order, the major pushed the chair back, sending it flying, and stood to his feet, eyes gleaming.

'But you know what, Jack? We are going to win this war. It's going to take some time. Those who think it'll be over quickly are deluding themselves, but we will win. Do you know why? Because our soldiers have heart, Jack. They won't be beaten. The Germans I've met are demoralised and their officers have trouble getting some of them to fight. One prisoner we took had been shot through the arm because he wouldn't leave his trench to attack. Our men are a mixed bunch, but by gum they can bear hardships as grim as any man has ever had to suffer and then get up and fight for their lives. They don't fight for King and country, Jack, they're mates from the same town or village, and that close bond means no man wants to let his mates down. So they fight and die for each other, and in this war of attrition that's what will win the day. The Germans don't have that camaraderie. Almost every day they throw messages over to our trenches asking us to stop fighting as they are sick of it. But we won't; no, we won't. Not until we've won and everyone can go home. So we need talks like this to make sure that we replenish the ranks of those brave men who have given their all and if that means I have to give them, then so be it, because if we fail, then what did they give their lives for?'

Jack didn't know what to say, so he said nothing and just looked at the man opposite him. A man whose passion, he realised, was likely to inspire the men around him to great things. Just as he was wondering what should happen next, the door burst open and Claudine Murray rushed into the room.

'There you are, Bill. Come on our lift is waiting to take us home. Everyone was so excited by your talk. Well done. Good evening, Inspector. I'm so glad there was no trouble.'

Then she spun round and, with a twirl of her skirt she was gone again. Bill Murray looked at Jack, smiled, gave a perfunctory salute and followed her. As he walked away, he shouted back over his shoulder, 'I've no doubt that with a few Claudine's in charge of organising the war effort, instead of some of our current generals, the fighting would be over before the summer ends.'

For several minutes, Jack stood still and reflected on his own position. When the war broke out he had spoken informally with a member of the Watch Committee about the possibility of being able to enlist for the duration of the fighting and rejoin the police after being discharged. He'd been informed that there was no chance of this, as his was a reserved occupation. Unhappy at the reply, he'd asked why two serving constables had been allowed to join up and been told that they had been on the army reserve list before the war. Disappointed, he had then decided to make a more formal approach to the chief constable, who, after listening to what Jack had to say, had indicated that he was not opposed to allowing serving police officers to volunteer but that each case would be considered individually. However, he was not minded to let older, more senior officers enlist as they were essential to the smooth running of a potentially reduced and less experienced force, and Jack fell into this category. During the meeting it became clear that whether or not the police fell into the category of a reserved occupation seemed to depend on the perceived importance of the officer's role and rank. Undeterred, his next stop had been the army recruiting office, where he had enquired about resigning from the police and enlisting as a private individual. The response had been perfunctory and unequivocal: not only were reserved occupations exempt from being conscripted, those holding such positions were prohibited from enlisting on their own initiative; instead, they were required to remain in post.

In the end he had accepted the situation with some reluctance, but meeting Bill Murray had reignited his frustrations, and as he followed the others out of the hall, he slammed the door in annoyance.

CHAPTER 18

Victoria Park, Carlisle

Afternoon, Saturday 3rd July 1915

Jack had wrestled Robert Brown twice before, and on both occasions he had won by two falls to nil. Each time the first bout had been hard-fought, but Brown wasn't fit and tired rapidly, so that he had taken him quite easily with a 'strike' on both occasions. Although more nervous than usual, Jack was expecting things to follow a similar pattern this time. The match was taking place in the nearby Victoria Park, which, despite the huge central bronze statue celebrating the Queen's long reign, was still commonly referred to as the 'Bitts'. Before being taken over for parkland, the 'Bitts' had originally been small parcels of land that were used for grazing. It was not one of the academy's usual venues, but, for a bout advertised as a 'Championship Eliminator', it was decided that somewhere central in the city was required, with good viewing for the large crowd expected. So the garden bowl beside the park's Lord Mayor's Walk and below the Eden Bridge had been selected. The 'hollow', as it was known, formed a natural amphitheatre, with grass banks surrounding a flat central area, within which a circular ring had been marked out with a single rope.

It was a beautiful summer day. The sun shone in the cobalt blue sky and wisps of horsetail clouds danced across the sky. The whole event had a carnival atmosphere. Men, women and children strolled along the park paths in their weekend best clothes. The men in dark suits and the women in long dresses with colourful bonnets on their heads or bright ribbons in their hair. Children raced between the trees, rolled hoops down the grass banks or sat on wooden benches under the arches below Eden Bridge to watch a Punch and Judy puppet show. A group of pensioners sat on the comfortable seats around the old bandstand listening to the St Stephen's and Foden's bands.

In the wrestling ring, a number of young men took part in a sequence of warm up bouts before the master of ceremonies lifted a speaking trumpet to his lips and announced that the main event would begin in five minutes' time. The luckiest spectators found a space to sit on the grass around the ring while hundreds of others stood on the adjacent paths or lined the bridge above, where they could look down on the two fighters. Many had never seen a wrestling match and had no idea what to expect but were eagerly waiting the 'match of the decade', as the local press had dubbed it. As the crowd settled, street vendors passed among them, selling bags of peanuts, biscuits, fruit and ginger bread slabs.

In a red, striped tent on the west side of the bowl, Jack and Brown stood waiting for the time when they would be escorted into the ring and introduced to the crowd. As usual, Jack wore his competition costume with the distinctive JJ on the front of his white, long-sleeved vest accompanied by dark blue embroidered shorts over white long johns. His opponent was similarly dressed but his shorts were red, as was the trim on his shorter-sleeved vest. With them stood a short, stocky man in a brown tweed suit with a straw boater on his head. Angus Kay had travelled through from Wigton to referee the match as an accepted neutral. However, Jack was a little nervous of the choice, as Kay had been a mediocre wrestler who had only recently decided to retire from competition and take up refereeing. Having only handled bouts at a few nearby country fairs, he was relatively inexperienced for such an important event. However, the Carlisle Academy had asked for someone from Wigton and when the nomination came through did not feel they could question the other 'Ring's' selection.

Neither man had spoken to the other since they had entered the tent to change into their wrestling wear, but as they waited just inside the entrance, Brown looked across to Jack and hissed, 'Forget what's gone before, Johnstone. Today you're going to feel some pain and I'm going to enjoy inflicting it. I'm wise to your tricks. There'll be none of your fast striking or dropping to loosen my grip, and when I win, I am going to enjoy the fact that half of Carlisle watched it.'

Jack stared at Brown but didn't respond. Normally he was excited by the prospect of a challenging bout, but today he was unusually nervous. He didn't know whether that was the importance of the event, the size of the crowd or the inexperienced referee. Or maybe it was because he couldn't take his mind off the continuing lack of progress tracking down the elusive saboteur. It certainly disrupted his concentration. There was still no news and he wondered if the man had perhaps left the area. The situation hadn't been helped by the fact that the Watch Committee had decided that it would be wise to extend the hunt to the villages on the outskirts of the city. This meant that for the best part of the last two weeks he'd had to pause his own searching to spend time liaising with his counterparts in the Cumberland and

Westmorland Force. Unfortunately they were sceptical about the presence of a German spy in the area and less than enthusiastic about the task of looking for him. He was constantly having to go back over areas they were supposed to have checked after he realised that they weren't going back to properties where they hadn't received an answer on their first visit. Perhaps, he reflected, it was the combination of everything. Either way, as the little group walked out to the centre of the ring and were introduced to the crowd, he pushed the concerns to the back of his mind. *It was,* he thought, *rather pointless worrying now.*

As the two wrestlers went to opposite sides of the ring and completed their warm-up stretches, the referee took the speaking trumpet and explained the sport's rules to the spectators. He was well aware that most people had little wrestling knowledge so kept the technical side of things brief.

'Ladies and gentlemen, today we will witness one of our county's oldest sports, demonstrated by two of our city's very best wrestlers. During the match, each wrestler will attempt to unbalance his opponent, or make him lose their hold, using methods such as lifting throws known as "hipes" and twisting throws such as "buttocks" and trips. If any part of a wrestler's body touches the ground aside from his feet, then he loses. This is known as a "fall". If both fall down at once the last to hit the ground is deemed the winner. If it is unclear which wrestler hit the ground first, the fall is disqualified and must be started again. This is known as a "dog fall". A win can also be achieved if either man loses his grip on the other while his opponent still retains his hold.'

He went on to give the crowd some information on the two wrestlers' competitive backgrounds before reminding everyone that the winner would take part in an exhibition bout with Douglas Clark, the unofficial county champion, later that summer.

'Although not officially for the World Title, the winner of that match might then, quite reasonably, call himself the best wrestler in the country.'

He finished this short introduction by stating that the match would be decided by the best of three falls and, without any additional fuss, called the two men together in the centre of the ring.

Jack expected Angus Kay to say something before the bout commenced, but, clearly nervous, he simply asked the two men to take up the starting 'backhold' position. This involved them standing chest to chest, grasping each other around the body with their chin on their opponent's right shoulder. The right arm of each contestant was then positioned under his opponent's left arm.

Taking a balanced hold at the start of a contest was one of the most frequent causes of dissention among wrestlers. Leaning to either side when the men were supposed to be on equal terms put the opposing wrestler off balance from the start and made it much easier to throw him. Normally referees were careful to ensure that both contestants were happy with their grips and stance before giving the signal to start the contest by calling 'en guard', then 'wrestle'. However, in this instance, Brown established his grip quickly and, dropping his weight to his right shouted, 'Ready'. To Jack's surprise, a somewhat startled Kay, shouted out the starting commands and he felt himself being dragged off his feet as his opponent twisted and spun him across his body before dumping him on the ground.

Immediately the referee's arm went up and a single finger pointed to the sky. 'First fall to Robert Brown.'

A howl of complaint immediately went up from a small group of wrestlers watching in the shade of a nearby willow tree. They had seen what had taken place and recognised the unfairness of what had happened. However, their protestations were drowned out by the clapping and cheering of the watching crowd, who acknowledged what they thought to be a clean and fair throw by the red-trunked combatant.

Rising to his feet, Jack stared directly at Kay but said nothing. The referee's face flushed red and he looked away before muttering, 'Gentlemen, get ready for the second fall.'

Brown bounced up and down on his toes before again quickly coming in to try and establish a hold. Jack stepped back and pushed him away. His opponent smirked.

'Frightened, Inspector. Not so cocky now, are you? In a couple of minutes your hopes of a championship tilt will be history.'

Kay stepped between the two men and tried to establish some element of control. 'Gentlemen, gentlemen. Please, there are hundreds of people watching you, including children. Can you please ready yourselves and establish your starting grip.'

This time a determined Jack was ready for Brown's rushed approach. He set himself to resist Brown's illegal move, but this time he found himself being dragged to the opposite side and only by using his extraordinary strength was he able to lift his opponent as he was falling, and both men hit the ground with a thud.

Brown leapt up and shouted, 'Yes, yes. I win. Two nil. I win.'

But to his dismay, Kay raised his arms and crossed them back and forwards above his head.

'Dog fall. It's unclear which wrestler hit the ground first, so the fall is disqualified and must be started again.'

A sweating Brown turned to the referee, but this time it was his turn for the protestations to be lost in the crowd reaction and as Jack walked over to the now heavy breathing constable, he could sense a change in the man's previously confident attitude.

'What now, Robert? Is that all you've got? You've tried your best tricks, but I'm still here, and I think now it's my turn and how I'm going to enjoy it.' He looked across to Kay and said, 'Let's get to it. I've other things to do today.'

Stepping back to his starting position, he put his hands on his hips and stood waiting. This time it was Brown's turn to approach cautiously, and as the two came together he felt Jack take a much firmer stance and tight grip behind his back which, despite his best efforts, he could not disrupt.

Throwing men by lifting them off the ground and rapidly placing a knee and the lower body between their thighs before flipping them onto their back was the most common way of throwing an opponent. Once lifted up, a wrestler was unable to touch the ground with his feet and was therefore easy to throw. Called 'hipeing' because of the use of the hip to execute the process, the technique had become popular after it was used with incredible success by Thomas Richardson from Hesket in the Caldbeck fells back in the 1820s. However, those with sufficient strength, on lifting their opposite number up, could simply throw their leg so high that he was turned by the action of the knee against the inside of his thigh and the simultaneous effort of the arms and chest. 'Striking' as it was known, was Jack's 'secret weapon'. Because of his size, many opponents who didn't know him expected him to try and throw them by 'hipeing' and set themselves to resist the move. Instead, Jack surprised them by attacking quickly and applying his considerable strength, developed through his hours of training, to lift and throw them before they really knew what had happened. As the bout began, Jack used this technique to devastating effect on Brown and the contest was over within seconds.

The final bout was also over quickly. Through years of practise and competition, Jack had also mastered many other ways to throw people, but it was often his defence and superior fitness that won him matches. Although smaller and lighter than his opponent, Jack wrenched his body from the other man's grasp by wriggling and shrinking low, causing his assailant to slacken his hold. This done, he was then able to drive forwards using his own, still-tight grip and execute a throw. Brown hit the ground with a thud and gasped as the air was knocked out of him. For a couple of minutes, he lay still, then grasped a hand proffered by Kay and was pulled to his feet. Reluctantly, he allowed the referee to steer him to the centre of the ring, where the three men stood side by side with Kay in the middle. After a pause to allow the cheers from the enthusiastic crowd to calm down, Jack's arm was lifted, and it was announced that, 'Third and final fall to Jack Johnstone. Johnstone wins by two falls to one.'

The cheering started again and Jack turned slowly round and waved at each section of the crowd in turn. He then faced Brown and offered a handshake as was the tradition after a match. Unwilling to respond but unsure what to do, the constable eventually gave the outstretched hand a brief slap before spinning on his heels and stalking off to the changing tent. Jack raised his eyebrows then shook Kay's hand and went to talk to his academy friends under the willow. Inside he couldn't help savour a deep sense of satisfaction and justice allied to relief after coming so close to defeat.

CHAPTER 19

Rome Street Signal Box, Carlisle

Early Morning, Wednesday 14ᵗʰ July 1915

Edwin Thomas bent down and rolled the constable over, then jerked back in horror. He was in a dreadful state. His face was covered in blood, the result of several deep wounds to the scalp, and his uniform was covered in a mixture of mud and gravel. The latter was presumably from being pushed down the nearby embankment onto the tracks. At first, he thought the man was dead, but with the movement he emitted a low groan. Thomas, a signalman in the Rome Street signal box, had noticed the body when, in the absence of an inside toilet, he'd gone outside to relieve himself. Although not quite dawn, it had been a clear night and there was enough morning twilight to make out something lying next to the railway line. Initially, he thought someone had tipped something down the embankment, a not-uncommon method of getting rid of rubbish, but an annoyance to rail workers as it needed to be removed in case a train hit it. However, as he'd approached it, he realised it was the body of a policeman.

'Are you OK, mate?' It seemed a stupid question in the circumstances, but he wasn't sure what else to say.

In response, the young officer opened his eyes and stared up at him. Then, with an effort, he raised his head and looked around. Gradually the realisation of where he was and what had happened seemed to come back to him. 'I need to contact the city police station urgently, help me up.' He tried to push up onto to his feet but sank back with another groan.

'Take it easy, fella. You look like you've just done ten rounds with Bombardier Billy. Let's sit you up slowly then get you back to my signal box and cleaned up, then we'll get a message back to your colleagues.'

It was a painfully slow struggle back to the signal box and the injured man could only manage to climb the steps up into the building on his hands and knees. Eventually Thomas got him sat down inside and, while he recovered his senses, gave him a couple of cups of hot tea. Blood was still trickling from the cuts so the signalman took out his handkerchief and tied it round the constable's head.

'You're lucky to be alive. Not many folk bump into a train and live to tell the tale. What the bloody hell were you doing on the railway at this time of night?'

'It wasn't a train, but it's a long story and I need to get a message to the police station on West Walls.'

*

The following morning, Jack arrived at the scene of the previous night's attack on PC Connor. Despite the early hour, there was already bright sunshine and a cloudless blue sky. It was hard to imagine that only a few hours earlier there had been an horrific attack on the young officer. Liam Connor was a proud Irish man from County Cork. He'd been in the force for almost four years and had a reputation of being a fearless determined officer. It wasn't surprising that he'd tried to confront the escaping villains by himself.

A close examination of the scene revealed signs of a struggle on both the embankment and railway line, with a large area of blood next to the tracks themselves. The evidence suggested that the initial fight had taken place on top of the bank before the officer ended up being knocked or dragged down the embankment to where he ended up unconscious. A short distance away he found the PC's helmet badly cut and bloodstained, with hair and skin sticking to it. He was lucky that he'd fallen beside and not onto the tracks.

'What do you think?' A chief constable didn't normally bother with a visit to a crime scene, but this was the third attack on a policeman in twenty-four hours and he was keen to ensure that everything that could possibly be done to apprehend those responsible was being done and, just as importantly, was seen to be being done. The previous evening he'd already received a visit from the chairman of the Watch Committee, who'd informed him of the general public's rising concerns over events. That was before this latest incident.

'I think Connor's a very lucky man. Not only did he survive the attack, but he was fortunate to fall beside the tracks rather than across them. If he'd landed on them, then it's possible that a passing train would have caused so much damage and disfigurement that his wounds would have been concealed and the whole thing could have been put down to a regrettable accident. I'll give him his due, he must be made of stern stuff to have limped his way back to West Walls without assistance.'

'The signal man says he wouldn't wait while he sent for help. Once he'd partially recovered, he just took off and left the man staring after him! Didn't even tell him his name. I've no doubt the Watch Committee will offer him some recognition for his bravery, perhaps a merit first class, which carries a shilling a week pay rise. That's assuming he fully recovers from his injuries. As well as the cuts to his head, it appears that his left knee is severely damaged where he was hit or kicked. The police surgeon doubts he'll walk properly again.'

The two policemen climbed back up the embankment and made their way back to the nearby road where the senior officer's car was parked on the road bridge that crossed the railway tracks.

'So, what next? Is it or isn't it our saboteur? If it is, then he's part of a bigger group. If it isn't, then we've got a second major incident going on and we were stretched to the limits with one.'

*

The first 'incident' had kicked off in the early morning of the previous day. At 5.30am a housemaid coming to start work at Willowburn Lodge near Longtown was surprised to find a side window open and the back door unlocked. As she was hanging her coat up in the rear vestibule, she'd been knocked to the floor as a group of men rushed past her, carrying a variety of canvas bags. Running upstairs, she'd found the owner, Major Sir Frederick Glendinning, sat on the floor of his bedroom, nursing a swelling on the side of his head behind his right ear. His sobbing wife was kneeling beside him, applying a cold compress. The couple had wakened from their slumbers to find a man going through the drawers of Lady Glendinning's dressing table. Sir Frederick had immediately thrown back the bedcovers and shouted a challenge. As he crossed the room to confront the thief, he was hit from behind and collapsed to the floor, unconscious. Whilst the wife went to help her injured husband, the two men had calmly continued to rifle through the couple's belongings until there was a cry of alarm from somewhere else in the house and the men had rushed off downstairs.

The Longtown police were called and, after a preliminary investigation, telegraphed nearby police stations, including the one at Carlisle, with details of the crime. It seemed one of the men had prised the window open and climbed in before unlocking the back door. Interviews with Lady Glendinning and the housemaid indicated that one of the men matched the description of the saboteur sought by the city police. Consequently, a decision was made that the Cumberland and Westmorland force would post look outs for the gang along the main road into the city and at various points to the north. At that time officers were unclear whether the culprit's aim was to attack and either kill or maim Sir Frederick, who had come out of retirement to work part-time as a training officer for new recruits, taking the opportunity to steal some valuables as well, or a genuine burglary.

Just before 9.00am Sergeant William Storey and Constable John Noble had attempted to stop three heavily laden men who were hurrying along the road at Kingstown. As they'd approached the group, one of the men had pulled out a gun and shot both officers. Storey received a superficial wound, but Noble had been seriously injured. Hearing the shots, another constable, Jacob Milburn, had run down the hill towards Kingstown from his post at Stanwix. As he approached Moorville, he'd come across the men who'd fired at him before they changed direction and headed west. Milburn had recognised one of the men as a local villain named Benjamin Rudd, although the officer's description of one of his accomplices again matched that of the individual wanted by the city police.

With the change of direction, senior officers in the city

police felt that the men were probably heading towards the goods yards at Etterby Junction to use the railway as a means to escape. From here, a line operated by the North British Railway Company circled the western side of the city. Large numbers of freight trains made use of this line in order to bypass the centre of Carlisle, making it an ideal escape route. Police officers were again hurried to various points along the tracks where the trains slowed down or stopped as they passed through the outskirts of the city. They were told to search stationary wagons and to keep an eye out for anyone jumping down from the rolling stock. PC Connor had been sent to the area around the Rome Street signal box to keep a look out for anything suspicious. Freight traffic was frequently held here to allow passenger trains to pass through or before switching tracks.

*

Jack didn't respond to his superior's comments immediately. He stood looking down onto the tracks below and then subconsciously pulled his pipe and matches from the inside pocket of his jacket. Lighting up, he puffed gently, the tobacco smoke drifting away on the faint breeze. For a few moments, deSchmid thought he wasn't going to get an answer, then the inspector took the pipe from his mouth and tapped it out on the heel of his shoe.

'I'm not sure. If it is our German sympathiser, then why attack Glendinning? If he knew where he lived, then surely, he would have known he was retired and, having stayed hidden for so long, why would you do something like this that's bound to draw attention to yourself? Also, in the past he always seems to have worked alone. On the other hand, the savage attack and callous disregard for life fits in with his behaviour elsewhere, and then there's the description.'

'According to Connor, he saw two men walking along the railway tracks towards Denton Holme. They were keeping to the shadows and, with no means of sending for help, he followed them hoping to see if they were looking for a place to lay low. Unfortunately, where the line passes behind the Cumberland Wrestler's pub just along from the signal box, he'd been spotted, and the men turned back towards him. He'd decided against a confrontation and started to climb the embankment when a third man came from somewhere behind him and struck him on the head with a heavy instrument. He'd collapsed to the ground where he received a savage kicking, he wasn't sure how many of them joined in, before losing consciousness. Presumably they rolled him down the bank onto the tracks and left him for dead. He's still very shaken and his memory of the incident is understandably vague and incomplete, but from the rough descriptions he was able to give us, one of the first two men looked like our man. Although the box isn't far from where it happened, the signalman seems not to have seen or heard anything.' As he spoke Jack put his pipe and matches back into the inside pocket of his jacket.

'So,' said deSchmid, 'if he is part of the group, he would have to be the third man, and the brutality of the attack would support that.'

The inspector nodded. 'In which case, if we catch the group, we catch him.'

At this point, a motorised police van crested the rise, coming from the direction of Carlisle. It pulled up in front of the two men and Sergeant Graham Gordon stepped out. He was breathing heavily, as if he'd been running, but as he got closer, it became apparent that this was in exasperation rather than exhaustion.

He looked directly at deSchmid. 'I'm sorry to interrupt, sir, but there's been a development. Around 6.00am a telegraph lineman who was called out to do an emergency repair on a connection just along from St Nicholas Bridge, saw three suspicious-looking characters slip into a tool shed next to the nearby LM&SR wagon repair shop. He reported it to his foreman, who went and got PC Fowler, who was patrolling the London Road Junction.'

'We've got them!' The chief constable's face broke into a smile, but his joy was short-lived.

'No, sir, I'm afraid not. Fowler decided to take things into his own hands and challenge the men by himself. The foreman saw him enter the shed, and after a couple of minutes he heard a loud bang and the three suspects came charging out of the building and ran off along the tracks towards the engine and carriage sheds to the south of the city.'

'And …?' The two senior officers looked despondently at the big sergeant.

Gordon's voice was tearful and emotional. 'When the foreman eventually plucked up the courage to go into the shed, he found Arthur – sorry PC Fowler – lying on the floor in a pool of blood; he'd been shot through the head. A doctor was called, but he was too late to do anything. Half his skull was missing. Death must have been instantaneous.'

The three men just stood and looked at each other, speechless. None of them were able to say anything until Jack broke the silence. With a solemn look and an angry voice, he asked his friend how long ago since the men were seen running off.

'About an hour after the first sighting by the lineman.'

'And they've not been seen at any of the other check points?'

'No.'

Jack turned and looked out over the railway lines towards the St Nicholas marshalling yards where the LM&SR freight trains brought steel to and from the local engineering works.

'So that would suggest that they've realised we're looking for them and have decided that the lesser of two evils is to lay low in the area rather than risk being seen again. They might even be in the engine or carriage sheds themselves.' He paused and ran his fingers through his hair, and then turned back to deSchmid. 'With your permission, sir, I'm going to go and have a look in the two sheds. I'll take Sergeant Gordon and two constables with me.'

'They're armed, Inspector and you're not. Perhaps you should wait while we send back to the station for some fire arms.'

'I think we do that as well, sir. If you can organise the weapons, we'll search the sheds, and if we find anything, we'll cordon them off and wait for support.'

deSchmid considered the proposal and nodded his agreement. He didn't want any more of his officers injured, but on the other hand, he didn't want to risk the men escaping.

Half an hour later Jack, Gordon and two other officers were stood outside the larger carriage shed. They were accompanied by the lineman and his foreman, both of whom held heavy metal bars as makeshift weapons. All five men were spread along the side wall, out of sight from anyone inside.

'Are you sure?' asked Jack.

'Certain,' replied the foreman. 'We knew they'd run off this way, so after reporting the shooting, Albert and I decided to investigate and summon help if we saw anything. We walked along to Upperby Junction, where one of your men is stationed. He hadn't seen them and there are open fields on either side of the lines; he would have noticed anyone trying to get away in either direction. So, they had to be hiding somewhere in between. The only buildings are the engine shed and the carriage shed. Both are open to the elements, so you can easily see inside. There's nothing in the engine shed and surprisingly only a set of freight wagons in the carriage shed. If they're hiding, it has to be in there.'

Indicating that everyone else should stay where they were, he beckoned the big sergeant forwards and the two of them crept stealthily around the side wall and into the shed. To the right, fourteen sets of tracks entered the massive structure, but only the farthest away ones were occupied. Three coupled wagons stood on their own, apparently empty. The doors of the nearest were closed whilst in the others they were open. Without saying anything, Jack looked at his friend and nodded towards the former.

'Bit of a giveaway,' he whispered.

The two men turned around and returned quietly to the others and recounted what they'd seen. There was a short discussion about whether to wait for the firearms to arrive, but the consensus was that if they weren't in the wagon, it would be wasted time, and if they were in it, then surprise now was better than the possibility of a long siege with a bloody end. The plan was simple. The two railway men would pull one of the double doors open as fast as possible and the four policemen, truncheons drawn, would rush the group.

Jack's biggest worry was that the men would hear their approach and come out shooting. If they did, then there was nowhere for his little army to hide. However, all went well, and they were soon stood next to the wagon, ready to go. When everyone was in position, he raised his hand and counted down with his fingers. Three, two, one, and his arm dropped. The doors were wrenched open with a screech and Jack jumped up into the truck. Although he had been hoping to find his quarry, he felt a mixture of surprise and relief to find the wanted men there. All three were seated with their backs against the far wall and, although initially startled, they quickly recovered their senses and scrambled to their feet. One pulled a revolver from the pocket of a grubby jacket, but, before he could raise it and fire, Jack brought his truncheon down on his wrist, and with a scream of pain it was dropped to the floor. The other two fared little better. A sweeping blow to the head from Graham Gordon's mighty right fist felled one man. The third launched himself at the two constables trying to grab him. After a brief struggle, he managed to extricate himself from their grasp and jump through the open door onto the trackside, whereupon the foreman hit him in the stomach with his metal bar. As he folded over, winded, the lineman grabbed him from behind. Eventually all three men were handcuffed and, when the armed reinforcements arrived led by Chief Constable de Schmid, were taken under escort to West Wall Police Station.

The next day Jack and his sergeant were called into the chief constable's office.

'I'm not sure I agree with your reasons for going ahead without armed support, Jack, but, at the end of the day it worked, so I suppose the approach was justified. One day, though …' But deSchmid just smiled and left the sentence unfinished before changing the subject. 'They'll hang for the killings. No doubt about it. Hang and be buried in an unmarked grave! A sad end to three sad lives.'

'There's nothing sad about it as far as I'm concerned, sir', replied Graham Gordon. 'They killed one of our officers and injured three more, one of whom may not recover. As far as I'm concerned, they should be burnt at the stake.'

'Er…quite,' muttered his senior before turning to his inspector. 'The other matter still remains unresolved. The men with Benjamin Rudd were both Irishmen he'd met in a pub. Both had come over looking for work but been attracted by Rudd's offer of rich pickings at Glendinning's house. A wealthy retired couple with only day servants. It was seen as an easy hit. According to them, they didn't realise he had a gun until he shot Storey and Noble. They were then terrified he might use it on them if they said anything. It was just a coincidence that one of them fit the description of our saboteur. That means that tomorrow we need to pick up where we left off before this unpleasant distraction. Dismissed.'

CHAPTER 20

HM Munitions Factory Near Eastriggs

Morning, Monday 26th July 1915

Heinrich stood beside the Butterdales Gatehouse and looked out in amazement at the developing munitions site. It was massive. Directly in front of him, in the distance, he could just about make out the wire fence that divided the emerging 'factory' from the beach. Beyond it, the treacherous Solway Firth and Irish Sea glistened in the early-morning sunshine. To the far south, the Lakeland Mountains reached up to a cloudless blue sky. Left and right, the site stretched out east and west as far as his eyes could see, and everywhere was a hive of activity. Hundreds of men were working on roads, laying train tracks or digging foundations for what he assumed would eventually be the factory buildings. Running directly through the site was a road. It was wide enough to allow two vehicles to pass each other and beside it a broad-gauge railway line was being constructed.

Most of the labourers wore collarless shirts under navy dungarees with a flat cap. Nearest to him, a group of men were toiling to lift iron rails onto wooden sleepers set in bed ballast. They had their sleeves rolled up and he noticed their shirts were dark with the sweat that had rolled down their backs and soaked through the rough cotton material. Some paused for a moment, using their cap to fan themselves or wipe the moisture on their brow. From well down the track behind them he could hear the clang of hammers as rail spikes were driven down through railroad ties to secure the rails in place. Ahead of the men laying the rails, another group was packing down a layer of ballast, on which adjacent sleepers would be set before the next length of track could be laid. From each side of these main arteries, at about 100-yard intervals, vegetation had been removed and rough tracks ran in straight lines to places where the land had been cleared and foundations laid in preparation for the construction of various buildings.

He hadn't expected anything on this scale and his stomach tightened as he realised that the idea of one man somehow sabotaging the new munitions works before it went into production was totally impractical. When he had suggested the idea to the meeting back in Berlin he had anticipated something on a similar scale to the Krupp's factories in Germany. Those in the Rhur were big, but if explosives were set off in strategic areas he knew that serious damage could be inflicted and production or transportation halted for a significant length of time. Here, even when the site was fully operational, it was clear that the layout was designed to ensure that damage to one area would not affect production in another. When finished, the buildings would be well dispersed and accessible by road or rail. Destroying a building, or part of the road or railway, would almost certainly be no more than a short-term inconvenience.

As he waited, he considered the possibility of large-scale damage from the air. He was aware that bombing from Zeppelins had achieved some limited success in the south and east of England, particularly on London, Hull, King's Lynn and Great Yarmouth, but he wasn't sure whether the craft could manage to get this far north. He'd need to gather as much information about the site as possible and then get this back to the Abteilung IIIb for consideration. The group might be sceptical of the suggestion, given the already-limited success of a mission he had outlined and which, despite the group's agreement, would be laid at his feet in terms of any failure.

His thoughts were disrupted as a young corporal came out of the red brick building that served as a guardhouse, stepped round the security barrier and, looking at his clipboard, said, 'No, you're definitely not on the list and your name hasn't been left anywhere else in the office. I'm sorry, but you've had a wasted journey. I can't let you in.'

Heinrich slipped his kit bag down on to the ground and spread his arms in a pleading fashion. 'But there must be a mistake. I spoke with one of Pearson's work foremen in Carlisle and he said that I should meet at the station with the other new men and get the 7.30am train to Dumfries, get off at Eastriggs and follow everyone down to this gatehouse, where we'd be met by him or someone else. I've handed my notice in at work and left my lodgings. I can't go back now.'

Heinrich knew that his explanation wasn't true, but he had hoped that, like the half truths about working on the ships and in the Globe, it would be accepted without question. In reality he'd overheard the drunken comments of a group of six men in the pub on Saturday night. The place had been busy with the usual mix of clientele, from old men playing dominos in one corner to labourers trying to drink away as much of their hard-earned money as they could, in the shortest time possible. The men, sat at a table near the rear of the building, had been talking loudly so that anyone who wanted to could have followed their conversation with little trouble. He'd easily picked up that they'd recently been recruited by Pearson's and Sons to work as navvies on the new munitions factory being built just over the border in Scotland. One of the men who was less inebriated than the others was obviously already employed on the site in some form of supervisory capacity and he outlined the arrangements for them to report for work on Monday morning. He was then at pains to ensure the men were clear about what would happen when they got there.

'Monday to Saturday working. Make sure you bring everything you need for the week. You'll be put up in one of the accommodation huts in nearby Eastriggs. There are twenty beds per hut and it's six pence for a bed for the night. Less if you sleep on the floor in one of the gaps between the bunks. It's up to you which you decide, just let the warden know when you arrive. Comes straight out of your pay packet. Saturday and Sunday night, you sort out for yourselves. Those with homes stay there, everyone else … that's your problem.'

As he was speaking, Heinrich stood up from his chair at the corner table from which he kept an eye on things and started to clear away dirty glasses. It was a task he normally wouldn't even contemplate but in this instance it gave him a chance to walk over to the men and listen more closely as he slowly picked up their empties.

'You'll be well paid. Five shillings a day, which compares well to anyone working in the local factories. Picks, shovels and wheelbarrows will be provided. If you damage or break them, you pay for the replacement.'

Heinrich bumped the table in feigned surprise and blurted out, 'Wow. I wouldn't mind being paid that. It's a lot more than I get here.'

The speaker paused for a moment and looked up at the well-built German. 'You shouldn't be listening, mate, but, if you're serious, we're always looking for hard workers. You don't have to stay here.' He turned back to the others and continued with his instructions. 'The work is hard, physical labouring. Most men new to the job can't manage to keep up with the experienced workers and often only manage the equivalent of half a day's work. If that happens, you'll only get half the pay until you gain the strength and stamina required to keep up.'

Heinrich shuffled away, keen not to be seen as over inquisitive but excited with the break through. After weeks of clandestine searching he'd stumbled on the information that he sought in his own pub. Thanks to the men's incautious conversation, he now knew where the munitions site was and had a potential way to gain access.

Early the following Monday morning, before anyone else was awake, he had packed all his belongings into his kitbag and left the Globe by the side door to walk up to the station. A light drizzle was falling from a washed-out sky and, when he arrived, he found four of the men sheltering under the arch over the main entrance. A couple nodded when he arrived, but no one spoke until the fifth man came out of the station and joined them. He looked slightly older than the others and was short and squat, with a round face and matching figure. At first, he didn't notice the German and started to hand out train tickets.

'These were left for us in the ticket office. Apparently they come out of our first week's wage. Normal practice, so the bloke behind the counter says. They deal with new workers every day. Pearson's have an arrangement with the railway company.'

Putting the last ticket into the top pocket of a well-worn jacket, he looked up and for the first time noticed Heinrich. 'You're from the pub aren't you?' When he received a brief nod in response, he asked, 'What you doing here?'

'I was told that they were always looking for hard workers. So here I am.'

'Well, there's no ticket for anyone else, and I'm not sure anyone expected you to simply drop everything and turn up.'

Heinrich said nothing and simply shrugged his shoulders.

One of the younger men interrupted. 'Just leave him alone, Frank. If he wants to try his luck, who are we to stop him. It won't affect us. From what I hear, there's more than enough work to go round. Come on, mate. You'll need to buy yourself a ticket. I'll show you where the ticket office is. One way to Eastriggs, second class.'

Eastriggs had proved to be a small Scottish village just over the border in Dumfries and Galloway. There were other small groups of men travelling on the same train, which was more crowded than might normally be expected on a rural line, and it was pretty obvious that they were all headed for the same place.

As they disembarked a sharp-faced, thin man in a shabby grey suit and matching cap was waiting for them outside the station platform. He shouted out in a deep and surprisingly loud voice which drowned out the various excited conversations. 'Move out onto the road and form a column in rows of three.' With that, he pointed to a narrow gap in a hawthorn hedge reached by a short but muddy footpath up a slippery bank.

Although straightforward, the instruction caused some confusion among the men with much pushing, shoving and sliding. As a result, it took nearly fifteen minutes before everyone was ready.

Their leader then walked to the front of the small column, which Heinrich guessed had between thirty and forty men in it, and shouted, 'Follow me, and don't get left behind. We won't be stopping to let folk catch up.'

With that, he'd marched off at a brisk pace, turning left onto a main road to head in a westerly direction, with the column hurriedly following on behind him. The rain had stopped and a warm sun was poking its way through the retreating clouds making the walk through the lush farmland a pleasant experience. After about a mile, they came to a small hamlet, which his new young friend from the station said was called Eastriggs. Almost immediately, they turned right down a narrow track, on either side of which building work was being carried out. A painted wooden sign on the side of the road indicated that the area bore the quaint name of Butterdales. The settlement, he was told, had originally consisted of no more than a few houses, but it was being expanded with purpose-built accommodation to house the growing number of workers based at the nearby munitions factory. Initially some of this would be in the form of wooden huts, but there was also the odd brick house and evidence of foundations being put down for more permanent homes. They quickly left the buildings behind as the road curved gently downhill towards the far-off-sea, but before they reached it, they arrived at the barricaded entrance to the fenced-off site and were told to wait on the grass verge. Their guide ducked under the red-and-white barrier across the road and spoke to a soldier who was stood outside a guardhouse apparently waiting for them, clipboard in hand. He took, what Heinrich assumed was a list, from the guardsman and returned to the column.

'When your name is called out step under the barrier and line up in threes again, just behind Corporal Jones. Matthew Kelly, Seamus Ryan, Rory O'Sullivan, Martin O'Connor ...'

He called out the names and ticked the clipboard until everyone except Heinrich was standing on the opposite side of the barrier.

'And who might you be?' he asked.

'Ricky Colman.'

'Well, Ricky Colman you're not on my list, so sod off...' And with that, he turned on his heels, ducked under the barrier again and shouted, 'The rest of you, follow me.' With that, he strode off down the road and into the site.

The German shouted, 'Wait,' but the group continued on their way without looking back, and after a couple of minutes they turned left and disappeared into the melee of other workers.

Heinrich wondered what to do next. He'd come too far just to give up when he was so close to his objective, but he was bereft of ideas to alter his predicament. At that point, fate intervened. Emerging out of the crowd of workers into which the column had only recently disappeared, five men came rushing into view. Four of them were carrying a dirty canvas stretcher on which a sixth man lay prone. As they came closer he could see that the man's left leg was roughly bandaged and splinted with what looked like a wooden pick handle. He held his left arm behind his head, but the other was pounding on the stretcher side, and from his cries it was clear that he was in some pain. However, it wasn't the injured workman that held the German's attention but the person leading them. It was the man who had spoken to the new workers in the Globe.

The little group hurried up to the gatehouse and stopped. Their leader took hold of the front of the stretcher from one of the bearers and then barked instructions at him. 'You! Run up and get the site doctor. At this time of day he'll still be at home. His is the first brick house as you turn into Butterdales Road. Get a move on.'

The man stepped round the barrier and set off up the hill towards the village at a rapid jog, his studded workman's boots clattering on the rough surface as he ran.

'Right let's get him inside and lay him down on the floor, away from the weather and prying eyes, until the doctor comes.'

The men shuffled through the doorway into the building and disappeared from sight for what seemed an age. When they came out there were only three of them, the two who had been carrying the back of the stretcher and the man who Heinrich now took to be some kind of foreman. The latter told the others to go back to work and then approached the corporal, who, like Heinrich, had been a statue-like observer to the whole process.

'OK. The doc' will come and see to him as soon as possible. I've left one of his workmates with him until then, although I can well do without being three men short this morning. Make sure the messenger and him,' he jerked a thumb at the door, 'come straight back to me as soon as he arrives. No waiting about "to see what happens" or any other excuse.'

'What did happen?' the soldier asked.

'While he and his gang were lifting a rail into place, the idiot manged to slip on the ballast that forms the bed on which the sleepers were laid. As he fell, he let go of it and the bloody thing fell on the bottom of his leg. Well and truly bust, and his own stupid fault, except that he's not the only one who's gonna suffer for it. I've a quota of track to lay by the end of today with one man short. Ruddy stupid bastard!'

He thumped the top of the barrier in frustration.

A smug look appeared on the young officer's face. 'Well, this might be your lucky day. A solution to your problem may be close at hand.'

The other man gave him a fearsome glare. 'What the hell are you talking about? Are you gonna take that fancy uniform off and do a bit of real work for a change? I doubt it.'

Continuing his annoying manner, the soldier shook his head and said, 'No, not me, but perhaps he will...' And he pointed slowly towards Heinrich.

The foreman switched his look to the tall man standing just outside the site, who, to all intents and purposes, had, until that minute been invisible to him. For a moment, he just stared, and then rubbing his jaw, he said, 'Don't I know you from somewhere?'

'The Globe at the weekend. You told me that you were always looking for hard workers and that I didn't have to stay there if I wanted to earn a better living. So here I am, but I'm told that I'm not on the list, so I can't come in.'

'Blow me, so I did, but I didn't really expect you to take me up on my offer. There's a proper way to apply for work up here, you can't just turn up.' He paused and looked Heinrich up and down. 'Or can you? I wonder? Where's the list?' Turning to the corporal, he held his hand out. The other man passed it over. 'What's your name?'

'Ricky Colman.'

He grabbed the pencil from the startled soldier, then turned and walked into the building where he had just deposited the injured man. After a couple of minutes, he came back out.

'I think someone's misread this,' he said. 'Ricky Colman is clearly here. It's the last name on the list. Let him in.' He thrust the clipboard at the surprised guardsman, who grabbed it and ran his finger down the list of names.

'But it wasn't there a minute ago,' he stammered.

'Well, it's bloody well there now. So let him in. Leave the list in the gatehouse and I'll sort his contract out later. Now you...' he pointed at Heinrich, 'move yourself, mate. I've a railway track to lay and I can't wait all day.' And with that Ricky Colman smiled and ducked quickly under the security barrier to join the hundreds of men striving to build a munitions factory the like of which had never been seen and which, if completed, might turn the course of the war against his German homeland.

CHAPTER 21

Globe Inn, Caldewgate

Morning, Friday 13th August 1915

The weather had been good for the first hour, a bright, crisp morning with clear skies. Jack had visited the pubs in the Denton Holme area, aiming to catch the landlords as they carried out their morning cleaning and would have time to talk without interruption, but as he crossed into Caldewgate it had turned dull and cold, with a chill wind. Shortly afterwards, a light drizzle began and as midday approached, this had turned into heavy rain. A damp tramp to the Pheasant, Jovial Sailor and Maltsters had revealed nothing of interest, and as he pushed open the door of the Globe, he was happy on two counts. It was the last place on his list, and to his right he could see a roaring open fire where he could warm up and dry his soaked clothes. As he crossed the room to stand in front of the flames, the landlord turned from his task of mopping the floor in front of the bar and nodded an acknowledgement.

'Morning, Billy. It's not like you to be doing the pot collecting and cleaning. I thought that was one of your "chucker out's" jobs.'

'It should be, but the bloody bastard just up and left without notice, leaving me in the lurch. Damn foreigner. You give the man a job when he's short and what do you get in return? Cleared his room and left without a word. I wouldn't mind but I bent over backwards with the odd day off when he asked and didn't kick him out when he couldn't work for a bit 'cos he was ill.'

Jack stopped rubbing his hands together over the open hearth and stared at the man. He wondered if, at the very end of weeks of fruitless searching, there might be a glimmer of light at the end of the tunnel.

'Tell me a bit more about this bloke, Billy. What does he look like? What do you know about his background and when were these absences from work?'

An hour later, a breathless and still-soaked Jack marched briskly into the West Walls Police Station and told the duty officer to find Sergeant Gordon and have him come to his office as matter of urgency. Ten minutes later, he'd just managed to light a small fire in the small grate and drape his damp jacket in front of it when there was a knock on the door and his friend walked into the room.

'Where's the fire?' joked the big man. 'Armstrong said it was urgent.'

'I think I might have found him, Graham. His name's Coleman ... Ricky Colman. Billy Dixon at the Globe says he employed a Canadian as his "chucker out" back at the start of April. There was a bit of a fracas at the pub and Colman stepped in and single-handedly dealt with four drunken navvies who'd attacked his soon-to-be predecessor. Billy said two of them needed to be carried out of the building by their mates. Says he'd never seen anything like it. At first, he thought the guy might be a professional boxer he was so fast with his hands, but Colman said he'd just left working on the boats down the coast and learnt to look after himself there. He's been living in one of his spare rooms ever since. However, here's what's interesting — '

'Wait ...' The big sergeant held up a huge hand to stop his inspector in full flow, '... I may have met him, Jack. In fact, I'm certain of it.' He went on to recount the events under the railway arches a few months earlier. 'It was me that showed him where the Globe was. He was just off a train from west Cumberland looking for work, but it was late and he was hoping to find lodgings for the night. I suggested he try Caldewgate and showed him how to get there.'

'Bloody hell, Graham. What else can you remember about him? Anything? Any detail, large or small. Did you check his papers?'

His friend pursed his lips and shook his head as his face slowly reddened. 'No. He offered to show me them, but he spoke perfect English and said he was hoping to work at the railway marshalling site. I knew they'd be thoroughly checked before they let him into the yard, so I didn't bother.' He stopped and lifted both hands over his face as if in prayer and then shook his head.

'What? What?'

'The other place he was looking for work was the munitions factory.'

'He knew about that?'

The sergeant nodded. 'The place is an open secret, Jack, and I didn't think anything of it, but now...'

Jack took a deep breath, then puffed out his cheeks and exhaled slowly. 'We need to talk to deSchmid. Come on.'

He grabbed his jacket and headed for the door. Fifteen minutes later, they were stood in front of the chief constable having briefed him on their suspicions.

'OK, Jack. I agree that there seems to be something fishy about the situation, but what you say is all circumstantial. There's no real hard evidence that he could be more than a deserter, conscientious objector, thief or any other of a dozen dubious types of character that we're currently having to deal with. These are strange times.'

'No. It's him, sir. I'm certain of it. Thinks about it. A stranger turns up, saying he's looking for employment having worked on the boats on the west coast. A plausible tale, but hard to check. Someone who is capable of dealing with four tough labourers on his own. The first attack occurs shortly after his arrival. The description matches the one given by the soldiers at the barracks and by Meakin and others following the Quintinshill crash. Then he suddenly disappears, in all probability because he thought someone might realise the same person was involved. There are too many...'

Jack paused in mid-sentence. Something else had suddenly occurred to him. The other two men looked at him waiting for him to continue.

'There's something else that fits as well,' he said. 'I've just realised that the period he spent laid up in his room coincides with the days I was in hospital after the Annetwell Street fire. The stranger who helped me disappeared after the event even though he must have received similar injuries to mine. The physical description fits. What if it was him?'

'A saboteur with a conscience?' replied deSchmid. 'Unlikely.'

'No. A soldier. Someone who'll target the military but not civilians. He's not a cold-blooded murderer. He's a raider who somehow has been dropped behind enemy lines to do as much damage as he possibly can and he's going to keep going until he's pulled out or until he's caught or killed. He'll accept civilian casualties linked to a military action but doesn't target them directly.'

'An interesting theory, although I'm not sure that it's supported by the events at Quintinshill. Assuming you are right, what's our modern-day reiver going to do next? He could be anywhere, planning to do anything. It's going to be like looking for a needle in a haystack if he's gone to ground.'

'I don't think so, sir,' Gordon interrupted. 'We know exactly where he's going to end up, although perhaps not when.'

Jack nodded in agreement. 'The munitions factory. He asked you about it on the first day and he also mentioned it to Billy Dixon. He's going to try and destroy it before it becomes operational.'

deScmidt leant forwards across his desk and looked at his junior officers. 'That's ridiculous. The place is massive. There's no chance he could do anything more than cause damage to a small section of the construction work. He might cause some disruption to part of the site, but that's all.'

'But he doesn't know that, does he sir? He won't have any idea of the impossibility of the task until he gets there. Security is pretty tight, so his first challenge will be to find a way to get in, and then when he realises the problem he'll need time to think about what to do. So...' He paused to think. 'How would you get onto the site and spend some time there so that you can plan a way to cause maximum damage?'

deScmidt looked at Jack and the two men spoke in simultaneously. 'I'd get a job there.'

The chief constable pushed his chair rapidly back and stood. 'I want you both on the site before the last shift today and the place shuts down. Use the paddy wagon, but keep it out of view of anyone once you get up there. Find out who's in charge and ask them if they can confirm that our man's working there. Given the size of the works, this may mean some clandestine observing. If he's there, don't approach him. I don't want him spooked or any bloodshed. Be discreet and make sure that everyone acts normally, but see if you can get a look at him to make a positive identification. If it's him, you remain and keep an eye on things Jack. Sergeant, you return here to confirm his presence, by which time I'll have arranged with the military for a detachment of armed soldiers to return with me to carry out his arrest and capture. You can lead us back to his location.'

Jack nodded and started to turn towards the door, ready to leave, but deSchmid lifted his hand to indicate the two officers should wait a moment. 'Jack.'

'Sir?'

'Be careful. Very careful. Both of you. Whoever this man is, he's complicit in the deaths of nearly 300 people. He has no hesitation in killing to achieve his objectives and I don't want one of my officers added to the total. Enough people were lost or injured sorting out the Benjamin Rudd fiasco.'

Nodding, Jack smiled at his chief. 'No, sir. Neither do I.'

Shortly after mid-day the two officers arrived at the munitions site. They parked the police wagon on the grass verge just outside the main entrance and Jack got out, indicating to Gordon that he should stay with the vehicle until called for.

'I don't want to advertise a uniformed presence until I've an idea what we're dealing with,' he said, and the big sergeant nodded his assent.

He walked up to the security barrier and spoke with the young soldier on guard duty, explaining who he was and why he was there. The boy looked shocked and asked him to wait while he went for the corporal in charge from within an adjacent gatehouse. He was back in a couple of minutes accompanied by an older man with a single officer's stripe on his arm.

'Lance Corporal Miller, sir. I believe there's a small problem we can help you with.'

Jack smiled at the typical military understatement. 'There is indeed, corporal.' And he explained the situation again.

Miller listened intently then turned to his colleague. 'Go and find Albert Richardson. Don't run or make a fuss, but make sure he knows it's urgent. If he asks why, just say I need to speak with him now about a security matter.'

As the private marched off in double time, he explained that, 'Pearson's contract the labourers for the site and George works for them as a foreman. He'll know whether your man is employed here and where he's likely to be right now. Do you really think that this bloke is a German saboteur? Seems a bit unlikely to me. I mean, how could he have got this far north?'

Jack said nothing in response. If the man had really been working on the local fishing boats with Canadian papers, it was possible that no one would think to challenge him. He could have been in the country for months and done all sorts of other unattributed damage. He shook his head at the prospect but then reconsidered the situation. Graham Gordon had come across him walking away from the station and looking for accommodation. So he must have just arrived in the city, in all probability by train. If, and it was a big if, he had had something to do with the boats down the coast, then he would have arrived from one of the three main harbours of Maryport, Workington or Whitehaven. It was unlikely to be Workington. Large amounts of haematite were mined in the surrounding area, and the town had developed into an iron and steel producing centre, with the Lonsdale Dock handling the trade. With the start of war, security had been tightened at both the steel works and the harbour. Maryport was the biggest and busiest port, principally handling coal and iron products. Once again, boats arriving and departing were carefully checked, as were the people arriving on them. That left Whitehaven. Although it was still exporting coal from the west Cumberland coalfields, its importance had diminished in recent years. However, its thriving fishing industry still existed. Someone arriving in the town having worked 'on the boats' might not be noticed. The more he thought about it, the more it made sense, and the more he was convinced that that was what had happened. He wasn't sure how he might have originally got onto one of the fishing vessels, but working that out was for another time and place. Perhaps when they caught him they'd find out.

His thoughts were interrupted as a deep, gravelly voice behind him said, 'I hope you have a bloody good reason for dragging me away from the site. Without me watching over them, the lazy Irish bog trotters will be taking an extended break and getting paid for doing nothing.'

Turning slowly round, Jack said, 'Oh, I do. I do indeed.'

CHAPTER 22

HM Munitions Factory near Eastriggs

Afternoon, Saturday 14th August 1915

It was a humid afternoon. Although warm, the grey sky threatened rain and across the Solway, the tops of the Cumberland Mountains were lost in the clouds. Heinrich was breathing heavily and his shirt was soaked with sweat. He'd been laying track ballast for most of the day. The ballast was made of crushed stone and new loads were brought forwards in tipper trucks, along track just laid, to be dropped where the next rails were to be put down. Shovelling it into place was hard, gruelling work. Despite the exhausting nature of the task, his mind had been on other things. Although he'd been at the munitions site for two weeks and used various excuses to explore the vast complex, quickly acquiring the nickname of 'pisspot' due to his frequent toilet breaks, he'd come up with nothing that was likely to cause any significant disruption to the building work. It was simply too big. Today would be his last day before he headed back to the coast for the hoped-for rendezvous with *U24* in three days' time and he'd thought about blowing up one of the tracks before he left. However, it would have limited impact and serve only to alert security to a saboteur, creating the possibility of being caught at the end of his mission. As the 16th August had got nearer and nearer, that was something that he had increasingly hoped to avoid. Instead, he had packed his kit bag and left it under his bed in the accommodation hut located on the road opposite the station. At the end of the day, he intended to collect it and join the groups of workers who would be catching the early evening train to Carlisle for a night out. He'd be lost in the crowds and, with luck, would arrive in time to catch the last train to Whitehaven or, at worst, find a solitary place to sleep in one of the waiting rooms before continuing early the next day. Once out west he'd return to the railway shack and hide until dawn on Monday morning. With luck, by the time anyone noticed he was missing, he would be on board the submarine and heading home.

'Hey, pisspot. You gonna stand there leaning on that shovel all day or do some work?' George Massey, his gang boss interrupted his musings and he realised that he'd been stood idle with his thoughts for several minutes.

'Sorry, George. Just thinking of picking up my pay packet at the end of the day and which pub I'm going to spend it in tonight.'

'Aye, well, if you don't get a move on, you'll not have any pay. You'll have to hand it over to the rest of us for doing your work.' Massey was a big, red-haired Scotsman with an untidy matching beard and a sharp tongue. Unusually, he lived in a small cottage just outside Eastriggs. He'd been a farm labourer until the building site had opened up and he swapped jobs to take advantage of the better-paid munitions work. By rights he should have left his tied dwelling, but he'd asked the farmer to take on his son as his replacement, allowing the family to remain in their home. The man had been happy to agree, since he viewed George as a grumbling, idle layabout who did everything he could to avoid a hard day's work. His boy, on the other hand, was young, cheerful and full of energy. Nothing was too much trouble for the lad. The farmer was well pleased with the swap. Heinrich had heard the tale from one of the other navvies; no one seemed to have any idea how Massey had ended up in charge of a gang, but he took advantage of the situation, pushing the other seven men in the group to exert themselves whilst managing to do as little as possible himself. He settled complaints with his fists and Heinrich suspected that if he'd been intending to stick around, the two would eventually have come to blows. As things stood, the need to keep a low profile meant that he simply did as he was told and got on with things.

He lifted his shovel to move another load of ballast and continued without stopping for several minutes until, out the corner of his eye, he noticed some hurried movement at the distant gatehouse. Putting his shovel down again, he squinted, trying to better make out what was going on. The foreman who had given him the job the previous Monday was being hurried towards the low building by one of the soldiers who stood on security duty. Another soldier was standing just inside the road barrier next to a smaller man dressed in a loose-fitting suit. The four of them chatted for a moment and then a fifth person stepped out from behind a dark-coloured wagon parked just outside the gatehouse. It was a man whose dress and features he immediately recognised. He would have known the tall police sergeant who had directed him to the Globe at twice the distance. The group stood talking for a moment before the munitions worker entered the building and returned after a couple of minutes with a clip board. Another discussion ensued before he pointed across the site in the general direction of Heinrich's work party.

At that moment it became a race against time. He knew that somehow his cover had been blown and these men were coming for him. Panic began to well up inside him and he fought to push it back down. He needed to stay calm and think. His immediate priority was to move before the men got closer. To his left, the land either side of the narrow Saugh-Hope Burn that ran north to south across the site had been cleared of vegetation in preparation for the start of various building projects. In the absence of cover, he could see as far as the wire security fence that formed a barrier between the munitions works and the Solway marshlands. Escape in that direction was a non-starter. To his right, the situation presented a better option. For about thirty metres the land had again been stripped back, but beyond that the original closely packed stunted trees and scrubland remained. He quickly made his mind up.

'I need a piss,' he said out loud, and without waiting for a reply, he turned and walked off rapidly towards the temporary safety of the dense thicket. Behind him he could hear the annoyed voice of George Massey, but he was totally focused on escape and the words washed over him without meaning. From a distance, the vegetation looked impenetrable, but a gap between two gorse bushes allowed him to slip out of sight more easily than he expected. Once inside, the undergrowth was dense and he was forced to move through similar gaps in the greenery until, to his surprise, he stepped out into an area of flattened land that bordered the northern security fence. The vegetation had obviously been cut down when the fence had been erected and as yet had not grown back. For a moment he paused and in the silence he could feel the thump of his heart and a sound like a drum beating in his ears. Closing his eyes, he sighed with relief and considered his options. He knew that if he tracked west along the barrier he would remain unseen and eventually arrive at the main gatehouse. With luck he would be able to sneak out, especially if the guards had accompanied the police contingent. The alternative was to head for the smaller east gate, but, although this would take him in the opposite direction from his pursuers, it also took him away from the accommodation block where he had left his kitbag which, given its contents, he was desperate not to leave behind. There was a chance that a guard had been sent to the hut, but he reasoned that this was unlikely if those looking for him had just arrived at the entrance and assumed he would be somewhere on site. It was more likely that, not being able to find him, they would only then ask to see where he lived. This gave him a short window of time to recover his possessions.

Decision made, he walked quickly in his chosen direction. Rising anxiety tempted him to run, but he forced himself to restrain the urge and keep to a fast walk. He had no desire to create more noise than necessary or to sustain an untimely injury through a careless fall. Even walking it took only a few minutes to reach his destination. Although the fence ran right up to the road barrier the gatehouse had been built just inside the site, leaving a narrow space between the two. Heinrich sneaked along the gap, ducking below a window that faced north along Butterdales Road in the direction of Eastriggs. At the edge of the building he peered slowly round the corner and was dismayed to see that one of the soldiers had been left on guard. However, as seconds passed it was clear that he was intent on looking down the road in the direction that his colleagues had disappeared. After a moment's pause, the German slipped out from his hiding place, stepped round the barrier and sneaked away, keeping to the right side of the road so that he was blocked from view by the gatehouse and the parked police van.

*

Jack bent forward and rested his elbows on the parapet of the sandstone bridge that took a narrow road over the Carlisle to Dumfries railway line before eventually disappearing northwards past the small local cemetery towards the remote hamlet of Creca. Below him to his left was the tiny station of Eastriggs, the single-storey structure more like a farm cottage than a stopping-off place on a major rail route. The domestic image was emphasised by the stationmaster who had stripped off his jacket, cap and tie, and was working, sleeves rolled up, in the vegetable garden at the far side of the site. In reality, the building was the man's house, with a waiting room and ticket office attached at one end.

It had, he reflected, been an unsatisfactory and frustrating afternoon. Albert Richardson had confirmed that a man known as Ricky Colman was working on the site. While he went into the gatehouse to find the work schedule detailing his whereabouts, Jack shouted for Graham Gordon to join him. Despite deSchmid's instructions, once he was certain Coleman was on site, he'd intended to arrest him then and there rather than risk anything going wrong while they waited for help. He couldn't imagine what a bigger group of armed men might achieve that he and his friend, accompanied by two armed guards, wouldn't be able to. The foreman returned with a list of working parties and their locations and had been sent off to check that their enemy was present while the police duo waited out of sight indoors. After only a few minutes, he'd returned to say that the Canadian had been with his group but had disappeared into the nearby bushes to go to the privy and not yet come back. They'd waited for him to return but when he hadn't appeared after an hour it had become clear that something was wrong. Richardson, accompanied by the sergeant and one of the soldiers, had been sent to check the accommodation block while Jack and the other had checked the area he had disappeared into. They'd found nothing and when the others returned to report that his sleeping area was empty and possessions gone, he'd realised that their quarry had evaded them. At first, he'd wondered how he could disappear at just the moment they had arrived and if he might have an accomplice who had tipped him off. However, when they'd talked to George Massey, he'd laughed the idea off and suggested it was more likely that Coleman had simply seen them arrive.

'Where we were working you can just about see the main entrance if you've a mind to look. I guess it would be the kind of thing yer man might be keeping an eye on if he were a spy.'

Graham Gordon had agreed. 'Nothing he's done so far would suggest he's got someone working with him, Jack. I think we've just been unlucky. Perhaps he saw us while he was looking about for a place to relieve himself. The question now is, where's he gone and what's he going to do next? We need to check the railway to see if he's been seen. Getting about in this part of the world isn't easy. He'd be quickly noticed if he was on foot. There's virtually no motor traffic, so someone wandering along the roads would stand out. Most of the land is given over to grazing, as such, he'll find it hard to conceal himself in the countryside.'

So the two of them had driven up to the station and questioned the stationmaster. He'd been adamant that no one had got on a train that afternoon.

'We've only had two trains through this afternoon. The 13.30 from Carlisle to Dumfries arrived at 13.50, but not a soul got on or off. The other was the 15.00 from Dumfries to Carlisle – it got in at 15.40. We had one person disembark. Maggie Williams goes up to Annan to check on her ailing mother and get the shopping every Tuesday and Saturday. Always catches the same early morning train and comes back at the same time in the afternoon.'

Jack had suggested that someone might have got on unseen, but the man was insistent that this was impossible. He stood on the small platform all the time the train was in and, together with the train's guard who travelled in the rear carriage, monitored people getting on and off. They then signalled to the driver when it was safe to depart. The fireman or the driver himself usually checked the blind side of the train. At Eastriggs, for anyone wanting to sneak onto a train, there was the added problem of having to fight their way through the hawthorn hedge that separated the line from the adjacent fields and nearby road, clamber down the sides of the cutting and then cross a set of tracks. It wasn't impossible, but he had to admit that it would be unlikely that someone carrying a heavy bag could do so without being seen or heard.

Sending Graham Gordon back with the paddy wagon, Jack had decided to wait for the early-evening train back to Carlisle on the outside chance that his prey might be waiting in hiding for the initial furore to die down before he risked getting on board. There was another arrival due just after 6.00pm but many of the workers from the munitions site caught this back into the city and they would be aware of the situation and on their guard for Coleman. The news about the German would have spread round the site like wildfire. He knew it was a forlorn hope, but he couldn't think of anything else to do and he wanted some time on his own to think.

Pushing himself back upright, he clasped his arms behind his head and stretched the stiffness out of his neck and shoulders. Turning round, he leant back against the stone work before pulling his pipe and tobacco out of the flap pocket of his jacket. To Jack, pipe-smoking was both a ritual and a relaxation. He got a certain satisfaction from packing the tobacco into the bowl just right, followed by the whoosh of the match and the wonderful aromatic smell of his favourite Condor Slice. It was a lighter, milder tobacco, yet had a rich flavour, and although he'd tried other types, none produced the same slow-burning, cool and satisfying smoke. As he puffed, his mind considered the situation. Where the hell had he disappeared to and where was he going next? The obvious place was back east to Carlisle from whence he had come, but he now knew that someone was after him and that almost certainly they were from that city. South was the coast, but escape across the treacherous Solway was unlikely. There was little of military interest to attract him north or west, although it was possible that his escape route lay in one of these directions. The more he thought about it, the more he felt the only option was for Colman to retrace his steps, despite the risks. If he'd come into Maryport, Workington or Whitehaven by boat, then it made sense for him to plan his escape the same way, particularly if he was assuming that he'd not be discovered. He decided to share his thoughts with deScmidt in the morning and suggest that the ports and railway stations be watched. A whistle behind him interrupted his thoughts and he turned to see the distant smoke of an approaching train. Tapping his pipe out on the bridge, he stepped through a gap in the adjacent hedge and, in a happier frame of mind, hurried down to the platform to await his transport home.

CHAPTER 23

Kingmoor Nature Reserve north of Carlisle

Night, Sunday 15th August 1915

Night was closing in when Heinrich had eventually arrived back on the outskirts of Carlisle wet, bedraggled and in low spirits. After his hasty departure from the munitions site, he'd returned to an empty accommodation hut and retrieved his kitbag before initially heading for the railway station. However, he realised that he was unlikely to be able to board a train back to the city unnoticed and those following would then be certain of his destination. Instead, as he stood at the roadside thinking, luck had been on his side and he'd hailed a lift from a passing farmer who was travelling to Gretna Green in a horse-drawn four wheeled cart for an evening drinking with friends. The man was tall and lean with a skin well-tanned from working out of doors. Happy to have company on his journey, he did most of the talking, complaining about the impact of the war on the local labour market. The number of men making themselves available for agricultural work was much reduced, he said, and there were worries that without sufficient men farms would be unable to gather the harvest.

'Yon bloody munitions site makes things even worse. Them that haven't gone off to war look to gain employment there. They're paying sodding ridiculous wages.'

Heinrich was happy just to listen, content that, other than his destination, he wasn't asked anything of consequence. The short journey took nearly two hours thanks to occasional stops to allow the horse to drink at roadside troughs. *I would have been quicker to walk,* he thought, but it was uneventful except for one heart-stopping moment when what looked like the police vehicle from the munitions factory roared passed as they reached the narrow bridge over the Kirtle Water. His host halted the cart to allow it to overtake and noted the German's discomfort as it approached and the way he turned his face away as it pulled round them.

'That bobby's in a big rush to get somewhere. That wouldn't have anything to do with you, would it?'

'Why would you think that?'

'Oh, no reason, other than you seemed pretty keen that he didn't see your face and you look like you've seen a ghost. Want to mention something before I ask you to get ootta my cart?'

The two men stared at each other before Heinrich held up his hands and replied, 'OK. I thought it possible that he was looking for me. I've been labouring at the munitions factory for the past few week, but my gang master, a guy called Massey, has been giving me stick since I arrived. Today I'd had enough, so I thumped him. Unfortunately I got a bit carried away and left him bleeding on the ground. I didn't wait to be sacked. Just picked up my things and legged it. I thought the police might have been looking for me for assault.'

'George Massey from Dornock, t'other side of Eastriggs? Used to be a labourer on Willie Richardson's farm? Big bloke with flaming red hair?' Heinrich nodded. 'They should be giving you a medal, never mind arresting you. Man's a bloody idiot. Nowt more than a loud-mouthed, lazy bully. There's a few round here that would have liked to be able to do the same.'

'Yes, well, unfortunately it's possible that the authorities don't share your views, so I'm heading back to the west coast to see if I can get a berth on one of the local fishing boats out of harm's way. I used to crew there before I decided to try my luck over here, attracted by the lure of big wages and a less dangerous way of life. Hopefully I can get work with one of the skippers who know me. There'll probably be someone going out on Monday morning, and if I get there early there might be something I can pick up last minute. With the war it can be hard to find a full crew.'

Eventually they had arrived in the village and pulled up outside what looked like an old coaching inn. The two-storey building had a distinctive black-and-white look with decorative half timbering and a steep slate roof. Next to it, a small field was accessible through an open gate through which the farmer guided the horse and cart before jumping down.

'I'm thinking you'll be wanting to buy me a pint by way of thanks for your lift before continuing on your way. I'll just unharness the horse first.'

That was not what Heinrich really wanted to do. He'd hoped to find his way back to Carlisle and sort out somewhere to sleep before it got too dark. On the other hand, he didn't want to offend the man in case it prompted him to change his mind about how he viewed the fictitious assault on Massey and decided to contact the police. It was still early and there was plenty of summer daylight left to complete his journey even on foot. So he smiled and said, 'Absolutely. A toast to old scores settled and new friends. My name's Ricky Colman by the way.'

'Jacob Irvine, at your service.' And with that the farmer pulled the gate closed, and, putting his arm round the German's shoulder, guided him towards the pub's embellished doorway. Inside the entrance porch were two doors, one to the left and one to the right. His new 'friend' pushed open the former and they entered a large room, well illuminated by the evening sun which streamed through the frosted windows and lit up the wisps of cigarette smoke from the all-male clientele. To the right of the door, a long bar ran the full width of the building and on the opposite wall was a magnificent enclosed but unlit fire place. Red leather bench seats extended along the length of each of the side walls, with dark wood tables and chairs facing them. Heinrich was guided across the busy room to the far corner where three men were playing dominoes together. In front of them each had a half-finished pint of a dark liquid that he took to be stout. Irvine pulled another table alongside the one they were using creating a bigger space and, as they adjusted their positions to allow the newcomers to join them, he introduced everyone.

'Bill, Jimmy, Harold… this is Ricky Colman. He's been working the munitions site but had a wee disagreement with our friend George Massey so decided to leave. He's joining us for a quick pint before heading off to Carlisle to catch a train to the west coast to rejoin one of the fishing boats out of Workington or Whitehaven.'

'Not tonight or tomorrow he's not,' said a voice behind them. Heinrich turned and his heart skipped a beat. Returning from the bar with a pint in his hand was a short man wearing what looked like the shirt, waistcoat and trousers of a stationmaster. He'd not noticed him when they entered the room and he was clearly part of the group.

'Ricky, meet Angus Scott. He's assistant stationmaster here in Gretna Green. You just finished, Angus?'

'Aye. Jimmy Pagan's on the morning and evening split shift this week, so plenty of time to wet me whistle this evening.' He looked at the newcomer. 'You hoping to catch a train out west this weekend?' The German nodded. 'Well, you're going to be out of luck, mate. The line's closed over the weekend so that engineers can make use of a special train to clear away the old overhead telephone lines and poles before installing a new underground system. Won't be anything until the first thing Monday morning.'

Heinrich felt his heart start to race and a rising nausea in his chest. He felt a queasy sensation in his stomach and for a moment he thought he was going to be sick.

'But I need to be in Whitehaven by dawn on Monday or I'll miss the boats going out. It's absolutely essential.' He stood up as if to go. However, Irvine put a hand on his arm to gently refrain him and explained to the group what had happened with George Massey and the concern that the police might be looking for Heinrich, hence his need to get away as soon as possible.

'Well, in that case,' replied Scott, 'walking that far isn't an option, even if you set off now, so you need to make sure that you're on the 5.00am train out of Carlisle on Monday morning and hope that it gets you there in time.'

'There must be some other way of getting there. I can't leave it to the last minute. What if I miss out? I'll be stuck.'

'It's around fifty or sixty miles to Whitehaven frae' here. If you started right now and you walked there at a brisk pace without stopping, it'd take yer' sixteen or seventeen hours. Realistically you'd need to pause and rest for a bit, so it's more likely to be well over twenty. That's assuming you're not picked up if you're wandering about after dark which, if you use the roads, is highly likely. You'd be advised to stick to the countryside, but that'll slow you down even more. Doing that I doubt you'd get there on Monday much earlier than if you caught the early train and there's always the possibility that you'd get lost on the way.'

Heinrich stood for a moment, unsure what to do. He cursed himself for leaving himself so short on time to get to the rendezvous. He should have anticipated the possibility of disruption or delay and planned accordingly. It was a stupid mistake to have made. His thoughts were interrupted by a shout behind him.

'Time, gentleman, please.' A man, presumably the landlord, draped a large towel over the beer pumps along the bar, then picked up a large bell which he proceeded to ring. On the wall above his head a large clock with a white face indicated it was approaching nine thirty. The new war-time closing times weren't popular and there were moans and groans from the various clientele, but slowly they drank up and made their way outside. To his surprise, neither Irvine nor Scott moved and their three friends also remained seated. When everyone else had left, the landlord stepped into the entrance porch and could be heard bolting the door. He then returned to the room and started pulling the curtains closed on the room's front-facing windows.

Irvine laughed. 'Don't look so confused, Ricky. Don't they have lock-ins in Canada? You didn't think I'd come all the way to Gretna just for an hour's drinking, did ye?'

'What if you get caught?'

'By who? More often than not Jimmy Mackay, our local constable, joins us, although you needn't worry, he's stuck at home with a sprained ankle at the moment. Twisted it chasing poachers down by the river last week. Besides, the landlord's allowed to have friends round, as long as he's not charging for his beer. Isn't that right, Malachi?'

'Aye, it is.' The landlord had finished his task and come across to the little group. 'Of course, I never say no to a donation to cover the cost of the drinks I provide for my visitors.'

'Now,' the farmer continued, 'sit yourself down and relax. It'll be tight, but you can still get to Whitehaven early on Monday morning.'

'But I need to get going if I want to reach Carlisle tonight in time to sort out somewhere to sleep.'

'Don't be daft, man. You've got all day tomorrow to get to there. Tonight just enjoy the company and have a couple of beers.'

'And then what? Where am I going to find somewhere to sleep?'

'Here, just like the rest of us. At least Bill, Jimmy, Harold and myself. Angus, if he doesn't fall asleep first, will toddle off to his wee cottage up the hill. You don't think I'm going to drive all the way back home in the dark and full of beer? Nay, lad. These benches are lovely and comfortable, and a rolled up jacket makes a more than adequate pillow. Tomorrow, if you head west, beyond the small hamlet of Springfield, you'll reach the mainline railway and you can follow it south towards Carlisle on foot. It'll be safer than using the road. Now, what do you fancy to drink?'

The next day Heinrich woke up feeling stiff and slightly hung over. When he looked up at the clock, he was concerned that it was nearly mid-day. Although padded, the narrow benches had proved uncomfortable and he'd transferred to the stone floor, where he'd dozed fitfully. He wasn't sure if this was due to worry or drinking more beer than he'd intended. Whatever the reason, he hadn't fallen into a deep slumber until the early hours of the morning and he was concerned at his late waking hour. The others were scattered around the room, still sleeping. He thought about waking them to say his goodbyes but decided not to. He wanted to be on his way.

After quietly slipping the main door bolts, he'd followed Irvine's directions and found the tracks with little difficulty. The line was direct and reduced the chance of becoming lost, but there was still an element of risk, not so much to do with the danger of being hit by a train, but because of the small but very real possibility of being seen and reported. He had no idea if there was a warning out to the general public, but once he'd got going he needn't have worried. The tracks ran in straight lines into the distance both ways, giving him an early sighting of the one north-bound locomotive that did roar past and plenty of time to hide behind the hawthorn hedge of an adjacent field. Despite this, the going was slow, and at one point he had to deviate from his route to avoid a group of rail workers doing maintenance work on telegraph wires running alongside the railway. At first, he'd slipped out of sight in nearby woodland and waited to see if they wouldn't be too long at their task. He decided that this was a better option than walking cross country, but when, after approaching two hours later, they showed no sign of packing up, he changed his mind and set off across the adjacent fields. Due to the late start and delay, it was now late afternoon and he realised that at his rate of progress it was going to be evening before he reached his destination.

Shortly after he had crossed the River Esk near Mossband, the weather changed. The sky darkened and clouds gathered from the west, bringing with them a light but persistent rain. His duffle coat kept the worst off, but eventually the cold and the damp worked their way through to his clothes underneath, making him shiver despite his exertions. He aimed to find or build a shelter close to edge of the city, where he could lay low overnight before continuing to follow the tracks back to the station and catch the early train back to Whitehaven in time for his rendezvous the next day with *U24*. He knew it would be a close run thing and constantly worried about the possibility of being too late.

*

He reached Carlisle at dusk, but unfortunately, on arrival he was concerned to find out that what he'd thought was a little-visited area of countryside adjacent to the railway line was actually a nature reserve. A sign pinned on a notice board at the edge of the woods stated that Kingmoor Nature Reserve had been established in 1914 and the area was now being managed by a reserve association on behalf of Carlisle Corporation. It gave details of the association's first annual report and a series of events that were currently taking place, including evening badger and bat watch meetings. Heinrich groaned out loud and inwardly cursed the situation, but he was tired, thirsty and in no fit state to wander around looking for an alternative place to camp. Earlier he'd passed a coaching inn which looked warm and inviting with its lights switched on as darkness approached and a smoking chimney, plus cheerful conversation coming through the open front door. He was tempted to wander in and ask for a room but reluctantly decided to stick to his original plan and find a quiet place in the woods where he could remain unseen. With a sigh he headed into the undergrowth, looking for a spot where he would be able to bivouac out of sight of even the most ardent nocturnal naturalist, but preferably not too far from a stream where he could get water.

His progress was laboured as he stumbled through the uneven undergrowth with branches whipping his face and catching on his loose clothing. The light faded and darkness slowly engulfed him until he could see virtually nothing, so that his first experience of the stream came when he slipped down a low muddy bank and ended up lying on his back in a couple of centimetres of cold, almost stagnant, water. Mud oozed through his fingers as he pushed himself up, and chilled hands made it awkward to untie the top of his kitbag and search for his torch. Using it was a risk, but then, so was floundering around in the dark, and a twisted ankle would put pay to his activities just as effectively as his arrest for spying. The rubber case made gripping the torch easier than it might have been and he used it to scan the area immediately around where he stood. To his relief, almost immediately to his left he saw a flat area of woodland which was free of trees and large bushes. He staggered across to it and, after clearing away a few broken branches and the smaller shrubs, stamped it as flat as he was able before looking around for someway of rigging up a shelter. It took him about half an hour to attach a length of cord from his survival kit between two silver birch trees and then hang his canvas sheet across it to form a tent-like structure, the sides of which he spread out and weighted down with stones scavenged from the stream. He then set about finding some drier wood and, after a considerable effort and several wasted matches, he was able to establish a smoky but welcome fire. Finally, he filled his water bottle from the stream and using a forked stick to hang it over the flames, boiled it to hopefully kill off any harmful bacteria or other gut-wrenching organisms. After allowing it to cool down, he drank greedily. It tasted disgusting and he wondered if the morning would bring with it diarrhoea, sickness or some other even worse affliction.

Thirst quenched but belly still gnawing with hunger, Heinrich stretched his hands out towards the small fire, trying to get both dry and warm. Away from the direct heat, his shoulders and back still felt cold and damp, and he gave an involuntary shiver. At least the rain clouds of the past few hours had slowly passed over and the sky had cleared. Countless stars shimmered in the vast blackness above him. The tinkling of the water in the nearby stream and the odd rustle as a small animal or bird moved through the undergrowth were the only sounds. He could have been in one of the fields beside the River Ammer near Oberammergau in Bavaria where he'd grown up. His thoughts drifted to his family and what they might be doing. His mother and father would soon be going to bed after another hard day on the alpine farm. His brother was somewhere on the western front, no doubt up to his waist in the mud and slime of the trenches. He shuddered at the thought. He had not seen or heard from any of them for over a year. Life with the intelligence service did not allow room for regular contact with family or friends. It was best for everyone if no one knew anything.

His reflections were broken by a thud to his right, a single sound followed by rustling in the bushes on the opposite side of the stream. He froze and a sweat broke out on his forehead. Instinctively he kicked the fire and extinguished the light, then stared into the darkness, gradually acquiring his night vision. This was a rural area in the north of England. The war had hardly affected some of the village and farming communities here, so it was unlikely to be some form of security night patrol. But he could see nothing and after a couple of minutes he began to relax again. *Probably a rabbit or feral cat,* he thought as he turned back to re-light the fire, feeling foolish at his nervousness.

'Now what's a young man like you doing out and about on a dark, damp night like this, I wonder,' said a broad-accented voice behind him.

Heinrich spun back around and could just make out a tall, stocky man in his late forties or early fifties, accompanied by a thin, younger companion of similar height. They had identical facial features, and it crossed the German's mind that they were probably father and son. Both carried shot guns, and as they moved slowly towards him, he could see that although the younger man's gun seemed to be unloaded with the action open, the other's was closed shut and, he assumed therefore loaded. Although he held the muzzle pointing to the sky, his fingers remained curled around the trigger guard, from where they could easily be moved onto the trigger itself. The older man gave him a false smile and repeated the question.

'I could ask you the same thing,' said Heinrich.

'Aye, you could, but then, you don't seem to be holding a gun, which would be a real encouragement for me to explain my presence, but I, on the other hand, do have one, so perhaps you could answer me. Without a proper explanation, me and the boy here will have to ask you to come down to the local bobby's house to chat to him.'

It took Heinrich a moment to decipher the man's words, which he took to be spoken in the local Cumberland accent, although it wasn't as broad as the one Sam had used when they first met, and he had to remind himself that bobby was the term for an English policeman. For a moment he said nothing and thought about the situation before replying.

'I don't think that likely. No lights and two guns. It strikes me that you two gentlemen are enjoying a bit of night-time poaching and I doubt the local police would look kindly on that.'

'Well, that might be true of the city police, but here you're outside the city boundary and it would be Joe Robertson, at the Harker police house, that we would be taking you to. Joe's very partial to a bit of rabbit, so he is, and I doubt he'll be over concerned if we drop you off with his morning brace. Now, I asked you a question and I want an answer.'

Heinrich stared at the man for a few moments before replying, 'Much the same as you, I suspect. I've been working at the Globe pub for the last few weeks as a live-in handyman, but Billy Dixon, the landlord, isn't so generous with either my food portions or wages. I decided a spot of poaching would solve both problems. A rabbit for me and one for the highest bidder in the pub.'

'You don't look much like a poacher to me, and that looks like you've made yourself a camp fire for the night,' the older man replied.

'I'm not normally, but when needs must I'll turn my hand to anything, and I've been lucky. It's been a good night. I've two beauties in my bag, one of which, as I'm starving, I was just about to cook when I heard you two and stamped out my fire. I'll show you.'

Keeping his eyes on the gun holder, he leaned forward, opened the top of his kitbag and rummaged inside as if looking for one to show them. Instead, his hand grasped the blade of his knife, which he'd put in there for fear of dropping it while he scrambled through the woods. In one fluid movement he swept it out of the sack and threw it. His action was violent and deadly. The weapon flew through the air and hit just below the breast bone, smashing a hole in the chest, from which burst a crimson spurt of blood. The man flinched with the initial impact and took a step backwards. As he recognised what had happened his eyes flashed wide with fear and his mouth went slack. He tried to speak, but nothing came out, and slowly he slumped onto his knees, then fell forwards, the knife driving deeper into his torso as he landed face first on the muddy woodland floor.

Heinrich stepped quickly forward, turned the figure over and pulled out his knife. Shocked, the boy looked from the prostrate figure to Heinrich. 'Pa,' he shouted fumbling to load his gun, but in panic he gave up and simply hurled the weapon at the killer, turned and ran. It was a lucky throw which saved his life. The solid wood butt hit the German on the side of the head, causing him to flinch and clench his eyes shut. For a moment he felt dizzy, his vision blurred and he thought he might pass out. The feeling quickly passed, but as his senses returned and he looked round there was no sign of the lad. Nor could he hear any distant movement. Clearly, despite his fear, or perhaps because of it, he was adept at moving through the countryside without drawing attention to himself.

Heinrich knew that he was in a desperate situation; in all probability the boy would head straight for the police house for help. He doubted that the local officer would be aware of the circumstances around his presence in the area, but as soon as he reported it to his seniors, they would be able to put two and two together and start looking for him. His best chance of escape would be to get to the railway station as fast as he could and hope to catch a train west before anyone realised his destination and tried to stop him. He searched the dead man for anything that might prove useful, but, finding nothing, gathered his belongings and packed them into his kitbag, before setting off through the woods in the direction of what he hoped was the quickest route into the city.

The first pale rays of dawn were fringing the horizon as Heinrich reached Carlisle Railway Station. He approached along the same road he had used when he first entered the city, this time moving cautiously in the opposite direction slipping in and out of the railway arches for cover. The few rough-sleepers hardly moved at his passing. As he neared the entrance, he crossed the road and slipped through a gap in the iron railings surrounding the gardens below the two sandstone towers guarding the south of the city. He was now aware that these defences were referred to as the citadel and the station itself was named after them. Concealing himself behind a low bush, he watched as dawn arrived, lighting up the square between his hiding place and the entrance to the building. At this early hour, there was little activity. A couple of vagrants slept in the shelter of the doorway. On the pavement opposite, a slim man, wearing a flat cap, suit and tie, and sporting a narrow moustache, was stocking the news stall he'd observed when he first arrived, with a bewildering range of newspapers and journals. He was helped by two young lads. One was aged around ten and smartly dressed. By the look of him, he could easily be the man's son. The other was younger, perhaps five or six, scruffily dressed and dirty. No doubt the second urchin was the seller's cheap labour.

There was no obvious police or military presence, and just as he wondered if the homeless men might be plain-clothed officers, a tall man in a stationmaster's uniform came out and roused them. Clearly he was unhappy with their presence and after a shouted exchange of words, the two men gathered their few belongings and shambled off towards the doorway of the adjacent Station Hotel. The stationmaster watched them until they settled on the entrance steps, then spun on his heels and went back from whence he had come.

Although apprehensive, Heinrich knew that to get back to Whitehaven in time for the rendezvous with *U24*, he had no option but to risk a train journey. Slipping out from behind his hiding place, he strode purposely across the cobbled square, nervously humming a tune his mother had sung to him at bedtime as a young child. In those days he hated the dark and the lullaby had helped him get to sleep; in times of stress he often found himself inadvertently singing it under his breath. Ten minutes later he was sat on the edge of his seat in an empty compartment, similar to the one he had arrived in, looking anxiously out of the window to see whether he had been followed. As a whistle was blown somewhere out on the platform, he relaxed, and, with a hiss of steam, the train pulled out of the station. It was only then that he felt his heart pounding in his chest and realised he was sweating profusely.

CHAPTER 24

Carlisle Police Headquarters

Early Morning, Monday 16th August 1915

'Wake up, sir. Wake up.'

Jack screwed his face and blinked his eyes open. Stifling a yawn, he scratched his head and looked up at the young constable standing in front of him. He'd been at the police station since getting back to Carlisle on Friday. Both he and the chief constable had remained awake all night, waiting for any news of their fugitive. By mid-afternoon on Sunday there was still nothing, so he'd decided to give it until early evening and return home to try and get some rest. Instead, exhaustion caught up with him and he'd fallen asleep in his chair, feet propped up on his desk.

'What time is it?'

'4.10am, sir but, the chief constable is still in and he wants to see you immediately.'

'What? At this ungodly hour? What's so important?'

'There's been a murder, sir. A poacher in Kingmoor Nature Reserve. His son saw it all. A bloke with a knife tried to kill the boy and his father, but the youngster escaped and managed to get to the local officer's house. He'd read the force dispatch urging everyone to report anything strange immediately, so he got on his bike and came straight down here. The night duty officer informed the chief and all hell has broken loose. He wants you now. At first they thought you were at home, but Roberts said he'd not seen you leave.'

'Sergeant Roberts to you young man. Excitement is no excuse for indiscipline. I presume that Chief Constable deSchmid is in his room?' Jack emphasised the words chief constable as he looked directly at the startled officer.

'Yes. I mean … Yes, sir.'

'Right. Well go and get me a cup of tea, no milk or sugar, then leave it on my desk and get back to whatever you should be doing.'

With that, he pushed his chair back and stood up. For a moment he stared at his visitor until he opened the door, allowing Jack to stride past him into the corridor and head up to deSchmid's office.

When he arrived, the door was open and a voice from within, presumably hearing his footsteps, shouted, 'Jack, is that you? Come in. Come in. Take a seat. I'm glad you're here. There have been developments. A murder, and it has to be our man. It has to be. The description fits. After we missed him yesterday, he seems to have managed to get himself back to Carlisle. Who knows how or why but it appears that two poachers disturbed him hiding in Kingmoor Nature Reserve and one of them paid for it with his life. The other, his son, escaped, and has given us an excellent description of the attacker. It matches Coleman's. We need to mobilise a hunting party to search the area between the attack and the city centre.

If we're lucky we might yet catch him before he goes to ground wherever he is headed for.'

Jack looked at his senior officer but said nothing. The silence was palpable until the chief constable said, 'Well, Jack, what are you waiting for? Time is of the essence. Get the search organised. I've already been in touch with the military for help. Lieutenant Colonel Machell is prepared to send down some of his men from the battalion at Blackhall. He just wants to know how many you want.'

'I won't need them, sir.'

'What do you mean, you won't need them? Why? It's unlikely that you'll be able to get a sufficiently large force together without their help.'

'I won't need them, sir, because, if he's back in the city, I know where he's going. I'm just not sure when.'

'Talk sense, man. How could you know where he's going?'

At this point Jack's theory about Coleman's intentions coalesced into a feeling of certainty and he explained his thoughts to the man who would undoubtedly hold him to account should he be wrong.

'And you think the destination is Whitehaven rather than Maryport or Workington? What if you're wrong?'

'Well he'll want to catch an early train in the hope that we won't have worked out what he's doing yet. So we simply have officers waiting at each station in case he gets off there.'

'Unfortunately that may take some time to organise. You're aware that the government has commissioned the expansion of the telephone underground cable network in order to improve our communications system and ensure that different areas of the country can be reached at a moment's notice. Well, the engineers are currently working in West Cumberland, and the telegraph lines, underground cables and overhead lines that the old trunk lines used are all down at the moment while the new system is installed. We've been sending daily dispatches to keep everyone informed of things. They're sent on the midday train and given to the stationmaster wherever the train stops before being picked up by a constable. It's an effective temporary system for day-to-day business but the earliest we can communicate ahead will be by the next train and how quickly the message gets to the local force will depend on when the message is picked up. In some ways it might be easier to send our own men and have them wait at each station, but we'd be out of our jurisdiction and I'd have to clear it through a senior officer in the county. That could take time and there's no guarantee that they wouldn't insist on using their own men.'

'Bloody hell,' said Jack. 'He could be getting on the early train as we speak. If I'm right, he'll certainly be gone by the time all that gets sorted out. We must be able to do something!'

'Well, I can organise our own officers to patrol the area around the citadel but if you think that he's likely to be on that 5.00am train west then you've got twenty minutes before it leaves. If you hurry, you might just make it. I'll try to find Graham Gordon and send him after you.'

It took Jack a couple of seconds to realise what deSchmid had just said before he turned, ran out of the room and, after taking the steps to the ground floor two at a time, raced out of the front door, heading for the station along the road that, unbeknown to him, Heinrich had taken less than an hour earlier. He raced through the entrance arch into the main concourse and arrived at the ticket office panting and gasping for air, his lungs burning with the exertion. The man behind the glass window looked startled, but Jack flashed his warrant card and after a breathless explanation, was quickly waved through with the information that the train he wanted was to be found on Platform Two.

The concourse opened straight onto a large concrete expanse split by two trainlines that passed through the station. Above his head, a large maroon sign with cream writing indicated that this side of the expanse was Platform Four and pointed to Platforms Five and Six, a short distance to his left. A stair-accessed footbridge crossed the tracks to Platforms One, Two and Three. Again taking the steps two at a time, he hurried across the walkway and ran through an arched gap between a café and a waiting room, arriving just in time to despair that the west coast train was slowly moving away. However, it was sluggish to gather speed and the carriages were of the old, compartmentalised type, meaning there was a door for every separate passenger area. Chasing the locomotive and trying to embark while it was moving would be dangerous, but Jack didn't hesitate and sprinted to catch up with the final carriage. As he got level with the last compartment, he felt his legs begin to give out and for a moment thought he'd missed his chance. However, at the critical moment, the door was flung open and a hand reached out towards him. He grabbed it and with an almighty heave pulled himself through the opening and collapsed on the floor.

He landed on the cold linoleum with a crash and the wind was temporarily knocked out of him, but as he gathered his senses he became aware of his surroundings. The worn compartment had clearly seen better days. The bench-type seating on both sides had well-worn brocade-style upholstery and the brass and rope luggage racks sagged from frequent use. In one corner sat his rescuer, a young serviceman in an immaculate private's uniform. He was small of stature, with a youthful face and a cheerful grin. Jack guessed he was in his late teens or early twenties, and he looked the picture of health, except that where his left arm should have been, the sleeve of his jacket was stitched back on itself.

The boy followed the direction of the policeman's eyes and said, 'Oh, this. Aye. It's a bit of a conversation-stopper. Teach me not to volunteer in future. That's if they let me go back, which I doubt. Happened at Neuve Chapelle back in March. I volunteered for a working party that came under fire. As I was going back to the trenches I heard a shell coming and dived into an old shellhole. I put my arm up to protect my head – daft thing to do, really – next minute I felt it jerk and go numb. I was taken back to the field hospital, where the arm was amputated, before I was sent back to England to recuperate. Now I've been relieved of duty. No longer fit to fight, apparently so I'm going home. Goodness knows what me mam will say. I used to work on the fishing boats out of Whitehaven and she thought that was risky. I can apply to go back but only as a non-combatant. I guess they might find me a job in the stores or medical corps. Who knows?'

Jack sat up and nodded. For a moment he didn't know what to say. Eventually he stood and held his hand out towards his helper, 'Thanks. I'm not sure I'd have managed without your help.'

'You're welcome. It seems everyone's in a rush to catch this train today. I thought the other bloke was cutting it fine, but you beat him hands down.'

Jack's curiosity was piqued. 'Someone else got on the train late? What did he look like? Can you describe him?' His enthusiasm was so palpable that his new companion was somewhat taken aback. 'Why do you need to know what he looks like? What's it to you?'

After introducing himself properly and showing his warrant card for the second time that morning, Jack explained who he thought the other latecomer was and what he looked like

'So this man's a German spy who's killed nearly 300 people in the last few weeks. That's … that's kind of hard to imagine.' The soldier shook his head in amazement. 'Well, there's no doubt that the fellow getting on the train before you matches his description. Height, build, hair colour, dress and he was carrying a sailor's kitbag. It could be him. What are you going to do if it is? Is there anything I can do to help?'

Jack found it hard to believe that he might be right and that he could actually be on same train as Colman. The question was … what was he going to do next?

'Until I'm certain I simply need to keep an eye on him. Once I'm satisfied that he's our man, I intend to arrest him and he'll be brought to trial. If he's found guilty, then he'll be executed. There is one small problem, though, I'm not sure which station he's going to get out at. I think it'll be Whitehaven, but I'm not sure, and I can't keep looking out of the carriage window to check because I think he may know what I look like. He's armed and if I'm seen it could lead to a confrontation and civilian casualties. He'll know what to expect if he's caught and desperate men can take desperate measures. I'm hoping that when he does disembark I can follow at a distance and deal with him away from the general public.'

'Given this bloke's past record that's a bit of a risk, isn't it? Have you got a weapon?'

Jack tapped the lower inside pocket of his jacket. 'I've got my truncheon.'

'Good luck with that, then. A stick against a knife, and probably a gun as well. No contest; you'll have no trouble.' It was a sarcastic response, but Jack realised it was probably appropriate in the circumstances.

'It's possible that I'll have time to call on help from the local police. If not, then I'll just have to deal with things on my own, but you can help. When we stop at each of the stations, you can lean out of the window and see whether he's getting off. If he sees you I doubt he'll be suspicious of an injured soldier presumably travelling home.'

'OK but if you do go after him, I'm coming with you. One and a half pairs of hands are better than one. By the way my name is Winfred Wilkes.'

'No, that's not going to happen, Winfred. You've not survived a German shell in France just to be killed at home. But if you want to do more, then when I follow him you can go for reinforcements. That way at least I'll know help is on the way and if something does happen to me at least there's a chance of him still being caught. That makes a lot more sense than both of us ending up dead.'

Wilkes looked at him and for a moment it looked as if he was going to refuse, but in the end he just nodded and for the second time the two men shook hands.

CHAPTER 25

Tanyard Bay Near Parton in Cumberland

Early Morning, Monday 16th August 1915

It was almost dawn when *U24's* kapitänleutnant had given the order to surface and the steel monster had risen out of the grey water. Pushing open the heavy hatch, he'd pulled himself up onto the small bridge on top of the conning tower and attached the rubber retaining strip along the series of stanchions screwed into the deck. When attached the band ran around the platform at chest height and reduced the danger of being washed overboard. The sea was choppy and the waves lashed the sides of the boat, sending spray cascading over the bows where it was caught by the wind and blew into his face. Even on a summer's morning, the droplets were bitterly cold and stung his face, forcing him to pull his cap down low over his brow. As far as he could judge, they were about a mile offshore and close to the point where Kohlmeir had been dropped off. For the first hour he'd concentrated on preparing to shell the United Coke and Chemical Works. The site was clearly visible on the cliffs opposite. Its three large and one small chimneys belched black smoke into an already-overcast sky. He'd ordered the three-man gun crew to set about laying the sights of the deck gun and bring up the 105 mm shells ready for the order to fire. As he watched them work, he hardly noticed the first watch officer join him on his precarious perch. Due to the limited space, he settled on the edge of the coaming with his legs hanging through the hatch.

'How long are we going to wait for him?' Schneider didn't respond and continued to stare landward. 'Rudi, how long? We've been surfaced for nearly an hour. There could be patrols in the area.'

'There are no patrols. The British and their Royal Navy arrogantly assume that none of our vessels could penetrate into the Irish Sea and launch an attack. They know we are capable of mounting assaults on their east coast fortifications and have established defences there, but there's nothing in this vicinity.'

'How can you be certain? Intelligence says the British have designated the benzene extracting plant as top secret. There's bound to be security.'

His senior officer smiled. 'Yes I'm aware that the plant has been designated top secret – a rather pointless gesture, seeing that it was a German company that installed it in the first place, but ...' he looked down at the his experienced colleague, '... you're right we shouldn't tempt fate. Kohlmeir was due to signal us between dawn and sunrise. It's hard to tell if the sun has breached the horizon with such a cloudy sky, but by my reckoning he's had long enough. Give the order to open fire.'

*

Heinrich had been nervous for the first few stops out of Carlisle.

What if the authorities had guessed where he was going and telephoned ahead? But the train halted at Dalston, Wigton and Aspatria, and there were no police officers or soldiers waiting on the platform, just the odd passenger disembarking or leaning out of the compartment windows for some fresh air. By the time the train passed through Workington he had relaxed and was contemplating what he would tell the High Command when he got back to Berlin. He knew he'd been fortunate with his successes at the Carlisle barracks and Quintinshill, but he was sure he could exaggerate the positives so that they reflected well on himself. However, the munitions works was another thing. It would be hard to get over to his superiors the size of the site and consequent difficulties of carrying out any effective sabotage. As far as he could see, perhaps the only conceivable weakness was to a threat from the sea. Shelling by battleship or submarine might be possible, but the Solway Firth was a treacherous waterway to navigate and he was unsure if the German Navy would have usable charts to allow either to get close enough to be effective. Still, it was an idea to take back. He was still working out how he might best present the suggestion when outside the carriage he heard what sounded like the distant sound of thunder. At first the locomotive continued, but as the noise continued and got louder he felt it slow down and gradually come to a halt. Immediately his heart began to race and an impending sense of doom forced its way into his thoughts. He recognised the sounds and felt the floor vibrate with each earth-shaking blast. It was the crash of shells exploding nearby.

'No. No. No. It can't be. It's too early.' But he realised it had to be. There was unlikely to be any other reason for the bombardment. *U24* had started to shell the chemical works.

Grabbing his bag, he reached forwards and twisted the handle before violently pushing the compartment door open. Leaping to the ground, his boots crunched on the track ballast and stones scattered behind him as he sprinted along the side of the carriages to the front of the train. He ran down the side nearest the sea and at first he couldn't see anything as the rolling stock to his left obscured his view. However, as he reached the stationary locomotive, his worst fears were confirmed. About a hundred yards ahead a short, fat individual in a dark railway uniform was walking towards them, waving a cap with one hand and a large red flag with another. Behind him a small wooden building stood by itself on a narrow platform. A white sign with black writing informed travellers that they had reached Parton, the station that served the nearby little cliff top village.

Heinrich grabbed the man roughly by the lapels on his jacket and shouted angrily into his face. 'What's going on? Why have we stopped?'

The man dropped his cap and flag and struggled to free himself before confirming Heinrich's worst fears. 'Calm down, marra. Don't git hysterical. There's a Bosche submarine out at sea and 'a think it's trying t' shell t' chemical works.' The man's accent wasn't as broad as Sam Armstrong's, but the west coast twang was unmistakeable. 'Doesn't seem to be having much success, though. Just south of the station the line runs almost on the seashore and most of the shells exploded on the cliffs behind, causing a landslide on t' tracks. There's no way round until the barrage stops and we can clear the debris. If thoo gits back on t' train you should be safe, though. It's a good quarter mile frey here and the feckless idiot firing doesn't seem to have much idea about where he's aiming. 'Av nivver sin nowt like it. I hope oor boys are better ower there in France.'

The flippant, apparently light-hearted response further inflamed Heinrich's already-agitated state and he pushed him forcefully away. The shocked rail worker staggered a few steps backwards before falling heavily and landing on his backside on one of the wooden sleepers. Bending quickly to pick up the discarded red flag, the German crossed the tracks and started clambering up the scrub-covered cliffs. He still hoped that if he could get a signal to the submarine it would pause the shelling long enough to send a boat to come and pick him up. It was only when he was nearing the top that he realised that in his panic he'd left his kitbag behind beside the train. His gun was in it. All he had were the clothes he was wearing and his knife tucked into the back of his trousers. A gradual despair enveloped him, but he scrambled upwards. Although the cliffs weren't steep, the climb was a struggle. Loose soil fell away under each step and vegetation gave way under his grasp, constantly causing him to slip back. His jumper and trousers frequently snagged on the rough brush, and his hands and face were soon scarred and bleeding as a result of the spikey gorse bushes that clung to the shallow earth. Eventually he reached the top and clambered over a wooden fence that ran along the clifftop to prevent a heard of black and white Friesian cattle, grazing in the field, from wandering over the edge of the bluff. Unbelievably, his mind was filled with a memory of his father telling him they kept the breed because it produced more milk than any other cattle. Blocking out the irrelevant thought, he turned to face seaward and ran southwards along the clifftop, frantically waving the flag to and fro above his head.

*

Back in the final compartment, Jack and Wilkes also wondered what was happening. At each of the stations they had stopped at so far, the young soldier had looked out of the drop-down window or stepped down onto the platform and stretched his arm whilst guardedly glancing around. The policeman had kept an eye on the opposite side of the tracks in case his fugitive tried to slip away unnoticed into the adjacent countryside. However, so far, no one matching Colman's description had left any of the carriages and Jack was beginning to think that he might have managed to journey the day before or for some reason was waiting for a later train. At the back of his mind he still harboured the worry that he was entirely wrong and his quarry was not heading west but at this moment was making good his escape in an entirely different direction. If that was so, then this was a wild goose chase that was giving his man time to make an untroubled escape.

The train had come to a halt a few hundred yards from the small station of Parton. At this point the line ran along the coastline on a narrow rocky beach that separated rounded cliffs from the Irish Sea. *Trying to pass at high tide on a stormy winter's day would be an interesting experience,* Jack thought as he glanced out of each window. The landward bluffs cast a dark shadow back across the tracks and the blue sky above was partially blocked out by steam from the locomotive that was drifting gently back down the carriages carried by the on-shore breeze. The overall effect was to turn an already-cloudy morning into a bleak and dismal day. He was wondering if this was an omen when his thoughts were interrupted by an excited shout from across the compartment.

'I think it's him. He's here. He's just jumped off the train.'

Jack rushed across the compartment and pushed Winfred out of the way to lean out the window. Up ahead he could see a tall, well-built individual running along the side of the carriages. As he watched the man reached the front of the engine and confronted a uniformed guard, knocking him to the ground. Stooping to pick something up, he then charged off out of sight inland.

'Try and get a message to the local police. Tell them what's happening and where.' Without waiting to see the nodded reply, Jack opened the carriage door, jumped down and raced after Coleman. So intent was he on the chase that he failed to hear the shouted, 'Good luck,' that drifted after him. The track ballast of loose stones made running difficult and by the time he reached the front of the locomotive he was breathing heavily.

The railway man was just getting to his feet, brushing the dust off his trousers as he straightened up. When he saw a second agitated stranger he threw his hands up and cried out, 'Calm down. Calm down. There's nothing to worry about. Just stay where you are and you'll be safe.'

To his dismay he was once again grabbed by the jacket and shaken.

'The man who knocked you down, where did he go?'

'He's up there,' a voice behind him replied.

Jack twisted round to see that the engine driver had climbed down from his cab and was walking towards him, holding a wrench in his right hand and patting it menacingly into the palm of the other.

'I'm a police officer and the man's a fugitive. It's important I stop him.'

The driver relaxed. 'He's up there.' And he pointed upwards to where a frantic figure could be seen scrambling up the cliffs. As they watched, he reached the top and disappeared over the brow.

'He dropped that.' The guard eased himself free of Jack's grasp and pointed to a canvas kitbag lying on the ground. For a moment the policeman wondered whether he should examine the contents but decided that the spy was more important.

'There's a soldier in the last compartment. He'll explain everything. Give him the bag and do what he tells you.' Without waiting for a reply, he ran off across the tracks in pursuit.

*

Although his arms were aching Heinrich kept waving the flag. The shelling had stopped, but the submarine had shown no signs that they'd seen him. He could just about make out two or three men standing beside the deck gun but no other movement. No boat was being launched, nor was there any blinking light or other signal to indicate something might be about to happen.

'It's over, mate. Whatever you've got planned isn't going to happen.'

The German turned to see a rather dishevelled individual approaching him from the direction he'd just come. The pair's footprints made a clear track across the dew-covered grass from where they'd both emerged onto the green fields above the tiny station. He was a slightly built man wearing a baggy suit that billowed in the light wind. The face looked familiar and then he remembered. 'You're from the house fire. You were trying to rescue the boy and it was you again at the munitions works. I thought the face was familiar, but I didn't make the connection then. You're a policeman.'

For a moment Jack was taken aback. 'So, it was you at the fire?'

'I was the one who pulled you both out.'

'And then you disappeared. Now I understand why. What I don't understand is why you'd risk your life to save two strangers when you could have just walked off but then you're happy to kill hundreds in cold blood. Why?'

'One is war, my friend. The other isn't. It's quite simple, really, and today I'm afraid, is war.' And with that he pulled his knife from within his trouser belt behind his back. 'I have no intention of being put in front of a firing squad, so this morning I'm happy to take your life. There may still be time for my friends to send a boat to pick me up. If not, then I am sure I can disappear for a while until I can figure out a way off this misguided little island and return to the Fatherland.'

Jack shook his head. 'Aye, lad. You can dream but unfortunately dreams don't always come true.'

'Of course, you could just walk away and no one would know or be any the wiser. You owe me. You could just say we fought and I managed to escape. Is the capture of a single man worth your life? Do they pay you enough for that, Mr Policeman?'

For a moment Jack said nothing and the German wondered if he was going to accept the offer, but then the Englishman did a strange thing. He reached into the outside flap pocket of his jacket and retrieved a pipe. Popping it into his mouth, he took out a box of matches and lit the bowl. For a minute or so he stood and puffed away as if nothing else mattered before taking it out of his mouth and tapping the loose ash out on the heel of his shoe. Putting both items on the ground, he straightened up and, from an inside compartment of the baggy suit, pulled a truncheon.

'I always think it's a waste to leave a pipe with half a bowl of tobacco in it waiting to be finished and ...' he pointed to the ground, '... that pipe's a good friend so I'd prefer that it didn't get broken.' He paused a moment, as if thinking, and then continued. 'No, they probably don't pay me enough, but then, that's not why I do the job. You see there's people who do good in the world and there's people who do evil things. In my simple mind, you need people like me to root out the evil doers and you, Mr Ricky Colman, or whoever you really are, are one of the worst I've come across. I'm going to arrest you or ...' He left the words unsaid. 'So let's be at it.' And with a nod and a resigned smile he moved purposefully towards the bigger man.

*

Turning his attention back to the cliff top chemical works Schneider noticed a plume of black smoke rising from a building behind the main chimneys.

'We appear to have a hit, but perhaps not a significant one. Commence firing again. Aim at the factory first and then widen the range to include the town.' He looked across to the grey buildings in the distance to his right. Along what appeared to be a harbour wall small groups of people were staring out to sea.

'But what about Kohlmeir?' asked his first officer. 'Someone was waving a flag on the cliff top. If that's his signal, he'll be right in the line of fire.'

'If that's his signal, then he's late and he was warned what would happen if he was late. We start firing and then we leave once we've hit the target and drawn attention to ourselves. Well, we've started firing, we've hit our target and that crowd over there certainly know we're here. So twenty more rounds over a wider range, including the town harbour, let's see if we can disrupt their unwanted curiosity, then get the men below and take us another mile seaward before we submerge.'

The first officer relayed his kapitänleutnant's orders and watched as the gun crew fired the first shell in the direction of their industrial target. The boat had drifted slightly with the current and so the gun crew's sights were now slightly out. He sighed as it fell short and exploded at the cliff edge.

CHAPTER 26

Eden Street, Carlisle

September 1915

Wilkes and the engine driver had been the first to arrive at the scene of the fight. They'd found the German lying on top of the unconscious policeman most of his clothes ripped from his back and a jagged piece of shrapnel sticking out of his neck. His right arm still held a vicious-looking knife, the point of which was driven into the ground inches to the side of the prone Jack. They'd lifted the body clear and at first thought that both men were dead, but the young soldier had sensed a slight pulse in his new friend. The Parton constable had arrived shortly afterwards on a horse and cart driven by the farmer whose field they were in. He was accompanied by the local doctor, who managed to bring the stunned man round. Although he was unable to walk without assistance and remained insensible to their questions, they'd managed to get him onto the carriage and take him back to the nearby Howgill Street Hospital.

Beyond those directly involved, the wider activities of the man known as Ricky Colman had been conveniently forgotten. Steps had been taken 'for the morale of all concerned' to ensure that those involved were clear that it was something that should not be spoken of again. A couple of weeks after the incident, a railworker had found a German dinghy in a railway storage shed near Whitehaven, it had quickly been disposed of and the man's silence ensured through threats under the Defence of the Realm Act. However, the attack on the chemical works couldn't be ignored. The official report released to the British press played down the event stating that, in the early hours of 16th August, a German submarine had fired several shells at Parton, Harrington and Whitehaven, but no material damage was caused. They praised the quick thinking of a plant engineer, who set fire to some tar and chemicals as a ruse to convince the attackers that the plant had been damaged, then went on to say that a few shells had hit the west coast railway line but the train service was only slightly delayed. No casualties had been reported. Not surprisingly, newspapers in Germany had put a different slant on things, reporting that the attack on the fortified port of Whitehaven testified to extraordinary boldness of the submarine commander and crew. It proved that the British Fleet was not even able to protect the coasts of the Irish Sea.

Jack couldn't have cared less about the conflicting reports. He was just happy that it was over and he was able to put the events behind him. After the confrontation on the cliffs he'd spent several days in the Whitehaven hospital before returning to Carlisle and finding himself back in the Cumberland Infirmary in the same ward as last time, with Lizzie Alexander once again fussing around him. His injuries hadn't been life-threatening, but the doctors had said they were serious and that he needed to rest and recuperate for at least six weeks before returning to work. He'd protested, but on his single visit, Eric deSchmid had made it abundantly clear that he was not to come back until the medics confirmed that he was completely recovered.

'I'd rather wait until you're fully fit and unlikely to have any relapses than rush things and end up being without you for an even longer period of time. A totally selfish position on my behalf, but one I'm not going to compromise on,' he'd said with a twinkle in his eye.

The issue then had become where he could stay after his discharge from hospital. The lead consultant was not happy for him to be home alone, at least for the first few days, in case there was a reaction.

'I'm not worried about the cuts and bruises, but the blow to the head may have done some unseen damage. I'd prefer it if there was someone around, even if it's only to periodically check you're OK.'

Over the weeks he had spent in hospital, he and Lizzie had talked a lot and become closer than they'd both expected, and so, at her insistence, he found himself convalescing in a comfortable wicker chair in the back garden of her Eden Street home. The sun was high in a cloudless sky and he could feel its heat beating down on his back through the collarless shirt he was wearing. Beside him his host sat on a similar chair holding a cream parasol for shade. In front of them was a round table on which were two empty glasses and a jug of homemade lemonade. Beyond that a small lawn was surrounded by narrow borders, in which grew a plethora of colourful flowers.

'My life's work appears to be to nurse you back to health after every reckless action you embark upon.'

'I hope it's not,' replied Jack.

'Oh! So you're not happy with me looking after you? You'd prefer that I didn't do it?'

'Pardon? No. No. That's not what I meant. I've really appreciated being here. You know I do. I —

His sentence was cut short as Lizzie smiled and then started to giggle. Jack looked at her for a moment and then slowly it dawned on him what her words meant.

'Your life's work? You really want me to be your life's work?'

She smiled and stood up, then nodded down at him. 'Of course, you idiot.'

For a moment he sat taking in the comment and then he rose up to embrace her.

As he did, he could still feel the aches and discomfort of his violent encounter but as she held him tight a warmth seemed to transfer from her body to his, spreading throughout his inner being, washing the pain away. The day of the reiver was past and the future seemed bright.

Historical Notes and Acknowledgements

Hopefully I have managed to acknowledge all the sources I have called on in each chapter. My special thanks to Bookcase Publications, Amberley Publishing, Pen and Sword Books, and P3 Publications, for giving permission for me to use the historical information in their books as the source for some of the events in this book. One of the problems in writing what is, in effect, a docu-fiction, is that I looked at so many sources, several of which refer to the same event often with only slightly altered wording, that it has been a challenge to try to write events so that my descriptions are different to other versions. In an age of technology, I did make use of the on-line plagiarism checker by Grammarly and was delighted that the system found no items. My apologies to anyone who still feels I haven't managed to fully avoid this or acknowledged a source. This was not my intention and I've strived hard to avoid this.

Maps

I would like to thank my friend Martin Sproul for producing the map of the Borderlands 1915 specifically for this book. Martin is a professional photographer from Lenzie near Glasgow. The story of how this ex-Glasgow policeman overcame a career ending serious illness to build an alternative successful business is an inspirational story in its own right.

The map of Jack Johnstone's Carlisle is from *Old Ordnance Survey Maps: Carlisle (NW) 1924,* the 2008 reprint published by Alan Godfrey Maps. Little changed between 1915 and 1924, so they give a wonderful insight into what Carlisle would have looked like around the time of World War I.

Prologue

Between the thirteenth and seventeenth centuries, lawlessness was endemic on both sides of the border between England and Scotland. The boundary itself frequently changed and in these 'debatable lands' people's allegiance was to their family or clan rather than their country. Feuding was common place and the Border Laws did little to prevent cattle-rustling and the destruction of property. Raiders or reivers showed no mercy to those they were attacking, murder was commonplace and victims' families were said to have been 'bereaved'. By the sixteenth century the situation was completely out of control and in 1525 Gavin Dunbar, Archbishop of Glasgow, decided to try and put a stop to it. He excommunicated the reiver families and issued a curse to be delivered from every pulpit in the diocese. It was treated with disdain by those with little time for the church and only when the English and Scottish crowns were combined under King James (VI of Scotland, I of England) in 1603 did things change. James was determined to put an end to this violent, criminal activity and ordered that offenders should be executed or deported. Slowly things calmed down and raids within the border lands became a thing of the past until … our story begins.

Source and further information

'Reivers' exhibit, Border Gallery, Tullie House Museum, Carlisle. Once an old Jacobean mansion, Tullie House was acquired by Carlisle Corporation and opened as a museum and art gallery in 1893. It's a fantastic place to visit, with something for everyone, and a primary source for border history. The galleries cover Neolithic times, the Vikings, Hadrian's Wall and the history of Carlisle and North Cumbria. On a broader front, other displays explore art, fashion, and natural history.

David Gopsill, 'Border Reivers: Turbulence in the Border Region' (2nd October 2018). A lecture given as part of Tullie House Museum's lunchtime lecture programme looking at the everyday life of the people along the English and Scottish border between the fourteenth and seventeenth centuries. David's fascinating talk looked at how the reiver culture of feuding and raiding developed and thrived for over 300 years.

'The Pele Towers of Cumbria and the Lake District' on the Visit Cumbria Website (https://www.visitcumbria.com/pele/).

Chapter 1

Heinrich's knife was the Mark I trench knife. This was an American trench knife designed for use in World War I by officers of the American Expeditionary Force (AEF). The double-edged blade was almost seven inches long, making it useful for both thrusting and slashing strokes. A cast bronze handle had a knuckle duster edged with spikes built onto it, creating a second weapon for use in hand-to-hand combat and also preventing an opponent from grabbing the knife during a fight. Heinrich could have been given one stolen from an Allied casualty or obtained it during his time in America. The Luger P08 semi-automatic pistol, mentioned in Chapter 5, served as the German Army's principal sidearm during World War I.

Source and further information

'Mark 1 Trench Knife' on Wikipedia.

Chapter 2

The Abteilung IIIb was indeed the intelligence section of the German Supreme Command and it was located at 76/78 Tirpitzufer, south of Tiergarten across the road from the Landwehr Canal in Berlin. Walter Nicolai, Max Bauer, Heinrich von Kirchberg, Heinrich Gunter and Hans von Haeften were part of this organisation in the roles described in the text. Heinrich Kohlmeir is a fictional character, but he is inspired by three colourful individuals who worked for German intelligence at this time. Anton Dilger was born in Ohio in 1894 but moved to Germany at the age of nine. Fluent in both languages, he trained as a physician in Heidelberg and went on to become the main proponent of the German biological warfare sabotage program. Dilger was in Germany at the start of World War I but at the behest of the German government he returned to the United States in 1915 with anthrax cultures which he intended to use for biological sabotage. Frederic Duquesne was born in South Africa in 1877. Working under many aliases, he gathered human intelligence, led spy rings and carried out sabotage missions as a covert field asset in South Africa, Great Britain, Central and South America, and the United States. Carl Hans Lody, alias Charles Inglis, was born in Germany, but before the war he worked for the Hamburg America Line as a tour guide and learnt to speak English fluently with an American accent. He joined German Naval Intelligence in May 1914 and the following August, having obtained a genuine United States passport from an American citizen in Germany, was sent to the UK with orders to spy on naval actitivity around Edinburgh and the Firth of Forth. Lody was eventually captured and on 6th November 1914 became the first person to be executed at the Tower of London in 150 years. He was also the first of a total of eleven convicted spies to be shot during the war.

Ernst Ludwig Kirchner was a German expressionist painter. His painting clashed with the social conventions of the time with casual love-making and frequent nudity within sessions. His life drawing used models from his social circle rather than professionals. So Bauer's joke at von Kirchberg's expense would be in keeping with the situation. Kirchner was based in Berlin and in September 1914 he volunteered for military service. However, there is no record of him actually serving and he may have remained in Berlin as a reservist. In July 1915 he was sent to train as a driver in a reserve unit of a field artillery regiment but was discharged after a mental breakdown.

The World War I Battle of Neuve Chapelle took place in the Artois region of France between the 10th and 13th March 1915. On the 10th the British carried out their first concentrated artillery barrage of the German trenches before attacking with the intention of breaking through enemy lines and exploiting the breach with a rush to the Aubers Ridge and possibly Lille. The British 8th Division did break through the German defences and reached the village of Neuve Chapelle. However, their success could not be exploited because the artillery were unable to keep up the levels of their initial bombardment due to a lack of ammunition. The Germans counter-attacked on 12th March, retook the village and trench warfare resumed. The expenditure of artillery ammunition on the first day was about thirty percent of the field-gun ammunition in the First Army. This was equivalent to seventeen days' shell production per gun. After the battle Field Marshal Sir John French informed Field Marshal Lord Kitchener, British Secretary of State for War, that the shortage of ammunition had forced a suspension of the offensive. News of the shortage led to the Shell Crisis of 1915 which, together with the failed attack on the Dardanelles, brought down the Liberal British government under the premiership of Herbert Asquith. He formed a new coalition government and appointed Lloyd George as Minister of

Munitions. It was a recognition that the whole economy would have to be adapted for war, if the Allies were to prevail on the Western Front. At the time the number killed or injured at Neuve Chappelle was reported differently by both sides, hence the conflicting figures reported by Max Bauer, Walter Nicolai and Bill Murray (Chapter 17). In reality, of the 40,000 Allied troops in the battle, 7,000 British and 4,200 Indian casualties were suffered. The German official history estimate of 'almost 10,000 men', was closer to 8,500, according to the records of the 6th Army.

Sources and further information

Information on the Abteilung IIIb, and the named officers above, was obtained from Wikipedia. Details about its offices at 76/78 Tirpitzufer were sourced from the Axis History Forum website (https://www.forum.axishistory.com/viewtopic.php?t=204629).

'Neuve Chappelle 1915: The BEF's first offensive' on the History Press website (https://www.thehistorypress.co.uk/articles/neuve-chapelle-1915-the-bef-s-first-offensive/).

'World War 1: Defence of the Realm Act' on the Gazette Official Public Record website (https://www.thegazette.co.uk/all-notices/content/217).

Chapter 3

Jack 'Smoking Joe' Johnstone started off as a fictional character based on my late father John (Jack) Routledge whose nickname was 'Smoking Joe' because he was frequently seen with a lit pipe in his mouth full of his favourite Condor Original Long Cut Tobacco. However, shortly before the book was completed I became aware that there was a real Inspector Johnstone working for the Carlisle City Police in 1915. Bob Lowther's book (see below) mentions that he was detailed to arrange identification of the bodies and inquests into the deaths following the Quintinshill Rail Disaster (Page 121). Not being able to find any other information I hope that the original officer would have been proud of his fictitious counterpart.

Sergeant Graham Gordon is inspired by Sergeant George Carlton of Carlisle City Police and later Cumbria Constabulary. An ex-Coldstream Guards sergeant who saw active service during World War II, he joined the police force in 1946 and achieved almost legendary status for his no-nonsense approach to policing. Bob Lowther's book expands on his time in the force and it's a pleasure to base Graham Gordon on such an iconic policeman as 'Mr Carlton'.

The Gilesgate pub in Durham is real and back in 1971 was much as described. It was the venue for many happy student evenings playing bar games such as shove ha'ppeny, darts and dominoes.

Source and further information

Bob Lowther, *Watching Over Carlisle: 140 Years of the Carlisle City Police Force 1827-1967* (P3 Publications, 2011). This is a highly informative and entertaining book about the characters and incidents that formed part of the life of the city's police force.

Chapter 4

Eric Herbert deSchmid was chief constable of Carlisle City Police from May 1913 until November 1928, and the circumstances by which he took over from his predecessor, George Hill, were as described. deSchmid spent twenty nine years in the Devon

County Constabulary, rising to the rank of Chief Constable before moving to Carlisle. He took over a police force still based in the old 1840's building on the city's West Walls. A planned move to new headquarters in Rickergate did not happen until April 1941 and in 2011 the city police moved again to a new building at Durranhill in the south of the city. The site is now a car park, but the Sallyport steps onto the West Walls still exisit.

The incident involving PC Brown and Sergeant Bone happened as described, although the actual event took place on 16th November 1914. I moved the date, as the opportunity to use this for the revenge attack on Jack was too good to miss.

Source and further information

Bob Lowther, *Watching Over Carlisle: 140 Years of the Carlisle City Police Force 1827-1967* (P3 Publications, 2011).

Chapter 5

Kapitänleutnant Rudolf Schneider, known as Rudi to his friends, joined the navy in 1901 and in June 1914 was promoted to kapitänleutnant. After becoming commanding officer of *U24* he carried out the first underwater attack at night sinking the British battleship HMS *Formidable* on the 1st January 1915 off Portland Bill. On 13th October 1917, he was lost overboard from the conning tower of *U87* during a storm and despite being rescued died of his injuries.

Source and further information

'Rudolf Schneider' on U-Boat.net website (https://uboat.net/wwi/men/commanders/304.html).

Alfred von Tirpitz was primarily responsible for the build-up of the German navy, including the submarine fleet, prior to the start of the World War I. He was a grand admiral and became Secretary of State of the German Imperial Naval Office, the powerful administrative branch of the German Imperial Navy from 1897 until 1916.

Source and further information

'Alfred von Tirpitz' on the Firstworldwar.com website (https://www.firstworldwar.com/bio/tirpitz.htm).

The sinking of the Cunard ocean liner RMS *Lusitania* occurred on Friday, 7th May 1915, *not* the 7th April as inferred in the book. It was torpedoed by a German submarine eleven miles off the southern coast of Ireland and 1,128 people were killed. The event raised concerns amongst merchant shipping and those working on the boats because until that time international naval 'prize laws', meant that ships were warned of a submarine's presence. However, Germany was concerned that British merchant and passenger ships were transporting both weapons and supplies from the United States to Europe. Consequently, Germany declared the waters around Britain a war zone and began attacking the transatlantic traffic.

Sources and further information

'RMS *Lusitania*' on Wikipedia.

'*Lusitania*' on the History.com website (https://www.history.com/topics/world-war-i/lusitania).

The tragic incident involving Crofts and Cassidy did indeed happen as described but in June 1890 *(not May 1915)* and off the coast at Harrington near Workington rather than the Mull of Galloway. Although it happened twenty-five years before the story is set, it provided a good background for the meeting between Heinrich and Samuel Armstrong.

Source and further information

Whitehaven News, on-line edition, 23rd July 2015.

Fishing did continue during World War I. At the outbreak of hostilities, the admiralty was concerned that unregulated fishing vessels might provide a convenient disguise for the infiltration of enemy agents and saboteurs. Therefore they issued instructions that no fishing boats were to sail for North Sea grounds. Fish supplies dried up and the country teetered on the edge of losing one of its major food sources. As a consequence, they changed their mind, but not before large numbers of fishermen had enlisted leaving the industry short of workers. This situation would have been ideal for Heinrich.

Source and further information

Seabreezes.co.im website.

Chapter 6

Heinrich would have been right to worry about travel during war-time Britain. The Defence of the Realm Act, or DORA was passed on 8th August 1914 only five days after the war began. Its aim was to help the war effort and 'secure public safety' by providing the government with emergency powers to implement a wide range of social, economic and industrial controls. These covered areas such as press censorship, talk about military matters, blackouts and the movement of foreign nationals. Heinrich's legitimate Canadian passport (an Allied country) and carefully fabricated background story were to avoid falling foul of the latter. At first, people accepted the restrictions, but laws were also introduced to outlaw strikes, extend the working day, limit pub opening times or trespass on railways, and eventually the mood changed. The public objected to the undermining of certain freedoms with what came to be seen as trivial and inconvenient rules.

Sources and further information

'Defence of the Realm Act 1914' on Wikipedia.

Amanda Mason, '10 Surprising Acts Passed During the First World War' on the Imperial War Museum website (https://www.iwm.org.uk/history/10-surprising-laws-passed-during-the-first-world-war).

'Domestic Impact of World War One – society and culture' on the BBC Bitesize website (https://www.bbc.co.uk/bitesize/guides/ztx66sg/revision/1).

'Copy of the Defence of the Realm Consolidation Act, 27th November 1914' on the National Archive Website
      (http://www.nationalarchives.gov.uk/pathways/firstworldwar/first_world_war/p_defence.htm).

The spectacular coastal railway line between Whitehaven and Carlisle still exists. In 1915 the London and North Western Railway brought trains to Whitehaven and people travelled on to Barrow courtesy of the Furness Railway Company. Whitehaven Station was jointly owned by LNWR and the Furness Railway Company. Carlisle Station today still retains the main features with which Heinrich was taken aback. It was designed by William Tite in what is referred to as a neo-classical style and opened in 1847. Initially it was one of several stations in the city, but by 1851 it had become the main one, expanding and extending to accommodate the new railway companies attracted to the area. The crenulated red sand stone towers he sees outside the building are the citadel buildings. Initially built in 1541 on the orders of Henry VIII as a defence on the town's southern border, they were demolished in 1807 before being later re-built to house the assizes courts and a prison. The arches underneath the north-bound railway lines still exist and have been converted to small business units.

Carlisle's city gates are no longer there, but their names live on. The Bochard Gate, which gives its name to the Botchergate area of the city, protected the southern entrance. Bochard were a Flanders family who owned the area immediately south of the gate. Beside it a sally port linked to the citadel became known as English Gate. To the north-east, the Scotch Gate or Richard's Gate (Rickergate) stood somewhere around the modern-day junction of Scotch Street and Rickergate. To the north-west, the Irish Gate stood where a modern footbridge spans the A595 (Castle Way) as it cuts through the city walls. Today it is more usually called Caldewgate as the road immediately crosses the River Caldew. The Globe pub where Heinrich worked still exists just over the Caldew Bridge on the corner of Bridge Street and Bridge Lane, although it is now an upmarket lounge bar and hairdressers.

Sources and further information

'Cumbria Coast Line' on Wikipedia.

Billy F. K. Howorth, *Carlisle History Tour* (Amberley Publishing, 2018). In this fascinating little book, readers are invited to follow the author as he guides them through the city's streets and alleyways, pointing out the well-known and lesser-known landmarks along the way.

Norman Nicholson, *Carlisle Lore and Mor'* (Bookcase, 2013). For fifteen years *Lore and More* was one of the most popular columns in the local newspaper, the *Cumberland News*. In this entertaining read, the author has chosen three dozen of his most entertaining articles about the city.

Dennis Perriam and David Ramshaw, *Carlisle Citadel Station* (P3 Publications, 1998). This colourful history book was written to mark the 150th anniversary of Carlisle's Citadel Station. It is full of photographs, diagrams and specially created images telling the building's story from the initial construction until 1997.

Chapter 7

Annetwell Street, Finkle Street, Holy Trinity Church, Parhambeck and Canal Bank were all well-known features of 1915 Carlisle. They are now either demolished and only a foot note in the city's history or have changed and are unrecognisable from the time of the story.

Finkle Street and Annetwell were once one of the main routes running east to west across the city. Rows of terraced houses fronted onto both sides of each road. Those on the north side have long since been demolished and replaced by Castle Way, a dual carriage way. The buildings on the south side are now home to numerous businesses, including a music shop, restaurant, Radio Cumbria and Tullie House Museum.

Holy Trinity stood opposite what is now the McVities Biscuit Factory on the site of the modern multi-use-games area. Head west up Newtown Road and you come to Canal Street on your left. Opposite this are a row of terrace houses which, together with the now-demolished buildings behind them, were once part of an area known as Canal Bank. From 1823 until 1853, the Carlisle Ship Canal ran from here to Port Carlisle on the coast. It was subsequently drained so that, from 1854, a railway linking the city to the Solway could use the canal bed for most of its route.

Today the Parham Beck runs from west to east through the Belle Vue area of Carlisle into Heysham Park where it disappears underground at Raffles Avenue to form part of the city's storm drainage system. Eventually after curving northwards it discharges into the River Eden beside the old Sewage Disposal Works at the end of Willow Holme Road. In 1915, except where it crossed Newtown Road via a hidden culvert, it was used as an open sewer until it disappeared behind Canal Bank. The area through which it ran before crossing Newtown Road was referred to as Parhambeck (one word). Roughly speaking, this is between Bower Street and Ashley Street.

Juvenile crime soared during World War I mainly for the reasons outlined in the book. Other factors included less school discipline, dark nights due to the lighting restrictions and the reduced numbers of police on patrol. Eventually it became so bad that the Home Office held a conference to look into the problem nationally and suggest ways to combat it.

Sources and further information

Old Ordnance Survey Maps: Carlisle (NW) 1924, the 2008 reprint published by Alan Godfrey Maps.

David Carter, *Carlisle in the Great War* (Pen and Sword Books, 2014). This excellent book has over 100 original black-and-white photographs of Carlisle at the time and features chapters that analyse the city before and after the war years.

D. R. Perriam, *Carlisle: an Ilustrated History* (Bookcase, 1992). A wonderful book that looks at the history of the city through illustration and photographs from collections in Cumbria County Library, Tullie House and private individuals.

Cumberland and Westmorland wrestling is more commonly known as simply Cumberland wrestling. Although an ancient and well-practised traditional form of wrestling, the sport continues today. The long-established costume for participants consists of long johns and an embroidered vest with a velvet centre piece over the top. Matches are usually decided by the best of three falls. For more information, see the notes for Chapter 18.

Douglas Clark was an extraordinary man. Born in 1891 in Ellenborough (a suburb of Maryport in what is now Cumbria but was then Cumberland) he began Cumberland and Westmorland wrestling when he was fifteen. It was a sport in which he excelled, winning the prestigious Grasmere Sports Cup in 1922 and 1924 and becoming three-time holder of the Cumberland and Westmorland Championship. It is this latter event that we have Jack preparing to beat him in. During the World War I, Clark fought on the front line in France, where he was wounded by shrapnel from a bomb and then badly gassed at Passchendale. Discharged in a wheelchair he returned to his unit less than a month later. In 1918 he was again discharged, this time with a ninety-five per cent disability certificate and awarded the Military Medal for valour during combat. He was advised to take things easy and responded by going on to become one of the greatest rugby league players of his generation, playing professionally for Huddersfield until 1927 and representing both England and Great Britain.

Sources and further information

Cumberland and Westmorland Wrestling Association website (http://www.cumberland-westmorland-wrestling-association.com/#)

'The Wrestling Heritage Number 1 Wrestler of the 1930s: Douglas Clark' on the Wrestling Heritage Website (https://www.wrestlingheritage.co.uk/douglas-clark)

'Douglas Clark' on Huddersfield Rugby League Heritage website
(http://www.huddersfieldrlheritage.co.uk/Archive/Written/Players/Douglas_Clark.html)

'Douglas Clark' on the Professional Wrestling Historical Society website
(https://www.prowrestlinghistoricalsociety.com/bio-0029.html)

Thomas Bewick was a British engraver and natural history author. He was born in Northumberland in 1753 and in his early career turned his hand to all manner of work, including engraving cutlery, making the wood blocks for advertisements and illustrating children's stories. Eventually he concentrated on the latter, illustrating, writing and publishing his own books. The one from which the illustration of two wrestlers was taken was not published until 1870, but dating the original engraving precisely has not been possible, although it's thought to be eighteenth century. Placing the picture in the Peter Street Gym is completely fictitious.

Source and further information

'Thomas Bewick' on Wikipedia.

Chapter 8

People often sought employment through the 'hirings'. Men and women looking for work would congregate in a specified place, hoping to be approached by a hirer. After selection, the new employer would give the hired person 'earnest money', sixpence or a shilling, to seal the appointment. In Carlisle, the hirings moved about. Initially they were held at the Market Cross, but they moved to outside the courts and then Lowther Street before, in 1901, moving back to their original venue, where they remained until 1953 when they ceased to be held.

Source and further information

D. R. Perriam, *Carlisle: An Illustrated History* (Bookcase, 1992).

Navvy was the term applied to 'navigational engineers' who laboured on major civil engineering projects such as the building of railway lines. Navvies were the men who laid thousands of miles of rail lines without the use of machinery. The process was very labour intensive and the standard tools of the navvies were picks, shovels and a wheelbarrow. A good navvy could shift twenty tonnes of earth a day and was well paid for his efforts compared to those who worked in factories. Usually they lived in shanty towns built beside the rail line they were building. Getting the job done quickly was far more important than employee safety, especially as there were plenty of navvies. Deaths while working were common and consequently many navvies chose to live for the day. Their drinking was well known and often towns feared the arrival of navvies in their area. 'Going on a randy' was navvy slang for going on a drinking spree that could last several days. Work on the rail line stopped and people in towns could fear for their safety. Only tavern owners were happy about the high spending on alcohol, although, like Billy Dixon, they worried about the possibility of damage should the drunkenness get out of hand. Drunkenness in Carlisle eventually led to the government stepping in to nationalise and control the brewing, distribution and sale of alcohol in the area through what was known as the State Management Scheme. The scheme ran from July 1916 until its abolition in 1971.

Sources and further information

John Anstey, 'The Greatest Munitions Factory on Earth' (7th August 2018). A talk given as part of Tullie House Museum's lunchtime lecture programme. For more details, see sources for Chapter 19.

'Navvies' by C. N. Trueman (31st March 2015) on the History Learning website (https://www.historylearningsite.co.uk/britain-1700-to-1900/transport-1750-to-1900/navvies/).

Chapter 9

The Border Regiment was also known simply as the Lonsdales, having been formed by the Earl of Lonsdale and a local executive committee. Its headquarters were based in Carlisle Castle, as were two regular and one reserve battalions plus two territorial army battalions. The barracks buildings still exist. At first all new recruits were also based here but as the numbers of volunteers increased tents were erected in nearby parkland, men were sent to fill spaces in other regiments around the country and others were signed up then sent home to await being called up to join a squad. Originally the Lonsdales recruiting centre was also located in the castle but as the flow of volunteers was initially slow, in April 1915, it was moved into the centre of the city to give it more prominence. Eventually things improved and an article in the *Carlisle Journal* on 19th November indicated that recruitment was thriving.

Sources and further information

The Lonsdale Battalion website (https://thelonsdalebattalion. co.uk/wiki/Main_Page).

'The Lonsdale Battalion, 11th (Service) Battalion of the Border Regiment: Timeline and Chronology – September 1914 to July 1918' on the Cumbria Archive website (https://www.cumbria. gov.uk/eLibrary/Content/Internet/542/795/4229216421.pdf).

Carlisle Journal, Friday, 19th November 1915.

David Carter, *Carlisle in the Great War* (Pen and Sword Books, 2014).

D. R. Perriam, *Carlisle: An Illustrated History* (Bookcase, 1992).

Carlisle's Norman Castle remains much as it was in 1915. It sits on the old Roman fort site of Luguvalium. Built on a bluff overlooking crossing points on the River Eden and Caldew it was an ideal defensive site. A motte-and-bailey wooden castle was initially ordered by William II in 1092 at a time of conflict between England and Scotland. In 1122 Henry I replaced it with a stone keep and high defensive walls. After the Border Regiment was formed in 1880, it became the garrison's HQ. The regiment continues to have offices in the castle, which is now run by English Heritage. It's open to the public and you can explore the mediaeval castle rooms, walk the walls, look at a variety of historical exhibits and, scattered around the drill square, recognise the barracks buildings that were the focus of Heinrich's attack. The small but excellent Cumbria Museum of Military Life is also on site.

Sources and further information

Billy F. K. Howorth, *Carlisle History Tour* (Amberley Publishing, 2018).

'Carlisle Castle' on the English Heritage website (https://www. english-heritage.org.uk).

Chapter 10

The Arrol Johnston bus Heinrich used for the rescue was real. The Whitehaven Hertofore website reports that the first regular bus service between Whitehaven and Cleator Moor was started by the Whitehaven Motor Service Company in October 1912. The first buses were a second-hand Arrol Johnston, called Lady Favourite, and a Commercial Car Charabanc, named Lady Florence. The company became the Cumberland Motor Services Limited in June 1921 and ran services between Whitehaven and Carlisle, Keswick, Cleator Moor and Egremont, and between Carlisle and Abbeytown and Maryport and Cockermouth.

Now closed, the former Arrol-Johnston Car Co. Ltd factory, opened in July 1913 on the northern outskirts of Dumfries in south-west Scotland. Car production ceased by the late 1920s, with the factory finally closing in 1931. The site was eventually bought by the North British Rubber Co. Ltd in 1946/7 and has continued in rubber production until the present day. The site is now owned by a subsidiary of the Gates Rubber Company.

Sources and further information

'Whitehaven Motor Service' on the Whitehaven Heretofore website (https://www.heretofore.co.uk/2019/06/whitehaven-motor-service.html).

Harry Postlethwaite, *Cumberland Motor Services 1912 – 2012: 100 Years of Service* (Venture Publications, 2012).

Chapter 11

The circumstances surrounding the setting up of national shell factories were well reported by the newspapers of the day, although, for the purpose of this story, developments in Carlisle have been brought forwards by three months. From the start of the war, the vast number of artillery shells being used led to an initial shortage and the article in *The Times* newspaper by Field Marshall Sir John French on the 27th March created a great deal of concern. The answer was for millions of extra shells to be made in new workshops to be created across the country. As a consequence, Carlisle MP Richard Denman called a meeting of local engineering businesses and trades unions at his home at St Nicholas View with a view to discussing if, and how, the city could contribute to the production of munitions. That initial meeting was actually held on 9th June *not* the earlier date of 22nd March and at it a Munitions Committee was formed, with Theodore Carr as chairman and Henry Campbell as secretary. After discussions with the War Office, the group eventually managed to obtain permission to set up a local munitions factory and in July a board of management was formed, comprising of Carr, Denman, a Mr James Morton and Mr J. B. Pearson of Cowans Sheldon and Co. engineering works.

Developments progressed rapidly and on 18th September

an agreement was signed, again with the War Office, to use the empty Rifle Drill Hall for free for the duration of the war. The factory recruited and started training women workers in November and on 15th December machinery began producing eighteen-pounder HE shell field gun ammunition at a rate of 2,000 a week. At its height it employed 136 women and sixty-eight men working shifts around the clock. In response to the 'shell crisis', Carlisle had managed to establish one of the first 'national shell factories' from start to finish in just five months.

The drill hall itself was built in 1874 opposite Carlisle Grammar School (now Trinity School) on Strand Road. Initially it was the headquarters of Carlisle Rifle Volunteers, part of a national part-time defence force, and in 1883 this unit became the 1st Volunteer Battalion, the Border Regiment. In August 1914 the battalion was mobilised and deployed to India, leaving the hall empty and available for use as a shell factory. After it was decommissioned, the building was used for concerts, political meetings (like the one in the story), wrestling events and as a sports centre. By the twenty-first century it was empty and dilapidated, and Carlisle College acquired it, demolished the old structure whilst retaining the front façade, and redeveloped the site into a digital and creative arts centre which opened in 2014.

Theodore Carr was a member of the Carr family who founded Carr and Company Ltd, biscuit manufactures (now McVities) and Carr's Flour Mills (Ltd). After attending Owen's College (now the University of Manchester) Theodore went into the business eventually becoming chairman of directors for both. Richard Denman was elected Liberal MP for Carlisle in January 1910 and represented the city until 1918. The two were close friends and political allies, and Carr, also a staunch Liberal, replaced Denman as the city's MP when he stood down.

The Munitions Committee meeting described is fictitious,

but I have no doubt that from its establishment in 1915 until the factory closed, many such meetings took place so that committee officials and then the board of management could keep the larger group aware of developments.

Sources and further information

'Theodore Carr' and 'Richard Denman', both on Wikipedia.

From June until November 1915 the *Carlisle Journal* included regular arcticles about the setting up of the East Cumberland National Shell Factory, notably on 11th June, 2nd July, 20th August, and 2nd, 5th, 16th, 19th and 30th of November 1915.

'The East Cumberland National Shell Factory 1915-19', a pamphlet published by James Beaty and Son/Northern Press of Carlisle. The pamphlet tells the story, with photographs, of the East Cumberland National Shell Factory from start to finish, and includes a final balance sheet and summary of accounts for August/September 1919, which is presumably the approximate time the publication was produced. It is held in the archive at Carlisle Library.

David Carter, *Carlisle in the Great War* (Pen and Sword Books, 2014).

'East Cumbria National Shell Factory' on the Tullie House Museum website (https://www.tulliehouse.co.uk/east-cumberland-national-shell-factory).

'East Cumberland Shell Factory' on the BBC World War One at Home website (https://www.bbc.co.uk/programmes/p022ypfc).

'Encyclopaedia – The Shell Scandal, 1915' on the Firstworldwar. com website (https://www.firstworldwar.com/atoz/shellscandal. htm).

'East Cumberland Shell Factory' on the Historic England Past Scape website (https://www.pastscape.org.uk/hob.aspx?hob_ id=1572916).

deSchmid's worry about losing officers to the military was a valid concern. As early as 1813 the cavalry staff corps were regarded as Britain's first standing military police force. However, it was in the World War I that the force really came into its own, with numbers expanding from around 508 to 25,000. Initially membership rose with the recall of all reservists, many of whom had been civilian policemen. These same men were also wanted to fill the gaps left by officers joining up.

Source and further information

'A Short History of the Royal Military Police and its Antecedents' on the Royal Military Police website (https:// rhqrmp.org/rmp_history.html).

Opposition to World War I was widespread, both before its outbreak and for the duration of the conflict. The Women's Peace Crusade expressed anger at conscription, the mounting death toll and attacks on personal liberties. Martha McNaughton was an active member in Carlisle. She was married to Daniel, who worked at the city's Hudson Scott and Sons tin manufactures making biscuit boxes for the local Carr's biscuit works. Martha was forty-one at the time of our story, with three young children living at 12 Crummock Street in the city. She died aged sixty-six, on 10th August 1941. Her attendance at the drill hall meeting is

HISTORICAL NOTES AND ACKNOWLEDGEMENTS

entirely fictitious but fits well with the Peace Crusade's anti-war protests.

Source and further information

'The Women's Peace Crusade in the North West' on the Documenting Dissent website (http://www.documentingdissent. org.uk/the-womens-peace-crusade-in-the-north-west/). Documenting Dissent is a community digital history project charting dissent and activism in the North West of England.

Chapter 12

The Molotov cocktail or petrol bomb was first used in the Spanish Civil War (1936 to 1939) but it wasn't until the Finns perfected the design for use against the Soviet Union, who had attacked them in November 1939, that the petrol bomb became a reliable weapon. They refined the fuel into a sticky mixture of gasoline, kerosene, tar and potassium chlorate, and used the bombs to great effect on enemy tanks setting fire to engine and gas lines, and getting into cracks and openings in the armour to roast the crews inside. The Finns named the bombs 'Molotov cocktails' after the Soviet Foreign Minister Vyacheslav Molotov. When questioned about the initial bombardment of the Finnish capital, Helsinki, he announced that reports of the bombing were a hoax and that in reality, the Soviets were dropping groceries and other humanitarian supplies. The Finns named the bombs as 'Molotov's bread baskets' and in return decided to send the red army a drink in the form of a 'Molotov cocktail'. However, although it was some time after World War I before petrol bombs came into common use, records show that sulphur-and-oil-soaked materials had been ignited and hurled at the enemy as far back as the tenth century. So it is plausible that Heinrich could have come up with the clever idea of a petrol based weapon.

Sources and further information

'Molotov cocktail' on Wikipedia.

'The Unexpected Origins of the Molotov Cocktail' by Matthew Gaskill (16th June 2018) on the Vintage News website (www.thevintagenews.com/2018/06/16/molotov-cocktail/).

Chapter 13

Stanwix was originally a village built on the site of the Roman fort of Uxelodunum, making use of stone from the ancient ruins. Uxelodunum was the largest and probably most important fort on Hadrian's Wall, as it was the administrative centre for the frontier. It was more generally known as Petriana after the Ala Petriana, the largest cavalry unit in Britannia who were based at the fort and whose commander was the most senior officer in the region. Over time the village expanded north, east and west but has always been separated from the main city by the River Eden to the south.

Sources and further information

Denis Perriam, *Carlisle's Suburbs Series: Stanwix* (P3 Publications, 2018).

Simon Forty, *Hadrian's Wall: From Construction to World Heritage Site* (Haynes Publishing 2018). An interesting book that presents a wealth of well-researched and in-depth information about the construction and purpose of the wall, how it was built, who worked on it and the lives of the people who lived on or around it.

Norman Nicholson, *Carlisle Lore and More* (Bookcase, 2013).

Lizzie Alexander is a fictitious character based on someone who was possibly real and whose journey to becoming a nurse may have been much as described. In November 2019, I organised and introduced a talk at Tullie House Museum in Carlisle by Gail Jefferson (a forensic radiographer) on the history and progression of forensic imaging. Amongst other things, Gail spoke about the role played by staff at the Cumberland Infirmary in the development of this specialist science. Afterwards, a member of the audience approached me to suggest that it would be interesting to have a talk on the history of the Cumberland Infirmary since the previous year we had celebrated the anniversary of the National Health Service (July 2018). The lady concerned had retired from the infirmary many years earlier and was interested in the history of the building and the people who worked there. She was keen to recount several stories collected over the years which she thought might be of interest to people. I listened and jotted down a few notes for future reference in case I was able to find someone to deliver such a talk. One tale was about a young woman who she thought had been at the forefront of treating the badly injured and traumatised soldiers returning from the Great War. The person concerned had moved to London to live with her wealthy unmarried aunt after her parents had died of typhoid. I've picked 1897 in the story because there was a series of significant typhoid outbreaks across England in that year. After training as a nurse, she moved back to Carlisle to work at the Cumberland Infirmary following the death of her aunt and the inheritance of a large sum of money. The storyteller didn't know the name of the woman but knew that she had lived in a town house somewhere in Stanwix and rented out rooms to those who worked with her at the hospital. Despite extensive research and the help of Carlisle Library staff, who spent one long Tuesday afternoon and early evening searching numerous publications and archive records, I have been unable to unearth anything more about the alleged character. However, in the *Cumberland Infirmary: Annual Report for 1915 (published by Thurnham and Sons)* mention is made of Miss Stead, Miss Beevor, Miss Creighton and Miss Doridd, all of whom paid subscriptions to the hospital and lived in Stanwix (unfortunately their specific address is not given). Whether these were donations, affiliation fees or some form of staff membership payment is unknown, but it is an interesting coincidence. Real or not, 'Lizzie' fit well into the story, and given Jack's sojourn in hospital it seemed a natural assumption for a fictitious meeting to take place between the two of them.

Lieutenant Colonel Percy Wilfred Machell and Major William Walter Riddell Binning were both heavily involved in the city's war effort in the roles described. Machell was persuaded out of retirement at the outbreak of war and served with the Lonsdale battalion from 1914 to 1916. He rose to the rank of lieutenant colonel and was the battalion's commanding officer until he was killed during the first day of the Battle of the Somme. Binning was his second in command and served from 1914 to 1918. Both men achieved their positions after Lord Lonsdale submitted a proposal to the War Office in September 1914 to create a battalion made entirely of men from Cumberland and Westmorland. The battalion comprised three detachments: Carlisle, Workington and Kendal. The former soon became the Lonsdale's headquarters and, over a period of a few short months, became the new force's bustling epicentre, with Binning and Machell at the helm. As such any military problem, such as the fictitious one in the book, would inevitably have been brought to their attention.

Sources and further information

'William Walter Riddell Binning' on the The Lonsdales website (https://thelonsdalebattalion.co.uk/wiki/William_Walter_ Riddell_Binning).

'Percy Wilfred Machell' on the Wikla.org website (https:// london.wikia.org/wiki/Percy_Wilfrid_Machell)

David Carter, *Carlisle in the Great War* (Pen and Sword Books, 2014).

Chapter 14

Cock-fighting, where birds are placed in a ring and forced to fight, usually to the death, was a popular blood sport in the 1800s and before. However, in 1849, the 'Act for the more effective Prevention of Cruelty to Animals' was passed and it became illegal for anyone to:

Keep, use or manage a place for the purpose of animal fighting, including cockerels.

Encourage, aid or assist at the fighting or baiting of an animal.

Breaking the law incurred a penalty of between five and ten pounds. As a consequence, the number of recorded incidents and prosecutions for cock-fighting declined significantly by the turn of the century, but the practice still existed. The problem was that for many people it was seen as a legitimate countryside sport and respectable citizens, including magistrates, attended the events. In the circumstances, police found it hard to bring prosecutions as reflected in the trial described in the book taken from a real event reported in the local paper. Meets were well organised, with lookouts and escape routes which participants used at the first sign of the police. Attempts to stop fights were seen as a waste of police time and in some cases rural officers colluded with organisers to ensure they went ahead or were not disrupted. Local papers took a very 'tongue-in-cheek' approach to the situation, as the following extract from the *Westmorland Gazette* (10th May, 1890, Page 8) illustrates:

'The South Cumberland and Furness Cock Fighting Club had a successful main *(meet)* on Saturday last, in the neighbourhood of Whitbeck. It is to be regretted that your contemporary was not in a position to publish the names of the hardened law breakers who took part in this disgraceful affair.'

I've used this extract in the story but adapted it to the Carlisle setting.

The trial description comes from an extract I came across then lost during my online research. Initially I thought it related to an event that took place a week later than suggested in the story at Carlisle Magistrates' Court. However, I was unable to find anything in either the *Carlisle Journal* or *Cumberland News* for that period. Consequently, I decided to contact Dr Guy Woolnough, who, as a lecturer in criminology at the University of Keele, researched extensively into blood sports in Cumberland and Westmorland at the end of the nineteenth and early twentieth centuries. On my behalf, Guy tried but failed to find any mention of the case in the on-line newspaper archives for the specified time frame. However, he suggested it was actually similar to a Petty Sessions Court Case held in Kendal during 1864 which he quoted in his article 'Blood Sports in Victorian Cumbria: Policing Cultural Change' published in the online *Journal of Victorian Culture* in 2014. In the absence of any alternative evidence, I am happy to bow to his greater knowledge and accept this as the source of the story.

Sources and further information

Dr Guy Woolnough 'Blood Sports in Victorian Cumbria: Policing Cultural Change' and 'Cock-fighting in Cumbria since 1850: contested popular culture' online PowerPoint presentations (www.guywoolnough.com).

Westmorland Gazette, 10th May 1890.

Carlisle Journal, 18th September 1862.

'Cock Fighting in Lakeland' on the Lakeland Hunting Memories Website (http://lakelandhuntingmemories.com/ CockfightingNew.html).

The origins of the term 'paddy wagon' or 'paddywagon' for a motorised police van are uncertain. One view is that it is linked to the derogatory use of the word paddy for an Irishman and, the English perspective in the late nineteenth and early twentieth centuries, that Irish immigrants were responsible for a high proportion of civil disorder through drunken brawling. A tendency towards resisting arrest meant that a police van was needed to take them into custody.

Source and further information

'Police van' on Wikipedia.

The discussion in the Kings Head with a local journalist could have taken place. The pub was and still is a popular meeting place for locals. It's thought to be the oldest pub in the city. The current building dates from 1879 but there are suggestions that a hostelry has existed on the site as far back as the tenth century.

By the end of the 1800s gambling had got out of control and eventually the government did take steps to try and control things. As with prohibition in the United States, it simply drove the practice underground.

Sources and further information

The King's Head website (https://www.kingsheadcarlisle.co.uk/about-us/history/).

'The History of Gambling in the UK' on the Anglotopia for Anglophiles website
(https://www.anglotopia.net/news-features/a-history-of-gambling-in-the-uk/).

'History of Gambling – The UK Viewpoint' on the Gordon House website (http://www.gordonhouse.org.uk/history-gambling-uk-viewpoint/).

'The History of Gambling, Betting and Bookmakers in the UK' on the Online Betting.Org.Uk website (https://www.onlinebetting.org.uk/betting-guides/history-of-gambling-and-bookmaking.html).

David Carter, *Carlisle in the Great War* (Pen and Sword Books, 2014)

Chapters 15 and 16

With over 200 deaths, the Quintinshill crash on 22nd May 1915 is the worst rail disaster in British history. The sequence of events was much as described, with one or two alterations to fit the storyline. For example, the gas cylinders from the Pintsch

Lighting System in the old wooden carriages were punctured during the crash and exploded entirely due to the spreading flames rather than to sabotage. The board of enquiry, referred to in Chapter 16, was held three days after the event and the two signalmen, George Meakin and James Tinsley, both admitted that their careless behaviour and failure to implement the correct changeover procedures caused the disaster. Probably the most critical error was that Tinsley, having moved the local train onto the south-bound mainline track, facing the wrong way, forgot about it and allowed the troop train to come down the same line. Eventually they were charged with culpable homicide by the Scottish authorities and manslaughter by those in England. Rather than hold two trials, it was decided that things should go ahead in Scotland and on the 24th September they were found guilty at the High Court in Edinburgh. Tinsley was sentenced to three years' penal servitude (prison with hard labour) and Meakin to eighteen months in prison. They were both released from prison in 1916 and amazingly were allowed to go straight back to working on the railway, Tinsley as a lamp man and Meakin as a goods train guard.

Sources and further information

The *Carlisle Journal* provides a first-hand report of the incident in the editions released on Tuesday, 25th and Friday, 28th May 1915. Similar information is reported in the *Cumberland News*, Friday 28th May 1915. Details of the subsequent trial of Meaken and Tinsley can be found in the *Carlisle Journal* for Friday, 17th September 1915.

Gordon L. Routledge, *The Gretna Railway Disaster 100 Years Age* (Bookcase, 2015). My namesake's book (no relation) is the definitive text on the disaster and covers every aspect in excellent detail.

David Carter, *Carlisle in the Great War* (Pen and Sword Books 2014).

'Quintinshill rail disaster' on Wikipedia.

As menitoned earlier when creating the fictitious Inspector Jack Johnstone as the hero of my story, I had no idea that such a person actually existed. My character was an amalgamation of my grandfather and father. The name and age were taken from Joseph Johnston (no 'e'), who was born in 1874 and worked as a foreman with the Carlisle Railway Company as war approached. The physical characteristics and habits were those of John (Jack) Routledge who worked as a Carlisle bus driver from 1947 to 1991 and was a habitual pipe smoker. It came as a complete shock when I read in Bob Lowther's book (Page 121) that Inspector Johnstone of the Carlisle City Police was detailed to arrange the identification of the bodies from Quintinshill and also the inquests into their deaths. I've been unable to find any additional information about the real Inspector Johnstone although an Andrew Johnstone of the city police was drowned on 3rd July 1915 (aged fifty-eight) in unknown circumstances after he had been on duty. It's proved impossible to find out if this was the same man. Perhaps a mystery for another story. Nor should Johnstone be confused with PC25 Johnston, who left the force to join up, was wounded in action and returned to police duties in 1918. Another real character in the story is PC Mackay, who was the constable at Gretna at the time of the disaster.

Source and further information

Bob Lowther, *Watching Over Carlisle: 140 Years of the Carlisle City Police Force 1827-1967* (P3 Publications, 2011).

The Aliens Restrictions Act 1914 required foreign nationals to register with the police providing details of their name, address, marital status and employment. In addition, under the act every person who visited a hotel or lodging house had to sign a register and the person keeping the house had to see that this register was kept up to date and available for scrutiny by the authorities. Unfortunately it was not uncommon for Carlisle landlords to fail to carry out this requirement and the *Carlisle Journal* of 19th November 1915 reports that two days earlier Mina Glendinning of Thomson Street had appeared before the magistrates court at the Town Hall charged with failing to keep a register. She was found guilty and fined fifteen (old) shillings.

Source and further information

Carlisle Journal, Friday, 19th November 1915.

Chapter 17

Lieutenant Colonel W.A. Murray (Bill) was appointed as Adjutant to the 1/1 Warwickshire Battery of the Royal Horse Artillery in 1911. In October 1914 he went with the Battery to France. He remained on the Western Front for the duration of the conflict where he had a distinguished war record. He was promoted to Lieutenant Colonel, mentioned in dispatches twice for gallantry in the face of the enemy and awarded the Companion (of the Order of) St Michael and St George, Distinguished Service Order and Croix de Guerre. Throughout the war, he regularly wrote home to his father William Senior and his half-sister Claudine Murray. The letters painted a vivid picture of the 1914-18 war years. Before she died in 1986 at the age of ninety-eight Claudine passed the letters on to Alan Michael Whitworth with a view to having them published. For a while the letters were stored away, until early

2013 when they were reopened and a decision made to put them into the public domain. In 2017 the letters were published in date order with his private diary entries in the correct sequence and supplementary notes added to set context.

The Thunder of Guns. An Artillery Officer on the Western Front 1914-1919 is edited and introduced by Alan Michael Whitworth and published by Bookcase Publications. Chapter 7 is based on information from this book. In the book Bill Murray's letters provide an insightful and poignant picture of the everyday life and camaraderie of the officers and men who served in an artillery battery during World War I. His story is both informative and inspiring, and deserves to be heard. Whether you are interested in this period of British history or not, I would recommend you read this book about a local man who was a true hero of that period. His time on the frontline took a toll on his nerves and periodically he required some respite and recuperation from the carnage and din of battle. In early June 1915, he made a flying visit to England for three days' rest in London. The journey to and from the front took over thirty hours each way and he didn't have time to travel up to Cumberland as the army insisted that he take it easy during the time away from his battery. However, for the purposes of the story I have him returning home during this short break to talk to the scout troop his sister supervised. As far as I am aware, nothing like this ever happened. However, comments within the drill hall talk are taken from letters written by him in March, April and May 1915, and one on 14th January 1917 when he tells his sister how well former scouts were doing at the front.

Source and further information

The Thunder of Guns. An Artillery Officer on the Western Front 1914-1919 edited by Alan Michael Whitworth (Bookcase, 2017).

The status of 'reserved occupation' is remarkably difficult to ascertain for World War I. Although there were instances of policemen who were military reservists being called up at the start of the war, there was a reluctance to allow police officers to enlist. For example, in October 1915 around thirty policemen in the North East enrolled as ready for military service. However, they were immediately placed on the army reserve and their army forms officially stamped as Reserved Occupation. It's possible that they, like others around the country, were placed on the reserve list because of concerns about the impact that large numbers of officers leaving the force would have on law and order.

The British government did not introduce conscription until March 1916, when voluntary enlistment could no longer meet the army's need for recruits. Under the terms of the Military Service Act, all medically fit single men between the ages of nineteen and forty-one were deemed to have enlisted in the armed forces from 2nd March. A succession of Military Service Acts were passed, which narrowed the way that exceptions could be identified. Rather than list specific occupations, the Acts said that exceptions had to be for work of national importance. Generally, being a policeman didn't fit this description.

In Carlisle, the attitude of the chief constable and the Watch Committee was supportive but initially cautious. As the war began, two serving constables, who were also reservists, were called up. Two others volunteered for military service for the duration of the war and were given permission to join the army. A number of officers followed them, with applications being considered on a case-by-case basis. It wasn't until 25th April 1915 that the Watch Committee directed the chief constable to post a notice to say that all officers enlisting would receive their full police pay on top of their military pay. The chief was then allowed to recruit replacements from retired officers or other suitable candidates. As a senior officer, it is unlikely that Jack would have been allowed to enlist at the start of the war and by the time conscription arrived he would have been approaching forty-two and too old.

Source and further information

Bob Lowther, *Watching Over Carlisle: 140 Years of the Carlisle City Police Force 1827-1967* (P3 Publications, 2011).

Chapter 18

Bitts Park lies to the north of carlisle city centre between the castle and the River Eden. 'Bitts' were originally small parcels of land on which cattle were allowed to graze. The area was the first public park to be established in Carlisle. At the western end, Victoria Park is part of the larger Bitts Park and comprises formal gardens and riverside walks around a central sunken 'bowl'. Built on a former rubbish tip, the park takes its name from the Victoria monument erected on 7th May 1902, a year after her death. I am not aware that any wrestling events took place in the formal part of the park referred to in the story, but the 'bowl' seemed like an ideal venue close to the city centre.

Source and further information

Billy F. K. Howorth, *Carlisle History Tour* (Amberley Publishing, 2018).

I found most of my information for wrestling on the Cumberland and Westmorland Wrestling Association Website. The site is a mine of information and the historical extracts in particular, provide an interesting insight into the sport's past.

The description of Jack's wrestling match is adapted from various descriptions on the site, including an excerpt that led me to William Litt's journal *Wrestliana,* published in 1823, in which he describes the wrestling holds and throws.

Sources and further information:

Cumberland and Westmorland Wrestling Association website (http://www.cumberland-westmorland-wrestling-association.com/#).

William Litt, *Wrestliana: A Historical Account of Ancient and Modern Wrestling,* originally printed in 1823 by Whitehaven printer R. Gibson but re-released by Wentworth Press in 2016.

Chapter 19

The incidents leading up to the arrest at the St Nicholas marshalling yards, although fictitious, are based on a similar incident that happened on 28th October 1885 described in Bob Lowther's book. Willowburn Lodge is imaginary, but the other locations existed at the time of the story. Half a mile south of the Citadel Station on the edge of the 1915 city, the marshalling yards were operated by the London, Midland and Scottish Railway (LM&SR). There was a huge upsurge in goods traffic in Carlisle during the war and the yard was heavily used, especially by the adjacent Cowans Sheldon Engineering Company. Cowans had a world-leading reputation for the construction of rail and dock cranes, and due to the high demand placed on heavy engineering for the war effort, production boomed. Some of the lines are now closed and, together with the buildings that supported them, have disappeared as Carlisle has grown and changed.

Sources and further information

'Cowans and Sheldon and Co Cranemakers' on the Tullie House Museuem website (https://www.tulliehouse.co.uk/collections/cowans-sheldon-and-co-cranemakers).

Bob Lowther, *Watching Over Carlisle: 140 Years of the Carlisle City Police Force 1827-1967* (P3 Publications, 2011).

Bombardier Billy Wells was an English heavyweight boxer. His full name was William Thomas Wells, and from 1911 until 1919 he was the British and British Empire champion.

Sources and further information

'Bombardier Billy Wells' on Wikipedia.

Chapters 20 to 22

The decision to build a new munitions factory beside the Solway Firth was taken in the spring/early summer of 1915 as a response to the developing shell scandal and Field Marshal Sir John French's remarks in the press about the acute shortage of ammunition. Several facilities were built but H.M. Factory Gretna was by far the biggest, growing to become the largest munitions factory in the world. It stretched nine miles from Dornock near Annan to Mossbank in what is now Cumbria. The site, which employed 20,000 workers, was accessed by thirty miles of road and 125 miles of rail track. The factory never made shells. The final product was cordite (an explosive) which was shipped to shell-filling factories all over the country. The land site was acquired by compulsory purchase from the local landowners and their tenants evicted. The main contract for the construction was given to the construction company S. P. Pearson and Sons, and the first sod was cut in early August 1915. Most of the workers were Irish navvies (around 15,000) and work began in earnest once they had built themselves a timber shanty town, the accommodation huts mentioned in the story. The labourers were well paid, but accidents were commonplace, so replacements were needed although there is no evidence to suggest that men were taken on in the manner described for Heinrich.

The first cordite was produced twelve months later in August 1916, and eventually production hit 800 tonnes a week, more than all the other sites across the country combined. Most of the workers were women, and two new townships, Gretna (not to be confused with Gretna Green) and Eastriggs, were built to house them. Cordite production was extremely dangerous work, involving mixing nitric and sulphuric acids, nitro-glycerine, gun cotton, mineral jelly, alcohol and either. The end product, referred to as 'Devil's Porridge', went into the shell cases. Very little remains of the factory today, but the site is occasionally opened for guided tours and commemorated by the award-winning Devil's Porridge Museum in Eastriggs. The tour accesses the site through the Butterdale entrance referred to in the story.

Sources and further information

John Anstey, *The Greatest Munitions Factory on Earth* (7th August 2018). John, from the superb Devil's Porridge Museum in Eastriggs, gave an excellent talk about the giant munitions factory and the navvies who helped build it (see Chapter 8). I also visited the award-winning museum which recounts the remarkable story of what was the largest munitions factory in the world during the World War I and the people who worked there. The museum uses artefacts, information panels, film and audio, photographs, and oral history to bring this aspect of border history to life. You can find out more from their website (https://www.devilsporridge.org.uk/about).

Gordon L. Routledge, *Gretna's Secret War* (Bookcase 1999). The best book available on the subject. This is the story of the factory, its workers and the towns that were built to house them. It also has an account of the Quintinshill railway disaster.

'World War One: HM Factory Gretna's vital munition role' by Willie Johnston (31st July 2014) on the BBC News website (https://www.bbc.co.uk/news/uk-scotland-south-scotland-28565239).

'HM Munitions Factory, Gretna' on the Scotland's War 1914 – 19 website (http://www.scotlandswar.co.uk/gretna_munitions.html).

'HM Factory, Gretna' on the Secret Scotland website (https://www.secretscotland.org.uk/index.php/Secrets/HMFactoryGretna).

Chapter 23

Kingmoor Nature Reserve is found to the north of the city. It is the oldest reserve in Cumbria and has been a public facility since King Edward II gave the original moorland to the people in 1352. As the story states the Corporation of Carlisle handed over the land to the newly formed Cumberland Nature Reserve Association in 1914. The sign Heinrich came across existed and, as specified, displayed the first annual report of the association giving details of the activity in the reserve.

Source and further information

Kingmoor Parish Council website (http://www.kingmoorparish council.org/about-kingmoor/kingmoor-amenities/).

Chapter 24

Winfred Wilkes' place in the book is a tribute to Wilfred Whitfield. Whitfield was a real but unlikely war hero, and his story is told on the 'Blesma: Limbless Veterans' website (see below). He volunteered to fight in World War I every week from the start of the conflict, but was sent home each time as he was shorter than five foot three inches, the minimum height for a soldier. Eventually the conflict's huge loss of life gave him his chance and he was allowed to sign up. Sadly Wilf lost his left arm at the Battle of the Somme and was then sent back to England. However, there was no hero's welcome, and when the war ended, along with other amputee service men, he found it hard to get work and his benefits were cut as the nation struggled through the Depression of the 1920s. Wilf, who died in 1958 aged sixty-two, and fellow amputees, battled again and again to improve employment opportunities, medical techniques, social support and public awareness of the struggles of wounded veterans. This was the catalyst for the formation of Blesma, a military charity for limbless veterans. Wilf was instrumental in setting up the Teesside branch of Blesma, then the Limbless Ex-Service Men's Association, to campaign for the 40,000 soldiers who lost limbs or eyes during the war.

Source and further information

Wilf kept a diary of his military and civilian campaigns, which his family edited into an incredible testimony of one man's war experiences and battle against injustice and discrimination. His story and extracts from the diary can be found on the 'Blesma – The Limbless Veterans' website.

(https://blesma.org/news-media/blesma-news/2016/ww1-war-diaries-reveal-how-a-war-hero-survived-losing-a-limb-during-battle-of-the-somme-and-helped-form-the-beginning-of-blesma/).

Chapters 25 and 26

Most German attacks on the UK mainland were on coastal communities along the east coast of England. However, the west coast also suffered at the hands of the U-boats. The British War Office reported that between 4.30 and 5.30am on 16th August 1915, a German U-boat did attack the chemical works at Lowca near Whitehaven. The attack was much as described, although in the story it takes place over two hours and not one. Submarine *U24* surfaced and fired fifty-five shells from its deck. The factory was attacked, because it extracted benzene, and other chemicals, such as toluene (an ingredient of TNT), from coal. Local legend has it that a quick-thinking worker opened a relief valve, which sent up an impressive plume of burning gas, so the submariners thought they had destroyed their target and left. Although the Lowca works were the target, most of the shells fell on the nearby hillside at Bransty. Apparently the only fatality of the incident was one local dog. There was no real damage sustained following the attack. A few shells hit the railway embankment north of Parton, but train service was only slightly delayed. Fires were caused at Whitehaven and at Harrington, which were soon extinguished.

Sources and further information

'WW1 Submarine Attack' on the Whitehaven Heretofore website (https://www.heretofore.co.uk/2019/06/wwi-submarine-attack.html).

'Lowca and Parton in Cumbria recall 1915 attack by German U-boat' on the BBC News archive website (bbc.co.uk/news/av/uk-england-cumbria-28668657/lowca-and-parton-in-cumbria-recall-1915-attack-by-german-u-boat).

'The day the "fightfulness of war arrived in Cumbria" on the Whitehaven News website (https://www.whitehavennews.co.uk/news/17157045.the-day-the-fightfulness-of-war-arrived-in-cumbria/).

General Source and Further Information

In many cases, my starting point for investigating various facts and events was 'Images from Carlisle in the Great War, 1914-1918: Munitions, Mayhem and Mobilisation', a major exhibition exploring Carlisle's Great War experience, developed and hosted by Tullie House Museum and Art Gallery in 2016-17 as part of the centenary commemorations of the Great War. The event was funded in part by the Heritage Lottery Fund and the museum website still details information from the exhibition:
(https://www.tulliehouse.co.uk/collections/carlisle-great-war-1914-1918-munitions-mayhem-and-mobilisation)

The Reiver Trail

For those who would like to explore Jack Johnstone's Carlisle in more detail, I would suggest that you use the 1915 map of to walk the city in the following order:

1. Carlisle Railway Station.
2. The Citadel.
3. The Market Cross.
4. The Kings Head Public House.
5. The Methodist Central Hall.
6. Peter Street Gym (now a row of shops and car park).
7. Finkle Street (from here you can look north across the River Eden towards Stanwix).
8. Carlisle Castle.
9. Annetwell Street.
10. Irish (or Caldew) Gate (now the site of the Millenium Bridge).
11. The Globe Inn (now a beauty salon and lounge bar).
12. The Biscuit Factory (originally Carr's but now McVitie's).
13. Canal Bank (all that's left is the Jovial Sailor Pub and the site of the old railway line that replaced the original canal).
14. Holy Trinity Church (now a multi-use games area).
15. To see the actual Parham Beck you need to visit Heysham

Park in the Raffles area of the city, but Canal Street and Ashley Street can be found a short walk past the multi-use games area)

16. Retrace your steps back to the Millenium Bridge and take the West Walls.
17. Dean Tait's Lane (still a short cut into the city from the West Walls)
18. The Cathedral
19. The Old Police Station (this is now a car park but the Sallyport steps still exist opposite Heads Lane and the Tithe Barn)

I've left the old Territorial Drill Hall off the walk but you can easily deviate from the route and within a few minutes cross the Georgian Way dual carriageway, which is roughly where Spring Garden Lane was, to find the facade opposite Trinity Sixth Form Centre (the old grammar school building) on Strand Road.

You'll enjoy exploring the historic parts of Carlisle, but it will be made even more interesting with a guide book. There are many you can get hold of, but for information presented in a clear and precise format with beautiful illustrations and pictures, I would recommend Billy F. K. Howorth's *Carlisle History Tour* (Amberley Publishing, 2018). I've never met the author and I'm certainly not on commission for recommending his book but I found this inexpensive, handy little paperback a great introduction to the city's historical sites.

Final Thanks

I want to thank everyone at Troubador Publishing for the support they have given me from draft through to publication particularly Hannah Dakin, Andrea Johnson, Jonathan White and Fern Bushnell, who were the constant, kind and helpful 'voices' on the telephone and at the end of an email.

MJR July 2020